How to Talk to Your Dog About Murder

How to Talk to Your Dog About Murder

A MYSTERY

Emily Soderberg

NEW YORK

Books should be disposed of and recycled according to local requirements. All paper materials used are FSC compliant.

This is a work of fiction. All of the names, characters, organizations, places, and events portrayed in this novel are either products of the author's imagination or are used fictitiously. Any resemblance to real or actual events, locales, or persons, living or dead, is entirely coincidental.

Published in the United States by Crooked Lane Books, an imprint of The Quick Brown Fox & Company LLC.

Crooked Lane Books and its logo are trademarks of The Quick Brown Fox & Company LLC.

Library of Congress Catalog-in-Publication data available upon request.

ISBN (hardcover): 979-8-89242-345-8
ISBN (paperback): 979-8-89242-346-5
ISBN (ebook): 979-8-89242-347-2

Cover design by Mallory Hayer

Printed in the United States.

www.crookedlanebooks.com

Crooked Lane Books
34 West 27th St., 10th Floor
New York, NY 10001

First Edition: October 2025

The authorized representative in the EU for product safety and compliance is eucomply OÜPärnu mnt 139b-14, 11317 Tallinn, Estonia, hello@eucompliancepartner.com, +33757690241

10 9 8 7 6 5 4 3 2 1

For Zack and Tommy

Chapter One

I sat in the car outside Mrs. Van Meer's mansion, trying to psych myself up to go in. I'd love to say my hesitation came from a sense of foreboding, a premonition that someone would die in this house, and soon. But I had no idea about any of that.

Mrs. Van Meer was a dog owner, just like any other dog owner, I reminded myself. I could talk to dog owners. They were good people. Dog owners in big houses were just good people in big houses, right?

I pulled out my phone to check the address again. It's not that the oversized house looked any different from the picture I'd seen checking directions earlier that morning, but I was stalling. The front lawn looked greener than it had any right to in mid-November. A formal circle drive cut across the front of the property, lined with evergreen topiaries in stone planters, and a long, winding driveway led around to the back of the house. I didn't know the etiquette dictating which one I should have pulled onto, so I'd settled for parking my old Corolla on the street.

The house somehow managed to fit in with the air of soullessness that marked the entire subdivision, and yet be uglier than its neighbors. Built of beige stone, it sprawled in all directions, more like a corporate campus than a personal residence, although I'd never seen a corporate building with turrets. Unless . . . had I heard somewhere that Cinderella's castle at Disneyland housed the administrative offices for the park? I rolled the question around in my mind, focusing on it as I hiked to the mansion's front door, which was dark green with a seasonal wreath of golden leaves and red berries and perfectly formed pinecones. Dredging up tidbits of real or imagined Disney trivia worked to distract me from my mission and kept me from chickening out.

A white woman in late middle age answered the door after a few seconds. If I described her outfit, you might get the wrong idea about her. She wore a pink sweatshirt, very pale blue jeans, and white sneakers, and had a white windbreaker tied around her waist. An outfit so dowdy that, on a teenager, it would have been recognizable as a Halloween costume of a certain type of older woman. But something about the absolute spotlessness of her clothes, the subtlety of her make-up, and her air of complete command meant she gave off an intimidatingly well-put-together impression. Like an elementary-school principal all the kids are scared of, but out walking her dog on a Sunday.

"Good morning," the woman greeted me without any enthusiasm. She gave me a quick once-over glance and craned around to get a look at my shabby Corolla. "You must be here for the dog."

Well. She didn't have to put quite so much disrespect on it. It's possible that this woman was trying to neutrally convey that the reason for my visit was known to her, but I don't think I was being a complete snowflake to bristle at her words. Sure, expressed simply, I was there "for the dog," but she could have phrased it differently. I was the one showing up to save the day after all.

And actually, was I there for the dog? They were the ones unable to communicate with a member of their family. They were the ones who needed help. They were the ones who couldn't cope. When people get to the point of calling me in, they usually have huge stress cracks in their lives. Their dogs' misbehavior is more often than not a reaction to the family's problems, not the cause of their problems.

Not that I said any of this out loud. I don't think I even let it show on my face. I barely had time to nod before the woman spun around and headed for the back of the house, calling over her shoulder for me to follow her.

I plunged into the marble foyer, trying to make up some of the lead Pink Sweatshirt Woman had already gotten. Before resolving not to look around like a slack-jawed tourist, I couldn't help noticing they literally had a sweeping front staircase. As in, their front staircase literally swept. Or figuratively, I guess. Like in *Gone with the Wind* or something.

After speed walking through a hallway wider than my living room, I caught up with Pink Sweatshirt Woman as the hallway widened out to what they probably referred to as a "great room." One end was a kitchen that looked like something straight out of a lifestyle magazine, with ornate whitewashed cabinetry, glossy white subway tiles, a stone-topped island the size of one-and-a-half regulation ping-pong tables, and a hammered-copper vent hood the manufacture of which had clearly been the primary driving force behind the skyrocketing cost of copper.

The rest of the room had plenty to catch the eye, too. Especially the patterned stone fireplace on the opposite end, the sparkling crystal chandelier suspended over a gathering of leather sofas, and the combination of floor-to-ceiling windows and French doors that seemed to make up the entirety of the back side of the house, and which made the whole space feel big and light and airy.

But I had no doubt as to why the kitchen end of the room made a stronger first impression. First was the smell. The most comforting combination of smells that could greet you when you entered a house on a dreary morning—fresh pancakes coming off the griddle, hot coffee, and I think, judging by the potency of the smell, they had even warmed up their maple syrup. I always got a warm fuzzy feeling when I smelled pancakes cooking. My husband, Jai, was a pancake fiend. He loved my just-add-water buttermilk pancakes, the fancy French crepes from our favorite brunch place, and especially the coconutty appam his grandmother makes. Jai would eat pancakes three meals a day, every day, if left to his own devices.

I stuck in that nice romantic bit about a warm and fuzzy feeling because of Jai and his love of pancakes, to maybe soften the blow if he ever reads this. The other reason the kitchen caught my attention was the incredibly hot guy doing the cooking. He was Black, about my age, so late twenties or early thirties, with a red ball cap and a gray T-shirt that fit him *very* well. At our entrance, he turned around to look, a coffee mug in one hand and a spatula in the other, and I caught my breath. Like in a soap opera. Of course, I had been speed walking, so maybe I was out of breath.

For just a second, we looked at each other, the incredibly hot man and I, and I thought, maybe we're having a moment. Maybe there's a small frisson of sexually charged energy in this giant, immaculate room.

Then I noticed the woman sitting at the kitchen island, a half-eaten plate of pancakes in front of her. She also had on a red ball cap, with a long, chestnut ponytail streaming out of the back of it. She wore a black crop-top-sports-bra thing, like it wasn't thirty-one degrees outside, and she was somehow tan. Not tanned like orange and leathery, but like she had just wrapped up her daily game of beach volleyball and was now enjoying a well-earned plate of pancakes before going jet skiing.

Because the beautiful man was making pancakes for her. He would eat some, too, but he was standing over the stove with a spatula in his hand in order to provide her with pancakes. They fit together, these two. I could tell.

They both smiled at me, and I pictured how I must look to them. I had on a green and blue puffy jacket, probably designed with an eleven-year-old boy in mind. But it was perfect for its warmth, and the fact that I could easily wipe off dog hair and muddy paw prints. Completing the ensemble were an orange pompom hat and my multi-colored Doctor Who-inspired scarf. Like I said, thirty-one degrees outside. But I was certain when the beautiful man and the beautiful woman went out, they would wear long, sleek, wool coats in black or gray or navy or camel, with perhaps matching plaid scarves for a sophisticated pop of color. Their coats probably had to be dry cleaned.

I pulled off the hat and unwound the scarf, thankful I couldn't see what the hat had done to my hair, which tends to defy the laws of gravity, even without interference from staticky hats. I turned away from the kitchen and the beautiful breakfasters, and toward the fireplace end of the room, where Pink Sweatshirt Woman approached an older woman on one of the leather sofas.

This end of the room looked as elegant as the kitchen. The leather sofas and armchairs. The fireplace, made of white-washed stones arranged in interwoven arches. Over the mantle hung a mirror that concealed a TV. Even on this overcast day, the chandelier fractured the sunlight into rainbows across the room. On a bright, sunny day, the effect must be dazzling. Nothing you could call "clutter," but every surface held a decorative element or two—a vase, a candle, a small statue of a bull I would call a doodad or a knickknack, but that had probably been called an "objet d'art" in whatever classy catalog it had come from.

Pink Sweatshirt Woman stood behind the sofa as the older woman rose unsteadily to her feet. I crossed and shook her thin hand.

"Good morning," she said. Her blue eyes were watery, but her voice proved surprisingly strong. "I'm Ruth Van Meer. Thank you so much for agreeing to help us."

"Of course! I'm Nikki." I took a seat on the sofa opposite, piling my winter gear beside me, then took a deep breath I hoped no one noticed.

I forced a smile, telling myself this was the same as any other consultation I'd been on when meeting a new client. Sure, this time the house was big enough that I'd need a map to find the bathroom. Sure, I was getting weird vibes from Pink Sweatshirt Lady, who still hadn't taken her eyes off me. Sure, these were the only clients I'd ever gotten who weren't directly referred by friends or family. Sure, before showing up, I'd decided that the success or failure of this particular job would determine whether I could make it long term as a pet behaviorist.

But hey, they'd called me, right? Out of the blue. If I could pull this off, there'd be no turning back.

Chapter Two

As soon as I sat on the sofa, the dog, curled into a plaid dog bed, became the focus of my attention. The humans around us faded into the background. He watched me, with no signs of being on high alert or feeling threatened in any way. So, a safe place for him. He seemed to be a mix of several different types of hound dog, with swinging tan ears and a long snout. He looked healthy at first glance, with graying hair around his muzzle and a hint of cloudiness in the eyes suggesting advanced age.

Forget about Mrs. Van Meer. This was my client. I slid to the floor and patted the ground next to me.

"Hello, old man! What's your name?" I looked away from the dog as Mrs. Van Meer introduced him as Reginald but kept my open hand lying invitingly beside me. Sure enough, Reginald got to his feet and plodded across to me, sniffing my hand before flopping down on the rug and laying his chin on my thigh. I scratched behind his ears in abject gratitude. Imagine if he'd been a Rottweiler whose problem was being overly aggressive to pet behaviorists! Whatever this little guy had going on, we were going to be OK.

"Can you tell me a little bit about why you called me in?" I asked Mrs. Van Meer. There'd been a change in her posture since Reginald had accepted me, a slight release of tension in her face. Pink Sweatshirt Woman, who still hadn't been introduced to me, left her post behind Mrs. Van Meer's sofa and drifted toward the kitchen, reminding me of a guard dog who's been waved off. I breathed more easily with her gone.

The younger man and woman joined us in the living room, bringing their plates of pancakes with them. When the woman approached, a domed belly protruded from her front. I bet people had been telling her she glowed, but I suspected she had glowed before getting pregnant and would continue to glow after the baby was born. She seemed like a natural glower.

Mrs. Van Meer didn't answer my question but waved to the two who had joined us. "My granddaughter, Ali. And her fiancé, Will."

I nodded politely at them, still scratching Reginald with one hand. They'd been so relaxed in the kitchen, alone in their own little world. Now there was a hardness around Ali's mouth, and she held her shoulders a little up and forward. She looked like a turtle who knew she might have to retreat into her shell at any moment. Will's expression hadn't changed, except for something in his eyes. Where before there had only been welcoming openness, a gate had clanged shut.

"They don't think I should have contacted you," continued Mrs. Van Meer. "They think this is a mistake."

Ali protested. "Grandma! That's not fair." She turned to me. "I didn't say that. I said I didn't know what good it could do." She looked back to Mrs. Van Meer. "That's not the same thing at all!"

Before Mrs. Van Meer could reply, another man and woman entered the room, about the same age as Ali and Will, but dressed for a boardroom, instead of a gym. The woman's dark hair was cut short, for a slightly more daring look than her conservative suit would have suggested. A heavy silver watch peeked out from one of her cuffs. Like everything else in this house, it was probably worth more than my monthly income. The woman stood a little taller than Ali. She would have been a little shorter than me, but I was sitting on the floor with a dog, so disadvantage me. The man was about her height, with a round face that made him look approachable, even though he wasn't smiling.

"And this is my other granddaughter, Teri. How was your run, dear?"

"Fine. My pace is up," Teri answered her grandmother without appearing to notice me.

"How nice. And Brett is our family's attorney. He grew up with the girls. Come meet Nikki, you two."

Teri made a big show of checking her watch before looking at me. "Oh, right. The dog whisperer. I can't believe you're going through with this."

Brett's eyebrows rose. "The dog whisperer?"

I sighed. The tiny surge of optimism I'd felt when Reginald dropped his head in my lap disappeared. Animal behavior is one thing. That's plain, easy to read, explicable. At least for me.

But now I was faced with a room full of people. To some degree or another, they were all on edge, for reasons that were totally hidden from me. Some were openly hostile to me, or at least snide.

And worst of all? They were family.

People are strange and unpredictable enough on their own. Get them around their family and everything is heightened to a ridiculous degree. Ali's comment to her grandmother could have been perfectly mild or even affectionate bantering. Or it could be a tiny wisp of smoke from an underground fire that's been smoldering for decades and could burst out at any moment. Teri's derision toward me could be par for the course, dismissed by the others as "just how she is," or it could be the deciding vote that would ultimately lead to me being run out of the house, tarred and feathered for some unknown transgression.

Put somebody around their family, and you can no long take any of their words at face value. Too many swirling undercurrents and emotional morasses. As far as I know, there's no good way to navigate family dynamics. Could be the reason I haven't seen most of my extended family for years.

If I hadn't thought I could actually help Reginald get past whatever he had going on, this is the moment I would have tucked my tail between my legs and run. But however unpleasant these people were, Reginald didn't deserve to suffer for it. Mrs. Van Meer had called in a pet behaviorist. In my experience, that's not something people do on a whim, at the first sign of trouble. If she was calling in outside help, something was at a breaking point. Reginald I could manage. But handling things with the human members of his family was a different story.

It was a daunting prospect. In a perfect world, I could have taken Reginald into the backyard, had a long talk about his life, his worries, and his anxieties, worked through whatever was going on with him, brought him back in fully cured, and gotten the hell out of Dodge.

In the real world, I was stuck dealing with these people. One, "good" behavior for a pet is subjective and is based on human expectations. Two, pet behavior is often a reflection of the animal's relationships with the humans in its life. Oh, and three, I guess, is that I can't actually talk to dogs.

Teri had opened her mouth to tell Brett all about the crazy pet whisperer hired by her crazy grandmother, then appeared to think better of it.

"I'll tell you about it later," she said instead. She rolled her eyes, dismissing me. "Sorry, Grandma. We've got a closing this morning. Ali, Will, keep an eye on . . . all of this . . . for me." Her hand gesture was the one you'd use to indicate a particularly foul mess that needed to be cleaned up. She tugged on Brett's arm. He had spotted me on the floor and looked at me with friendly interest but followed her out of the room like an obedient puppy.

After they left, I let the silence stretch for a few moments. Reginald's relaxed breathing filled the room, a small drool spot developing on the leg of my jeans. He really was a very good boy.

"Mrs. Van Meer?" I asked again. "Could you tell me what it is you and Reginald need help with?"

The older woman gazed behind me, toward the wall of windows at the back of the house. "I lost my husband about a month ago," she said after a few seconds.

"Oh, I'm so sorry for your loss." I didn't know what else I could say, so I waited.

"Reginald is grieving. That is, we're all grieving, and Reginald is no exception. He was my husband's dog. But I'm not sure he understands what has happened. He just mopes around. No life or spirit. Not like when Frank was alive. I was hoping you could . . . fix that, in a way I can't—to put his mind at ease. A little, at least."

Well, shit. I was way out of my depth.

Not with Reginald's behavior. Of course his behavior had changed since his beloved owner had passed away. I understood why Mrs. Van Meer was concerned, but it was really no biggie. Hopefully whatever was going with Reginald would have a straightforward solution.

But how was I supposed to have a rational discussion about dog behavior modification tactics with a grieving widow? One who was asking for a dog grief counseling session? While I am widely known within my friend group as one of St. Louis's premiere pet behaviorists, I am not equally renowned for my tact. What if I said the wrong thing and Mrs. Van Meer dissolved into tears?

I patted Reginald's soft head, to cover while I drew a deep, calming breath.

"Dogs do feel grief very deeply," I told her. The words sounded inane, banal, but she wiped an eye. "Could you . . . If it's not too painful, could you tell me a little about his passing?"

Mrs. Van Meer looked a little taken aback, and I felt my cheeks get hot. She probably thought I was trying to satisfy my morbid curiosity. Or worse, that I was overstepping and thought I was in a position to give *her* grief counseling.

"I mean—no, I'm sorry. I don't mean like a play-by-play, or anything like that. I'm sorry. I mean, does Reginald even know that he's dead?" That deep calming breath hadn't helped for long. I tried another. "I'm sorry. I'm having trouble expressing myself right now. Dogs can understand death, but only as a thing they observe. Did your husband pass away at home?

Was it sudden? Was he in the hospital for a long time? Home on hospice? That's all I was trying to ask."

Mrs. Van Meer nodded. "I understand. It was cancer. Fast. Once they found it, I mean. He hadn't been right for months, but Frank hated doctors. Hospitals. Got to a point where he couldn't ignore it any longer. I think he knew." She looked at her hands. "It was too late. Too aggressive. He was admitted that same week. He wanted to be at home, but it was too fast. He never . . . he didn't come home again after that."

Ali moved over to sit beside her grandmother and put an arm around her. "Like she said, we're all grieving," she told me. "It's only been a month since he died."

"How has Reginald's behavior changed since then? How is his grief manifesting itself?"

Neither woman answered, so after a moment Will spoke up in a reassuring, steady baritone. "He wanders around sometimes, looking for Mr. Van Meer. His appetite's not as good as it was, and he's a little more listless."

"Don't forget about the howling!" Mrs. Van Meer prompted him.

Will nodded but took a sip of coffee before continuing. I'm sure his deliberate pace was calming for Ali and Mrs. Van Meer, but I could have done with a fast-forward button. "That was new. Two nights ago, in the middle of the night, he started howling at nothing. It's not like he'd never howled before—he's a hound dog—but this was eerie, mournful. Like he could sense something we couldn't. Like a presence. The sound of it set everyone on edge."

I could imagine the sound. In the right atmosphere, pretty spooky. Even now, with the sun streaming through the wall of windows that formed the back of the house, I felt goosebumps rise on my arms. Something about Will's calm recitation of the facts was creeping me out more than if he'd had a melodramatic reaction. He sounded like the audience-proxy character at the start of a horror movie, who explains why we shouldn't get too worked up about all the strange happenings in town, but you know he's going to get proven wrong, because he's a character in a horror movie.

"It was exactly one month since my husband's passing. Exactly one month to the day. I was in a dead sleep, and Reginald started this horrific howl out of nowhere. It went on and on, and he wouldn't stop for anything." Mrs. Van Meer shivered and pulled an afghan off the back of the sofa and onto her lap. "I finally took him to Frank's study and sat with him there, until we both fell asleep." She shook again, but this time like a dog shaking itself dry. Her voice, which had taken on a hint of a dream-like quality, was firm and matter-of-fact again. "That was Sunday night. The very next day, yesterday, I called you."

I nodded to her, trying my best to look like I was up to the task. I focused on Reginald, whose eyes had almost closed. My heart broke for him. "Well, old man. You heard what they told me. What do you have to say for yourself? You like the study? I bet it smells like Frank—makes you remember when he was here. I don't blame you for wanting to spend time in there."

The next question was obvious. Ninety-nine percent of the time, when there's a change in a pet's behavior, they're responding to some other change. It's either something physical going on inside their bodies, or a disruption of their routine. A simple question most pet owners could answer with a little bit of reflection. But I couldn't make it sound like I was accusing them of neglect. Who knows what family dynamics were swirling around the question of Reginald's care?

"I assume Reginald's daily routine has changed quite a bit in the past month."

Mrs. Van Meer flushed. "He was Frank's dog. We've been doing our best, but . . ."

She showed no sign of continuing. I let my hand trail down to massage one of Reginald's front paws. The nails felt longer than they should. "Was it your husband who used to take him on walks?"

Reginald, who I would not describe as terribly alert, had noticed my use of the word "walk." His eyebrows rose, and without moving his head, he watched me for further promising signs. Dogs are so easy to read. If more people would just pay attention to their animals, they wouldn't have to bring in pet behaviorists in the first place.

My human client hadn't noticed Reginald's reaction. "Yes, Frank walked him every morning. All around the neighborhood. But he has free range of the grounds!" She pointed at the dog door set into a pane of the French doors, and I noted the defensiveness in her voice.

"That's good! But if there's any way to get back to regular walks, that would be better. He must feel like his territory has shrunk."

We were interrupted by the doorbell ringing. I'd forgotten about Pink Sweatshirt Woman, who must have been in the kitchen this whole time, just out of my line of sight. Now she crossed the room and headed for the front of the house. None of the others watched her go, but we all fell silent until she returned with the new arrival.

"Mrs. Van Meer? I'm Patty Reubens? Debbie Schluester told you I was coming by? To consult about the staging? Ten-thirty this morning?" She pulled a phone from her pocket and checked the time, seeing the blank look on Mrs. Van Meer's face.

"Oh, Debbie? Yes, of course. I'd forgotten. I'm so sorry." Mrs. Van Meer stood and shook hands. "Bonnie," she finally addressed Pink Sweatshirt Woman by name, to my relief, "Patty is here to consult about the staging. Patty, I'm in the middle of an earlier appointment, but I'll be with you as soon as I can. Just know I'll trust whatever you and Debbie recommend. Bonnie will take you upstairs to start looking around, and I'll join you shortly."

When Bonnie and the stager had left, Ali leaned forward. "Grandpa always used to give Reginald table scraps, too. We always told him that's bad for dogs, so now nobody's been doing that. But we're right, aren't we?"

I turned my attention back to Reginald. "Did you used to get treats from the table?" As I spoke, I ran my hands over his body, trying to get a feel for his muscle tone and joint health. "Oh, I bet you loved that!

"How old is Reginald?" I asked Mrs. Van Meer.

She referred the question to Ali, who looked toward the ceiling and did a calculation.

"Seventeen," she said. "Grandpa got him my freshman year of high school."

I tried to answer as honestly as I could. "Any vet would tell you that Reginald is better off with no table scraps. Dog food is healthier. But that food was part of his routine with Mr. Van Meer. And continuity is good." I went back to scratching the dog's droopy ears. "I know if I had a seventeen-year-old dog, I would not be worried about the long-term health effects of some table scraps. I'd like to see him happy."

Right on cue, Reginald wagged his tail. Everyone in the room noticed that, and I felt the mood lift.

Before the mood could come crashing back down, sudden inspiration showed me a temporary escape hatch. "When we're done here, if you'd like, I'd be happy to take Reginald on a short walk around the neighborhood. I always like to try to get some time alone with the pet, if I can, to see if he behaves differently away from any other influences." I winced, aware that I was right back to blaming them.

Thankfully, Mrs. Van Meer just nodded. "Of course, of course. I really do appreciate your help. You've given us some things to think about, and I think Reginald is calmer, just from having someone who really understands him." She stood. "It was so nice to meet you. I'll have Bonnie arrange for our next consultation."

I scrambled to my feet but hadn't made it all the way upright before she was gone. Ali looked lost in her own world, maybe thinking about her dead grandfather, but Will smiled at me.

"She can be abrupt sometimes. But she likes you. C'mon, I'll help you find a leash."

Chapter Three

Leaving that fraught living room and striking out with Reginald was a breath of fresh air, figuratively and literally. I'm a seasoned dog walker. Clients in need of a pet behaviorist are few and far between, so I kept my schedule full with dog walking. At this point, I'm not sure which one is the side gig and which one is my bread and butter. For a single consultation, I can charge my pet behaviorist clients easily four times the price of a simple walk, but real money is much better than theoretical money.

On my own in an unfamiliar neighborhood, I let Reginald show me where to go. We weren't likely to stumble into a bad part of town out here in the land of the super-rich. I'd have to be alert for a wayward fox hunt, instead of a drive-by.

We'd gone out the French doors at the back of the house, past the pool, and followed a concrete path toward the driveway. I unlatched a heavy iron gate to let us continue around the side of the house. When we reached the end of the long driveway and stepped onto the asphalt, Reginald turned right without hesitation. As a seventeen-year-old dog who hadn't been walked in at least a month, he didn't move super quickly. He alternated between a nose-to-the-ground stance that looked like something straight out of a bloodhound training manual, and glancing around in all directions, like the first dog to show up at the dog park, searching for all his friends.

"Did you used to see other doggos on your walks, Reggie? I bet if you went at the same time every day, you saw the same dogs most days. I bet your friends have missed you."

Fact: when I'm walking a dog, I keep up a steady stream of conversation, unless I think another pedestrian might be within earshot. Compared to my normal dog-walking routes, the population density here was something akin to Montana in the offseason, so Reginald got to hear my thoughts on a wide variety of topics. He proved a receptive and patient audience, if somewhat distracted.

I hadn't paid a ton of attention to the neighborhood as I drove up to the Van Meers' address that morning. Fixated on house numbers and not much else. But I've found that even with familiar streets, you notice a different set of details walking than driving. Certainly, walking emphasized the distances between the houses here. I was more used to city houses from the early twentieth century, not quite attached row houses, but more like townhouses than suburban-style ranch houses. The houses here boasted enormous lots, with huge expanses of lawn keeping them all spaced out from each other. No sidewalks, so I walked on the street, but with basically no traffic, that was fine.

At the first intersection, Reginald guided me left along the sweeping curve of another identical-looking street. This turned out to be the hopping street. We met a French bulldog with a floppy white flower attached to its collar, being walked by a couple in their sixties, and then a Labradoodle accompanied by two preschool-aged children and a very young woman who I assume was their nanny. The dogs were all very well trained, so engaged in some friendly sniffing, but no barking or leaping. The humans and I exchanged nods, but chose, on this occasion, to forgo sniffing each other.

When we got back to the house about twenty minutes after we'd left, I followed Reginald up the driveway, through the latched gate that led into the back of the property, and along the edge of the pool. From this direction, the size of the property struck me. More than a house, it reminded me of a picturesque European village in the Alps somewhere, with all the buildings clustered in a half circle on the edge of a lake. The scale was all off, of course, because here the buildings all loomed over the pool. There were two garages, one big and one ginormous, and two mini houses. Over the time I would spend with the Van Meers, I'd learn that the family referred to them as the pool house and the carriage house, respectively, but I never did understand their purpose.

When Reginald and I reached the patio, I unclipped his leash, expecting him to head for the French doors we'd used to exit the house; I'd seen a dog door set into one of the panes of glass. But he had other ideas. He turned and trundled farther along the house, following a flagstone pathway.

I retraced my steps back toward the driveway, looking for a trash can for a small green plastic bag off a roll that Will had found stored next to Reginald's leash. The bag had been empty, and now it wasn't, and I needed to throw it away before entering the beautiful house decorated mostly in white.

No trash can along the driveway. If the trash cans weren't along the driveway, the garage was the next place to look, but I had no idea how to apply this rule with more than one garage. Besides, all the garage doors were down, and I didn't see anyone around.

I turned around again and followed the path Reginald had taken, around the perimeter of the house. A six-foot-tall brick wall jutted out from the house and formed the eastern end of the patio. Once the path led me past the wall, the house continued on for what seemed like an impossibly long way, with windows and French doors running the whole length. Glass glittered in the weak sunlight for as far as I could see. Well, almost. The glittering was interrupted by a small furry butt disappearing through a dog door set into one of the French doors, just like I'd seen in the great room.

Reginald had gone where I could not follow, leaving me clutching a bag of poop. I turned around again. On my second time retracing this ground, I saw that what I'd taken for a head-height brick wall was actually two parallel walls, with a four-foot-wide space between them. Here at last were the trashcans, along with the air conditioner, a spigot for a garden hose, and what must have been the pool's filtration system. All the things that made the house work but that couldn't be made decorative enough to be installed in view of the rest of the yard. No labels on either of the wheeled bins, so I crossed my fingers that the green one was for recycling and dropped my plastic bag into the brown one. That felt appropriate.

"Looking for the trash cans?" The shout came from across the yard.

I turned, as if caught in some unspeakable act. A man in an oversized tan canvas coat and paint-splattered navy-blue pants exited the smaller of the two garages. He waved at me across the pool and pointed behind me. "They're right there," he called, helpfully.

"Thanks," I called back. Should I pretend I had something else to throw away, so he could continue in the delusion that he had helped me find the trash cans? By the time I'd formulated the question, the man had moved on with his life, heading toward the back of the property with a pair of massive hedge clippers.

My great commission discharged, I circled back to the patio and let myself through one set of French doors and into the great room.

No one except Reginald greeted me. He must have come through the house from wherever his entrance had led, to wait for me in the huge, deserted room.

Now inside someone else's house, with no idea where they were, I stood rooted to the spot. I could have left, or gone poking around for them, or checked the kitchen for leftover pancakes, or I suppose, sat down on one of the couches that stood six feet to my left, but I wasn't raised in a barn. So instead, I stood stock still just inside the door and resolved not to move until someone came to find me. Thankfully, Bonnie came into the room less than a minute later.

Funny, but I felt much more warmth toward Bonnie, now that I knew her name. When I only knew her as Pink Sweatshirt Woman, I felt some hostility toward her. Now she was

"Bonnie," a fellow human, trying to live her life like the rest of us. I still didn't like her sweatshirt, but now I found it easier to forgive.

"How was the walk?" she asked.

"I think Reginald enjoyed himself," I answered.

"A dog? Enjoyed a walk?" She cocked her head to one side. "Will wonders never cease?"

I never liked the name "Bonnie."

"Ha, ha," I said, very deliberately, so it couldn't be mistaken for laughter. "That's funny."

"Hmm." She pursed her lips and stared at me. Why, oh, why had I tried to out-awkward a woman who was clearly the master of awkward interactions?

"Anyway," I said, more to break the silence than anything, "I think the walk did Reginald good. I've already talked to Mrs. Van Meer about the value of routine and minimizing disruption in cases of loss. Specifically, giving Reginald the same treats Mr. Van Meer used to give him and taking him on a daily walk."

I was about to explain another benefit of the daily walks. They would give Mrs. Van Meer a chance to bond with her late husband's dog. Half an hour alone together every single day, exploring the neighborhood as a team? It would do wonders for their relationship.

Like I said, I was about to explain all that, but Bonnie was already nodding impatiently through the three sentences I managed to get out. As soon as I paused for breath, she jumped in.

"Yes, yes. Ruth told me all that. Therefore, Mrs. Van Meer would like you to walk Reginald daily, as Mr. Van Meer previously did. Your website indicates this is a service you offer.

Do you have a different rate for dog-walking than for your professional consultations?"

I considered briefly. It really wasn't worth my time to drive out here every day to walk a dog. "I do," I said, "but my other dog-walking clients are concentrated in the Tower Grove area, where I live. I'm able to walk multiple dogs at the same time. Besides," I ventured, "wouldn't it be nice for Mrs. Van Meer to walk Reginald herself? Build a relationship, you know?"

Bonnie drew herself up stiffly. "None of us has any idea how much time has been granted us. If Mrs. Van Meer chooses not to spend whatever time she has on this green earth walking a dog, that's her prerogative."

Ok, then. The pink sweatshirt and the white sneakers were a blind. She was the ominous butler in the gothic horror film. If and when they got around to making a biopic of Mrs. Van Meer, they'd probably try to cast Vincent Price as the Bonnie character.

"However," she added, "I completely understand that we're away from your normal route."

Phew. My shoulders relaxed. I'd worried she was going to try to guilt me into adding Reginald into my schedule. I'm a sucker for a good animal-based guilt trip.

"Therefore Mrs. Van Meer will pay your regular consultation rate for a daily walk. We'll see you tomorrow. The same time?"

I'd been sandbagged. Instead of politely declining, Bonnie mistook my words for haggling. Now it was taken for granted that I'd accepted. But, of course, I would. With the amount of money they were offering for a simple walk, I would have commuted out here by unicycle in a blizzard.

"That works for me," I replied, trying to sound nonchalant.

The consultation had gone well. Or at least, not terribly. I'd given my opinion of Reginald and had inadvertently turned it into a lucrative dog-walking gig. And I'd only made a handful of glaring conversational blunders.

Of course, and I cannot stress this enough, at that point, no one had died yet.

Chapter Four

The rest of that week flew by. In addition to my regular dog-walking clients, I now had Reginald to worry about. A large order had come in through my freelance calligraphy business, from a bride who wanted not only hand-addressed envelopes for her invitations, but the invitations themselves to be hand-lettered. A well-paying job, but a time-consuming one. A couple of small orders came through for the catnip-filled cat toys I sold online, but I was able to fulfill them with existing stock. I don't think I touched my sewing machine once that week. Jai was busier than normal in the evenings. He coached a collegiate mock trial team, and they crammed in last minute practices in the week running up to a tournament. That weekend they would be in Kansas City, at one of the universities there.

On Thursday, two days after my initial consultation, I was walking Reginald along his regular route, enjoying a slightly warmer day. I'd left my jacket in the car. We hadn't seen any other pedestrians, although a few cars, invariably shiny and expensive, had driven past. Eventually, as we turned onto a short lane leading along the local country club, a jogger came from the opposite direction. She wore black shorts and a black top and had a black phone strapped to her upper arm. The only pop of color came from her neon pink sneakers. Although the road was plenty wide here, I shuffled a little to the side and choked up on Reginald's leash, clear communication to the jogger that we'd stay out of her way.

Instead, she changed her course and headed right toward us without slowing down. As she neared, I was able to see her face more clearly, red with exertion and shiny with sweat. It was Mrs. Van Meer's older granddaughter, Teri.

"Hey, dog whisperer!" she shouted as she came up to us. Turns out, maybe her face wasn't red just with exertion. The anger in her tone was unmistakable. I looked around as she jabbed a finger into my chest. We were alone.

"You're just like all the other vultures, hovering around now that Grandpa died. My grandmother is a grieving widow, not your next payday."

I was blanking on a way to get away from this onslaught. Obviously she could outrun me. Then my knight in shining armor appeared.

No, really.

A shiny silver pickup truck had turned onto the street. It picked up speed as it came toward us and skidded to a halt with its bumper just inches from Teri. In ordinary circumstances, I wouldn't welcome a jacked-up truck with oversized tires on chromed-out rims and an intentionally noisy exhaust system hurtling at me, but at least it was a witness. It really felt like Teri might attack me otherwise.

The tinted driver's-side window rolled down, and I recognized Brett, the lawyer I'd last seen at Teri's side, in the driver's seat.

"Everything OK here, Teri?" he called through the open window, a little hesitantly. Teri didn't acknowledge his presence. She jabbed her finger in my chest again. "You take advantage of my Grandma, I come after you! Got it?"

"OK. That's probably enough of that," Brett said, climbing down from the truck. He took Teri's arm and guided her away from me.

I didn't stick around to see what happened next. Reginald and I did an about-face and headed straight back to the house. Presumably this was part of Teri's regular route for her morning runs. Reginald and I would pick a different path for our walks. No need to risk a repeat of that confrontation. The encounter with Teri might explain why I felt caught off guard when I got back to the house and Teri's sister, Ali, almost immediately invited me to a party.

"It's not a formal thing. More like a barbecue. All our friends and everybody in the neighborhood, they all just know to stop by on Sunday nights during football season." She and Will met me as they crossed the backyard, sweaty and carrying tennis rackets. I craned my neck as unobtrusively as I could manage. Did they have a tennis court back there somewhere? How big was this place?

Will nodded in agreement. "It's chill. Bring somebody, if you want to." He pointed toward the patio. "We cook a bunch of food and have the primetime game playing. The Chiefs this week, of course. But if you're not into football, you can still come. Plenty of people just hang out."

A feeling akin to whiplash hit me, dealing with Teri and then Ali in such quick succession. I tried to smile. "Thank you so much. I'd better not."

"Oh, you should!" Ali clapped her hands. "I always think 'the more, the merrier.' Besides, Reginald would be so happy to see you!"

A low blow. I've told you about my susceptibility to animal-based guilt-trips.

"I wouldn't want to intrude." I could tell the usual polite refusals weren't going to work here, so I got a little more specific. "I don't think Teri would want me there."

Ali frowned quickly, but Will nodded. "Don't worry about her," he said. "She'll relax eventually. She's protective of her grandmother."

"I'll think about it."

Ali clapped again, and I grinned. Her enthusiasm was contagious. And, while I really did prefer to avoid Teri, the invitation tempted me. Jai would be out of town until stupidly late Sunday night. The game would be a good one, between two teams with playoff hopes. I'd be watching it one way or the other, so why choose to watch it alone in our apartment? And I couldn't imagine what a house party might be like among the filthy rich. Would there be ice sculptures? I thought it unlikely, but there was only one way to be 100 percent sure.

The question of the party came up again the very next day, on Friday. I'd finished walking Reginald, successfully avoided Teri, disposed of what needed to be disposed of, and put away his leash. On my way down the driveway toward my car, Brett came running after me.

"Nikki! Hey, Nikki, wait up a minute!"

I stopped to wait for him, looking behind him for Teri to emerge around the side of the house. But he was alone.

"Hey, I heard that Ali and Will invited you for Sunday night."

It was a statement, both in content and inflection, but he stood waiting for an answer. After a few seconds, I nodded.

He nodded, too. "Good. You should come."

I laughed. I'd recovered from the sting of Teri's hostility but didn't want to invite another onslaught. "Sounds fun, but I know when I'm not welcome."

"I'm sorry about Teri. She'll come around."

This felt overly optimistic. I didn't say anything, but Brett seemed to read my mind.

"You have to understand. The second word got out that Frank—that's Mr. Van Meer—had died, all kinds of people have come out of the woodwork. Some guy from the local classic car club says he and Frank had a handshake agreement for him to buy Frank's Studebaker for, like, a quarter of its value. His Elk Lodge is after Ruth to honor some pledge he supposedly made to fund a scholarship. A shady tuckpointing place one of the neighbors used a year ago has called seven times, claiming they'd given Frank a quote, and he was just about to sign the contract, and if she doesn't act on it right away, the house is going to crumble away to nothing. Even the country club is telling her that the dues for the year are outstanding, and we're pretty sure those were paid up last spring. It's been nonstop. A real nightmare for me and Ruth to sort through. Some of the claims are probably legit, so we can't ignore anything."

I nodded slowly, empathizing with the pressure all this must be putting on Mrs. Van Meer, but not really sure what it had to do with me.

"So when Ruth announced out of the blue that she was hiring some dog whisperer to come in for private consultations, Teri figured you were selling bunk services to a vulnerable widow." He held up a hand to stop my protest. "But that's coming from a place of grief and stress, not logic, so there's no point in trying to talk her out of it. Give it time. Really, she'll warm up to you. I think the party might be the perfect opportunity for her to get to know you. Low key, low stakes, you know."

"Yeah, or she'll throw a drink in my face and then have me thrown off the property."

Brett took a step backward, almost as though I had slapped him. "Teri? Oh, no. You clearly don't know her at all. The last thing she'd ever want to do is cause a scene." He cocked his head to one side, considering. "Not in front of people, anyway. Family's different, of course. You're much safer with an audience." He grinned. "Not 'safer,' I didn't mean that. Teri's got a temper, but she's also got great self-control. I've known her since we were kids. Trust me, a relaxed party atmosphere is exactly right for letting her get to know you."

I wondered again about their relationship. When we'd first met, I'd guessed business partners, and then at some point I'd started to assume they were romantically involved. But something about the way Brett had said "I've known her since we were kids" didn't feel right for a romantic relationship. Whatever the truth, I did get the feeling that Brett knew and understood her well. Maybe he was right.

Sunday morning, I remained officially undecided but leaned toward attending the party. Jai had left for the tournament in Kansas City on Friday afternoon and could be gone until sometime around midnight. If things went really badly, their team might get eliminated early and leave Sunday afternoon. But unfortunately, this crop of kids was really hardworking and talented, so they'd probably be stuck there til the bitter end.

Despite the sunny skies, when I arrived at the Van Meer house for Reginald's daily walk, temperatures hovered in the mid-forties, and my weather app said they would fall rapidly as the day went on, ending up below freezing and with a chance of sleet in the overnight hours.

So, I was shocked to find the pool in use. Mrs. Van Meer stood in chest-deep water, mimicking the motions of a woman with a blond ponytail. I'd never seen anyone doing water aerobics before. Their movements reminded me of a group of elderly men and women who meet in the park near me to practice Tai Chi. Tai Chi with foam noodles.

As I crossed the patio, Mrs. Van Meer noticed me and waved. The blond woman broke off her string of encouraging words and turned around to watch me cross the patio.

"Good morning, Nikki!" called Mrs. Van Meer. "Reginald's looking forward to his walk!"

I waved and smiled and headed into the house. Reginald perked up as soon as I appeared at the door, and he escorted me as I grabbed the leash, pressing his body against my legs with such enthusiasm I almost fell over a couple of times.

I waved to Mrs. Van Meer again as we passed the pool. Rich people were so weird. She paid me to walk her dog and paid the woman with the blond ponytail to lead her in water aerobics. She could kill two birds with one stone and save a heck of a lot of money if she'd just walk her own damn dog. But that was none of my business.

Almost out of the yard, I heard her call out to me again. I stopped and turned back toward the pool. She glided to the edge with a strange combination of swimming and walking. She lifted herself a few inches for conversation by planting her elbows on the concrete lip of the pool. Almost immediately, she dropped back down, at this time of year, better to keep as much skin as possible submerged in the heated water.

"You're coming to the kids' party tonight!"

I nodded and decided that I'd made up my mind. "Yes, ma'am. Ali invited me."

"I'm so glad you're all getting along!" She waved again and returned to her personal trainer.

Maybe a more assertive person would have corrected her, and explained that "all" wasn't exactly right, given Teri's hostility. How childish would that sound? "Teri doesn't like me." I couldn't even think of a way to word it that didn't sound whiny. But it made me feel better to know that, as the others warmed up to me, Teri would find herself more and more in the minority. She'd have to give up and like me, eventually.

Chapter Five

I was in a crappy mood when I turned up for the party Sunday night. Midafternoon, Jai had called to warn me that they might not make it back at all that night. His kids had breezed into the final round of the tournament, and the weather forecast for the Kansas City region predicted freezing rain to start about an hour before the trophies would be handed out. Now, a rational person, looking at the situation from the outside, might expect the tournament organizers to end things early, to give their guests a chance to get home safely. There did not appear to be many rational people at the helm that weekend. If the weather reports were accurate, they'd extend their hotel stays and drive back Monday morning.

Cars stood everywhere around the Van Meer house. I ended up parking pretty far up the street. The equivalent of six or seven doors down, in my neighborhood, but here I was barely to a low hedge that marked the property line between the Van Meers and their closest neighbors.

As I hiked toward the house, I regretted not bringing someone along with me. Sure, Jai wasn't available, but I could have called someone. Anyone. A big enough group converged on the Van Meer place that I could have shown up with a whole entourage in tow, and no one would have batted an eye. Now I had no buffer. I would have to talk to the Van Meers, virtual strangers to me, by myself. Or I would have to talk to people I had only met for the first time tonight—literal strangers.

In that instant, the smell of the food hit me. I could tough it out. I resolved to sit quietly and watch the football game and stuff my face. If my mouth was full, wouldn't I be excused from conversation anyway?

I followed a small knot of people up the driveway and rounded the back of the house. The party was in full swing, although I'd made it with plenty of time before kick-off. A massive, but somewhat blurry, version of the pregame coverage was being projected on the side of one of the garages. Closer to the house, three big-screen TVs showed the same footage, much more sharply, their sound routed through hidden speakers that blanketed the backyard with coverage.

Brett and Will manned the grill, and a long table behind them stood ready to receive the food. The grill, bigger than any I'd ever seen in person, was the centerpiece of an entire elaborate outdoor kitchen. I hadn't really noticed it before, presumably because it was normally shrouded in the matte black grill cover now flung over the top of the six-foot tall brick wall behind the grill. The incredible smells were so mouth-wateringly powerful I was tempted to stand between the grill and the food table, to intercept anything and everything coming off the flames.

Instead, I pulled a bottle from the six-pack I'd brought and dropped off the remainder in an open cooler already filled with ice and drinks, then drifted toward one of the six or seven patio heaters arrayed around the space. It hadn't gotten as cold as predicted, but it wouldn't have been possible to spend much time at all outside without the tall, remarkably effective gas heaters. As it was, they made things not just bearable, but comfortable. Leaning over the grill, Brett's face flushed red with heat, both he and Will were sweating.

I didn't recognize any of the other guests. They mingled in pretty distinct groups, and I got the sense they were regulars at these watch parties. Was it too early to hover near the food table? Probably. I didn't see anyone else eating yet. I sat on the end of a red-cushioned lounge chair near one of the TVs and watched the pregame coverage with about half of my attention. Kansas City's all-star left tackle was questionable to play after a hamstring injury two weeks ago, and the five commentators did their best trying to guess whether he would make it onto the field and what effect that might have on the game.

Ali joined me after I had only been sitting alone for a minute or two. Her oversized Chiefs sweatshirt hid her pregnant belly, but she seemed to be suffering more tonight than any other time I'd seen her. She groaned and laid a hand on her stomach as she maneuvered into a seat on the end of the chaise lounge next to me.

"I'm so glad you came, Nikki! Brett told me he thought he'd talked you into it. Getting people to show up the first time is always the hard part. After that, they always seem to come back." She leaned in. "I doubt many of these people are even football fans. We always get at least a couple people wandering into the yard the week before the season opener, and a few years ago, one really confused guy showed up the week after the Super Bowl. I don't think he ever understood why there wasn't a crowd here."

Brett came over to join us, beer in hand, and plopped down next to Ali, flinging an arm around her shoulders. She promptly shrugged it off, scooted to one side, and rolled her eyes at me. I decided maybe the flush in Brett's cheeks hadn't just been from the heat of the grill. If he was noticeably drunk before kickoff, it was either going to be a very long or a very short night for him, depending on how well he could pace himself. I resolved to keep my distance whenever possible. A guy who's handsy with an engaged, pregnant woman gave me very clear red flags.

"Hey! It's the dog girl! What's your name, again?" he asked, more loudly than necessary, I thought.

Ali agreed with me. She looked around, then patted him on the knee. "I don't think you know that you're yelling. Her name is Nikki, and we're talking about football. What's your prediction for the game?"

He drew a deep breath, ready to dispense wisdom. "Well, it's going to be a battle, that's for sure. Real smashmouth football. Whichever team can stay ahead of the chains is going to come out ahead. But I'm expecting them to air it out. Watch for some chunk plays, especially in the secondary. And lots of RPO. The Chiefs' front four have been a nightmare for dropback offenses all year, so I'm watching for a sack-fumble." He sucked in air, and I thought he was finished, but then his brain offered up one more tidbit. "And special teams!" he yelled, stabbing a finger into the air.

Ali patted his knee again. "Very good. We'll have to wait and see, but I bet you're right. Now, go back and help Will. You've left him all alone over there."

Brett nodded to himself a few times, then rose carefully and wandered back toward the grill.

After he was out of earshot I turned to Ali. "You know that was all nonsense, right? He sounded like the AI version of a color commentator."

She grinned. "Yeah. One of the great things about Brett is that he's the world's best bullshitter. You ask him about any topic on earth, and you'll never get him to admit he doesn't know anything about it. I've never even caught him hesitating. He just launches in, sounding exactly as authoritative as if you'd asked him what he ate for breakfast that morning. It's fun. Give it a try some time."

"Is it safe for him to be near the grill? He seems a little out of it."

Ali frowned. "Yeah, Brett's gotten pretty drunk at these the last few weeks. Last week, it really sucked, because Kevin was out of town, so it was just us setting up and cleaning up, and Brett was basically useless. I don't know what's going on with him. He's not usually like this."

"Who's Kevin?"

"You haven't met Kevin?" Ali looked surprised. "But he's always around." She swiveled her head as if she wanted to pick him out in the crowd. "Oh, well, not right now. But he's always around. Surely, you've seen him."

I shook my head, and tried to get her back on topic, worrying about Brett being so close to fire.

Ali laughed when I told her my concern. "Will can keep an eye on him. Will's worked in restaurants his whole life. If he couldn't keep a handle on stoned or drunk line cooks, he wouldn't have lasted very long."

"Oh? Where's he working now?" I sipped my beer, and then we both directed our attention to the nearest TV screen for the kickoff. A touchback. We resumed our conversation.

"He owns a couple of places in The Grove—The Barnhouse and Afterhours—and Oil & Vinegar in Clayton."

I took a moment to rearrange my thinking. In my world, if someone said they "worked in restaurants," they were a waiter, or a host, or a bartender, or a cook, or a dishwasher, or a busser. Apparently, in this world, "working in restaurants" could also mean owning multiple restaurants. Two of the restaurants Ali named were fine dining establishments, with prices to match. I'd never been to Afterhours, but I knew it was in the same block as a much less upscale bar where I sometimes picked up bartending shifts. I felt like I'd heard about it recently, like one of my friends had mentioned going there, or I'd seen a posting for an event there, or something.

Ali leaned over to me, speaking in a low voice. "Hey, you seem really nice. I want to warn you." She looked around again. "Teri thinks the whole idea of a 'pet behaviorist' is bunk. She thinks you're trying to bilk Grandma."

This wasn't news to me, since, you know, Teri had said exactly that to me herself, but I appreciated Ali giving me the heads up. If nothing else, it was a good indication that she didn't agree with her sister. I nodded a couple of times, trying to decide how to frame my response. Ali was looking at me, expecting something from me. She hadn't asked a question, but I think she needed to hear me deny the allegation.

"Brett said the same thing. I don't know . . . you guys know that *she* called *me*, right? I don't go around cold calling widows or anything."

Ali patted my knee. “I know. I wasn’t accusing you. I just wanted to warn you. But even Teri would have to admit that Reginald has been happier since you’ve been around.” Then her smiled dropped, and she shuddered slightly. “At least we haven’t had a repeat of that one middle-of-the-night howling session. Thank god. That was really creepy. Poor Reg.”

I tried to imagine what that had sounded like. Late at night, the house hushed, and one grieving hound dog pouring out his desolation and loneliness. It had been a night just like this one. Despite the warmth pumping from the nearby heater, I shuddered.

Chapter Six

The first possession was a three-and-out, and the ensuing punt another touchback. A mix of rain and sleet and ice poured down at the stadium, and the players on the bench wore giant hooded coats that looked more like tents than jackets. No way we'd see a riveting game of football, after all. I excused myself, wanting to check out the food, and Ali stood, too.

"I should probably go relieve Will. He has the patience of a saint, but nobody should have to deal with drunk Brett for too long."

I trailed her toward the grill, where a couple of things had made it to the food table, but no one else was helping themselves yet. Fine. If they could hold out, so could I. Probably.

Nobody paid any attention to me, which was fine. I sipped my beer, standing within the warm bubble created by one of the tall patio heaters, and stared into the pool. The near side of the pool looked like any other pool, with wide cement steps leading down into the water, but the far side was styled like a natural grotto, with artistically arranged rocks creating miniature waterfalls. The underwater lighting changed color gradually, cycling slowly through blue, green, purple, and red. It must be fantastically expensive to keep your pool open throughout the winter, unless you live somewhere tropical. Freezing rain poured down four hours west of here, and I was standing poolside, watching tendrils of steam curl off the rippling water. Thank god these people had a recycling bin, otherwise I might have judged them for how stupidly wasteful and bad for the planet it was to heat a pool this time of year.

I hadn't heard from Jai yet with a final decision about whether they were driving back tonight. Surely, they weren't going to try it.

I texted him. *Watching the Chiefs game. Sleet looks miserable. Be safe.*

As I waited for an answer, I noticed movement at the far side of the pool. Surely rich people don't have to worry about raccoons, the way we peasants do! But no, it was Reginald, his tail wagging as he waddled toward the back of the property. With no human interaction to keep me, I wandered after him. Jai will tell you, if you ever lose track of me at a party, you'll find me chilling with the host's pets.

Reginald led me around to the backside of the smaller of the two garages on the property. One door stood open, light spilling out of it. With the garage between us and the party, the sounds from the TVs and the smells from the grill had faded. They'd been replaced by the sounds of a first-person shooter game, and the strong smell of cheap weed, both coming from inside the garage. Before I'd given myself even a second to contemplate the situation, I trotted inside, right on Reginald's heels.

I had stumbled into the lair of the handyman, whom I'd seen from a distance a couple of times but never spoken to. He wore the same paint-splattered clothes as when I'd last seen him, and was just as badly in need of a shave. His face had a weather-beaten look that made it impossible to tell whether he was in his early forties or late fifties. He sat on a folding chair, playing his game on an old, boxy TV set on the floor. When Reginald trundled in, he glanced over and then did a double take when he saw me.

"Oh!" He dropped his controller without pausing, almost instantly dying in a splatter of blood that covered the screen. "Shit."

"I'm sorry!" I cringed, feeling as though I'd been seated in the audience and, right in the middle of the play, I'd stood up and walked backstage to have a look around. "I was following Reginald. I didn't mean to interrupt. Sorry!"

As I turned to leave, he waved a hand to another chair. "Fuck it. Want a hit?" He held out the tiniest roach I'd ever seen.

I shook my head, holding up my beer, in some kind of feeble display of my own vices. But I did sit down.

"Reg comes by every time they have one of these shindigs. He's after my treats." As he spoke, he stood up and fished around in one of the cabinets mounted over a pristine work-bench. He pulled out a Tupperware container, opening it awkwardly one-handed, to avoid putting pressure on a bandage around his left palm. Reginald watched his every move, standing at full attention. Well, as much at attention as a droopy hound can manage.

"Are you going to the party?" I couldn't think of what else to ask.

"Ha! Not me! They just need me to help with set-up and tear-down. It's not worth it to drive home for a few hours just to turn around and drive right back." He doled out a small handful of treats, and Reginald went to work, snuffling and crunching with noisy satisfaction.

"And they won't let you come to the party?"

"Ha! Wouldn't want to. Spend time with those people when I don't have to? No thanks." He nodded to the TV. "I'm just fine in here. But I guess you're all chummy with them now."

Chummy? I opened my mouth to reply and closed it again. I guess he'd seen me around as the dogwalker and knew I didn't really belong at the party, either. "Will invited me."

He nodded. "Will's OK." Then his mood turned, and he frowned at the ground. "The rest of them can fall in the pool and drown, far as I care. We'd all be better off."

I was no stranger to people complaining about their bosses, and it's not like I knew any of them well enough to feel like I needed to jump to their defense. I took a swig of my beer and nodded. "I think Teri hates me, but Mrs. Van Meer's OK."

He stared at me. "Teri's the only decent one out of all of them. She loves this house. The others can't wait to get rid of it. Mr. VM was only in the ground a week before his poor grieving widow was talking about selling and moving into a condo. No concern about anybody else! Do you think anybody needs a landscaper when they've moved into a condo? Hell no! I'd be out on my ass, after all I've done. Don't care about anybody else."

"You're a landscaper? I wasn't sure what you did around here." I didn't know how to address his anger, so I ignored it.

"I do everything around here! I was gone for one week, one lousy week, and the whole place went to hell. Annual hunting trip, you know, with some buddies. Just got back this week, and I've been working my ass off all week to try and catch up, because nobody did anything while I was gone." He waved his bandaged hand in the air. "And this doesn't make it any easier! But they all count on me for everything. When they need something, it's, 'Oh, Kevin, could you please' and, 'Oh, Kevin would you please,' but when they're thinking of selling the whole thing, does anybody think about Kevin? Ha!"

My conversation with Ali suddenly made sense. This was Kevin, who was always around, but whom I hadn't officially met. I felt like I'd solved a riddle.

Kevin pulled an old Altoids tin from his shirt pocket and extracted a fresh joint, lighting it with a bright green Bic. Seemed like a good idea. He needed something to calm down. But the rant kept going.

"Even Teri, though! It's not like she's against selling out of concern for my livelihood. Don't think that for a second! She's just pissed because she thought she'd get the house when her grandparents croaked. She thought she had it in the bag." He looked up at me for the first time since starting on this topic. "Do you want to know the sad thing? These people've got no idea how to fight. My family, your family, it'd be a knock-down, drag-out fight in the front yard, or at least good old-fashioned screaming in the other person's face. Everybody'd know where everybody stood, and they'd get it out of their systems. These people, they fight by being a little colder, or a little more polite, or just a remark here or there, and it'd make me lose my mind if I was part of it."

I didn't hear the end of his rant, shaken. This guy had me pegged. Kevin the landscaper had me pegged. He had only known me for five minutes, and he was coming out with things like "my family, your family." He must have been able to smell my South City background, hear a trace of it in my accent. Because he was right. That was exactly the kind of the family I came from. As he said the words "knock-down, drag-out fight in the front yard," I remembered a specific Fourth of July when I was eight or nine. It fit his description perfectly.

My entire life since my late teens had been a more or less constant effort to distance myself from the type of life I'd grown up with. I still talked to a handful of people in my family, but most of the others would only drag me back into those circles, those situations I'd worked so hard to get away from.

Reginald had finished his treats and snuffled his way across the garage, making sure he hadn't missed any. The two old cars behind us both had an air of disuse, although clean and in good repair. I knew without having to be told that these were Mr. Van Meer's cars, and likely they'd be sold before being driven again. Reginald focused on a small gray ball lying partly under one of the old cars, but he abandoned it after a short investigation revealed that it was not a treat. He located a spare tire leaning against the far wall and decided it was a giant chew toy, even though he couldn't really get his mouth around it. I watched as he tried from multiple angles, letting the silence between me and Kevin stretch. Finally, Reginald gave up and we both headed back to the main house. I heard Kevin's game start back up as we left. Probably relieved to be rid of me.

Chapter Seven

The food was ready. Oh, my god, was the food ready. You're probably picturing hamburgers and hot dogs. But this was so much classier. Grilled artichoke and shrimp skewers, garnished with lemon wedges sporting their own perfect-looking grill marks. A pile of steaks surrounded by ramekins filled with an array of compound butters to suit individual tastes. Instead of the potato chips from a more pedestrian menu, partygoers grabbed chunks of twice-baked sweet potatoes, crispy and salty on the outside, creamy and sweet on the inside. Several people took eager bites and then blew ferociously on the rest of their portion, so I took their cue and was able to avoid burning the roof of my mouth.

I grabbed another beer, piled my plate high, and chose a seat with an end table next to it. Steak is delicious, but not particularly manageable with a plate balanced on your knees. Teri sat in the next seat over, her phone to her ear and her eyes on the TV screen. I nodded politely at her when she glanced over, but didn't get any response.

The game was still scoreless, but the Chiefs had managed to get something of a run game going, so they now strung together a couple of first downs before having to punt. Oh, wait. That's not fair. I forgot a missed field goal in there somewhere, set up by a bad punt.

"The shrimp is delicious," I said to Teri, who'd put down her phone.

She nodded but didn't look my way.

I tried again. "Thank you so much for having me."

This time, I got more of a reaction. She sighed deeply and turned to face me. "Look. I'm not trying to be rude. Ali tried telling me earlier how much better Reginald is since Grandma hired you. But that doesn't prove anything. What was your advice? Give him more attention? Try to get back into the routines he had with Grandpa? Daily walks? That's not anything she needed to hire somebody for. That's not anything you need an expert for. That's just common sense."

I squinted at her, momentarily unsure how to respond. If we'd had this exchange right at the beginning of the party, I might have defended my methods, trying to dress the whole thing up with some jargon about animal behavior. But my second beer had given me a little courage. And I had Ali in my corner, so it's not like Teri could pretend to be speaking for the whole family.

"Right. It's all common sense. I completely agree with you."

Teri froze, her beer bottle halfway to her mouth.

I pressed on. "So do you mind telling me why the hell none of you did anything to help Reginald until I came in and told you to? You saw a grieving dog and shrugged your shoulders and did nothing? And I'm the bad guy? Really?"

Teri's face flushed. "We've had a lot to deal with," she said, the steel gone from her voice.

"I know. I understand, really I do." I let my tone relax, too. "And that's why it's helpful to get outside help once in a while. Because nobody can take care of everything. You've got Brett to help with the legal stuff. You've got that real estate agent lady to help with the house. You've got me to help with Reginald."

With impeccable timing, Reginald trotted over, hearing his named bandied around. He really was a good boy. His long ears swung like pendulums as he came. He ignored Teri and stared up at me. I slid out of my chair and rubbed his cheeks and ears with both hands.

"Hello, old man. You enjoying the party?"

Reginald's tongue lolled out of one side of his mouth, and I swear he smiled at me. He was a complete sucker for ear scritches.

Part of me wanted to focus completely on Reginald and forget that Teri existed, but I also thought she and I were making progress, and I didn't want to lose the momentum. Reginald gave me an idea for a conversational gambit.

"What's the plan for Reginald? I mean, long-term, if your grandmother sells the house and moves into a condo?"

Teri gave no sign that she'd heard me, staring into her plate. She crammed an enormous bite of steak into her mouth and chewed ferociously, washing it down with a swig of beer.

I gave Reginald a last scratch and pulled my leg out from under his head. He got back to his feet and wandered toward the house, and I climbed back up into my chair.

"Ali told you about the house?" She was still looking at her plate, not at me. Her tone was back to its normal stridency, but somehow I sensed that I was no longer the target of her displeasure.

Sure, that sounded better than admitting I'd been gossiping with the disgruntled landscaper. These kinds of people don't like being reminded that the help talk behind their backs.

She ate another couple of bites of steak before continuing. Either buying herself some time to collect her thoughts, or maybe she was just really hungry. I let her eat in silence and started watching the game. They went into an injury timeout and the broadcast cut to commercials.

When Teri spoke, her voice was even, as though she was recounting facts of no personal interest to herself. "Ever since our grandfather passed away, Grandma's been talking about selling this house. She owns a condo in Clayton, and her plan is to downsize and move in there." She stopped briefly, and I glanced over, expecting to see someone wrestling with extreme anger. Instead, amusement played on her face. "When I say it out loud to someone, it sounds like the rational thing to do, the only sensible thing to do. But I can't help feeling like this house is being sold out from under me. Like I have some right to it, which of course I don't, except that I consider it home."

"Did you grow up in this house?" If I could just keep her talking, maybe I could find some common ground to convince her that I wasn't the enemy.

"Mostly."

She'd clearly intended it as a complete answer, but you know, I've found you can sometimes get to the really fascinating stuff by pushing past those kinds of soft conversational barriers.

"Oh?"

I thought for sure she wasn't going to answer. She finished her steak and laid her knife and fork on the plate. She readjusted herself in her chair, leaning back, and allowing herself to relax.

"Since I was six or so. Our mother's always been in the Foreign Service, and she took Ali and me with her when we were little. We spent three years in Norway, a year in Greece, and some time in Bolivia, but I don't remember anything about Bolivia. When we were a little older, she wanted us raised in the US, so she dropped us off here."

"Oh, wow. That's so cool! What about your father?"

She shrugged. "Divorced."

I nodded. "Mine, too." Not a rock-solid connection upon which I could forge a relationship with her. I mean, who doesn't have divorced parents? Now, if my mother had been the ambassador to Norway, then we'd be in business. She'd probably have had to get a passport first, though. But I did think Teri was softening, just a little.

"You said you don't remember anything about Bolivia. Does that mean you do remember Greece and Norway? I've never been out of the country."

She smiled then, suddenly and quickly. "My strongest memory from back then is when we got to meet the King of Norway. I don't remember meeting him, but I remember all the fuss about getting ready, and the excitement, and my new dress, and learning how to curtsy."

Now, in the moment, I was 100 percent sure she was making things up to mock me. I Googled it later, and Norway really does have a king. Who knew? The thought had never crossed my mind before. I still have no idea if Teri really met him, but I don't have any concrete reason to believe she lied to me.

Teri opened her mouth, maybe to make up a story about dueling the Archbishop of Greece. But she changed the subject. "Oh, why can't she just leave him alone?"

I turned in my seat to follow her gaze. Brett and Ali stood at the grill. As we watched, Ali took a pair of tongs out of Brett's hands, turning something that had probably been on the verge of burning. Will was nowhere to be seen. Brett put an arm around Ali's shoulder again, maybe just to steady his balance.

"I talked to him earlier. He seemed pretty hammered."

She snorted. "He hasn't had so much that he can't stand on his own two feet. My sweet little sister just wants an excuse."

It sounded like she was intending to say more, but she stopped herself and turned to the TV, where we both watched an incomplete pass bounce harmlessly to the turf and kick up a spray of water.

I wanted to keep the conversation going, on whatever subject. I needed to get Teri to like me. Well, I guess I didn't *need* her to like me, but things would be so much more comfortable if she weren't so hostile. And besides, everybody likes me. I'm likable, dammit.

I pointed to Ali with my beer bottle. "When's she due?"

Teri sighed and rubbed her temples. "End of January. Then she and Will are hoping to move into the new house by April, then get married in September. They've got all the elements of the traditional life lined up—marriage, house, baby—but they've screwed up the order."

I shrugged. "I don't know if the 'traditional' order is normal anymore. Does Will's family have a problem with it? Or your grandmother?"

She let out a loud, single burst of laughter, then took a huge swig of beer. "That's not Grandma's problem with it." She stood from her chair without looking at me and stalked off.

I was left sitting alone, my mind casting around for other reasons for objecting to Ali's relationship with Will. Was Teri implying that Mrs. Van Meer was racist? Maybe old Mrs. Van Meer wasn't comfortable with her little white granddaughter having a child with and marrying a Black man? Maybe my mind leaped to that option because of my experience with Jai's family. His parents were supportive, but some of his extended family didn't try to hide the fact they thought he should have settled down with a nice Indian girl.

But there were other possibilities. Maybe Mrs. Van Meer's objection was a class thing? I didn't know anything about Will's background. Ali had said he'd always worked in restaurants, and that he owned restaurants. Conceivably, he could have a rags-to-riches story, where he started as a dishwasher and worked his way up to ownership.

All assuming Mrs. Van Meer actually objected to their relationship. Whatever it was, it couldn't be that serious, because she'd let Will move in at some point. Maybe I'd misunderstood Teri.

My phone buzzed with a text from Jai. I read it and groaned with disappointment. The sleet wasn't letting up, so they'd decided to stay in Kansas City for another night and drive back tomorrow. He would have told me sooner, but he'd been down in the lobby of the hotel, dealing with the front desk. Driving back in sleet would have been a stupid decision, but one I'd been selfishly hoping for. I could cope with Jai being away. Jai being away longer than scheduled left me off-balance.

Probably the right decision, I replied. *I'm watching the Chiefs game, and the weather looks awful.*

Some of us are watching, too. Miserable game.

Complete waste of time.

Was it supposed to be a good game? Jai didn't really follow football the way I did.

Yeah, but nobody can get anything going in this weather.

He didn't reply for a while, probably talking to some of the students. I imagined them, with the happy energy leftover from winning the tournament, and then the restlessness from being stuck in their hotel, not able to get on the road and home to their own beds. I wished I was watching the game with them. Even a terrible game would be fun with people in such giddy moods. Instead, I was at a swanky but low-energy party with people I barely knew, who kept hinting at drama and gossip that didn't interest me.

Drive safe tomorrow, I told Jai.

He sent me a thumbs up. I stuck my phone back in my pocket and stood up to get a soda. Time to leave soon.

Will stood at the cooler, fishing around for a drink. "Hey, are you OK? You look a little down." He looked at me with genuine concern.

I smiled, wanting to reassure him. "Yeah, I'm fine. My husband's been in Kansas City all weekend, and they've decided not to make the drive back tonight because of the weather."

He nodded. "That sucks. I don't blame him, though. Seventy's a bitch when it gets icy. A work conference? Or he's at the game?"

"If they'd gone to this game, I bet they'd be driving back now, just to get away from it. Ice be damned." I grinned. "No, he coaches college mock trial, and they had a tournament this weekend."

"Oh, for real? I've got a good friend who did that in college. My business partner, MacKenzie Valdez. I think she judges sometimes."

"I bet they know each other. And if she's anything like Jai, we couldn't get them to talk about anything else, if they were here."

Will laughed. "No, probably not."

"It's a great party," I said, with a wide gesture that took in everything happening around me and ended pointing at the food table. "I'm so glad you and Ali invited me. The food was amazing."

He gave a quick, modest grin. "We go pretty simple. Not too much prep. You need to come back next week. You ever have grilled pineapple?"

I nodded, even though I didn't think I had. I could imagine it.

Will nodded along with me. "Amazing, right? That's usually on the menu, but Bonnie helps us with the prep, and she had to run out. Something about her mom. So it got dropped. But next week, next week you'll see."

Now that he'd mentioned it, I realized I hadn't seen Bonnie during the party. She'd been so ubiquitous every other time I'd visited the house, but tonight she was nowhere to be found.

"Something about her mom?" I repeated. I couldn't guess Bonnie's age. Anything from her early fifties to her late sixties was plausible. How old must her mother be?

Will shook his head. "I'm sure she's fine. I mean, she's not fine, but I don't think whatever happened tonight was a major crisis. She's in bad health, and Bonnie's always getting called over to deal with her."

He started to say something else to me, but then something happening at the grill caught his attention.

"Brett! You've got a flare-up!"

We both watched as Brett looked around helplessly, unable to cope with the four-inch-tall orange flame threatening to scorch a rib-eye. Will made it to the grill in three long strides and took the tongs from Brett's hand, shifting the steak out of the danger zone.

I fully intended to leave before halftime. The game sucked and the party sucked, leaving no reason to stay. However, as the second quarter wound to an anticlimactic conclusion, the food table was cleared off. I watched with a sense of loss as Will and Brett carried the picked-over platters of steak and sides into the house. What an odd thing to do.

Surely, even though most guests would have eaten their fill, they might wander back over for a refill as the game wore on. Something about their actions seemed so out of place that I stayed just to see what happened. Was this their way off avoiding guests overstaying their welcome, indicating that the party had a time limit?

Nope. An array of desserts, fancier than the fanciest dessert spread at the fanciest wedding you've ever seen pictures of on the internet, appeared. I'm not joking. A spread I will dream about for the rest of my life. Cheesecake slices and chocolate-covered strawberries (in November!) and even these fancy little composed s'mores with brûléed marshmallows on top of chocolate and speculoos tarts. No way they should sit there going to waste, so I stayed. I ate three of the s'mores things, and I have no regrets.

Midway through the third quarter, I sat alone and stared at one of the TVs. The game hadn't really improved after halftime, but the effects of the food meant moving seemed like a terrible idea. Reginald had made his way back over to me at some point and curled up against my legs.

"Reginald! Here, boy!" Mrs. Van Meer called out from the door to the great room. Reginald lifted his head when he heard his name, then jumped to his feet and allowed her to lead him into the house.

I hadn't talked to Mrs. Van Meer that night, although I'd caught sight of her a couple of times through the glass windows on the back of the house. She let the young people have their fun without intruding. That impression was confirmed by the way she called out her good night.

"You kids have fun! I'm going to bed."

A general chorus of good nights rose from the group, and then everyone turned their attention back to the game, or their conversation, or their food. I thought her announcement might be an agreed-upon signal to turn down the volume of the backyard sound system, but the party continued with no noticeable change. The game also didn't improve. I didn't stay to the bitter end, but I lasted until the two-minute warning, which came right after yet another punt. That's when I threw in the towel and headed out, already dreading coming back in less than twelve hours. I didn't know it at the time, but Reginald wouldn't get his walk the next morning.

Chapter Eight

Our building was an old, shabby-looking duplex about two blocks off of Tower Grove Park, in South St. Louis City. It's an eclectic neighborhood, partially gentrified, mostly catering to youngish, hipsterish people like me and Jai. We'd lived on the top floor of the duplex for a couple of years, dreaming of the day when we could buy a place of our own. I mean, the area's great, the building's fine, and our landlord, Dwayne, was OK, but both of us wanted to stop renting at some point before it was time to move into a nursing home.

When we first moved in, a young family lived downstairs. The parents were Guatemalan, and were wonderful neighbors. Their twin girls were sweeter than they were loud, so we missed them when they moved out, having found a place in a better school district.

Next came an elderly Bosnian woman, there temporarily while her son built an addition to his house to create space for her. She'd lived in South City, just a few blocks away, and in anticipation of no longer being able to live on her own, sold her home to finance the expansion of her son's previously one-bedroom house. The day she moved out was a celebration, her whole family on hand to help, with an air of bringing her home from exile. I went down to help carry boxes, and let me tell you, I ate well that day. Before everyone arrived, she'd made a giant pot of something I would have called polenta and they called *pura*, which she dished up to hungry movers (and hovering neighbors) in bowls with dollops of sour cream. We got her place cleared out within a couple of hours, just in time for lunch, some kind of beef-and-cabbage-filled pastry packets. Delicious, but I ate mine with one eye fixed on a platter of baklava waiting for dessert. Before meeting Mrs. Medunjanin, I'd never had homemade baklava, a decades-long deprivation she took it upon herself to remedy over and over again in the year or so we shared a building.

By now, the downstairs unit had been vacant for a couple of months. But at about 8:30 that Monday morning, I heard the unmistakable sounds of a new neighbor. First came the alternating engine noises and beeping of a moving truck trying to maneuver in our street, lined as always with bumper-to-bumper parked cars on both sides. Next, several people clomped up the wooden porch steps, and then I heard the outside door to the other unit open. I toyed with the idea of hunkering down and pretending I didn't exist. Jai wouldn't be home for a few hours, I'd spent the whole night before socializing with strangers, and I hadn't expected to have to do so again so soon.

But I'd have to leave in a little bit anyway, and they'd still be carrying boxes in, and I couldn't count on being able to sneak past them. I'd have to pretend I hadn't heard, and it would be awkward. So I steeled myself, changed out of my pajamas, put on shoes, and went downstairs onto the porch.

I'd timed it wrong. When I made it outside, no one was visible. Our new neighbors and the movers were either inside the apartment, with the door shut, or maybe at the moving truck. My plan for this encounter had been based on creating a chance meeting. I would come out our door and run into them on the porch, introducing myself and welcoming them to the building. Now I was left standing by myself, trying to decide what to do. Should I knock on their door? Surely, they'd be back out any minute.

I suddenly wished that I smoked. How convenient it would be to reach in my pocket and light up a cigarette right now. That would be the most natural scene in the world. I'd be on the porch smoking, and we'd bump into each other and fall into conversation. The threat of future lung cancer seemed preferable to the other alternative I seriously considered at that moment, which was going back inside and crouching on our stairs, just on the other side of the door, until I heard the new neighbors come out, and then stepping out with oh-so-natural perfect timing.

Instead, the new neighbor came out onto the porch while I was standing there, unable to make up my mind. A white woman, younger than me, maybe in her early twenties, with almost waist-length wavy hair. She wore a blue billowy top that looked like something you'd expect to see on a medieval minstrel, with cuffs that gaped open to reveal dozens of beaded bracelets and bangles on each wrist that clanked and jangled when she moved.

"Oh, hi, there," I started. "I'm Nikki. My husband, Jai, and I live upstairs." I pointed, apparently worried that this concept might be foreign to her. "Welcome to the building."

She grinned, a genuine smile that made her whole face light up. "Nikki! Oh, I'm so glad to meet you! I'm McKayla. We're going to be best friends!"

I think I took a small step back. On the new-neighbor spectrum, "loner with serial-killer vibes" and "clingy, needy, desperate for interaction" were at opposite ends, but equally bad. But McKayla seemed sweet. I told myself that maybe she comes on strong as a first impression, but settles down as you get to know her. I decided to give her a chance, while cautiously keeping her at arm's length.

"Where are you moving from?" A polite question but nothing too personal. That was the way forward.

The answer came in a flood. "Oh, I've been staying a few blocks down, kind of at Spring and Chippewa, you know? It was a nice place, but my mom owns it, so it's kind of like living at home, you know? So I was like, 'Mom, I need to find my own place,' so she found this place, and I'm so excited! I love this building—do you guys have an awesome stained-glass window in your bathroom, too?—I love this block, and I'm closer to the park, which is awesome, because I love to go there and recharge my batteries, you know? And then I met you, and you're so nice—" She clapped her hands excitedly. "This is going to be so much fun!"

All right, now was the time for lying. She made it sound like living downstairs from us was going to be a super exciting slumber party. I did not have the energy to deal with her.

"It was so great to meet you, McKayla, but I was just running out! Good luck with the rest of the move!" This last part I called over my shoulder, already hurtling down the porch steps at breakneck speed. Thank god I'd stashed my phone, wallet, and keys in the pocket of my hoodie before leaving. If I went back upstairs now, I risked getting trapped up there all day.

Too early for my weekday morning group walk, with a Doxie named Lady, a German Shepherd named Princess, and a mutt with lopsided ears named Maniac McGee. I went to a neighborhood coffee shop and bought myself a cardamom latte. If you get exiled from your own home unexpectedly, you're allowed to treat yourself. That's the law.

The group walk was as uneventful as a group walk ever is. Lady spent most of her time trying to get Princess's legs tangled in the leash, and Maniac McGee took it upon himself to alert me every time a leaf fell off a tree or blew across the ground. But we survived.

Once I got each of them delivered back to the correct home, it was time to make the trek out to the county for Reginald's walk. I headed west, leaving my historic, interesting, and poorly maintained city neighborhood for the soulless Stepford mansions of the suburbs.

As I made the long hike up the driveway, Bonnie came out of the larger of the two garages. I hadn't been inside that one, but I assumed everyone parked there. She wore a white windbreaker that I'd already seen her in often enough that I thought of it as her uniform, and had the long strap of a red purse slung over one shoulder. I slowed my pace as she made her way around the other side of the pool, so we met on the patio.

"Good morning, Bonnie! I was surprised I didn't see you last night!"

"Nikki! Good to see you!" She, at least, had warmed up to me. She sounded friendly and genuine. "Yes, I was sorry to miss the party! We should all cherish whatever little bits of joy we can find in this life." She dropped her voice, although no one else stood within earshot. "I certainly would have had more fun with you kids. I was called away on very short notice. My mother. She's in a nursing home, you know, and they were a little worried about her and decided they wanted to send her to the hospital, where they could keep a better eye on her. She gets real agitated sometimes, so they wanted me to go with her, of course." She affected a yawn. "You know how hospitals are, though. We got there at four o'clock in the afternoon, and then we waited until the wee hours of the morning for her to be admitted. By the time I got home, it almost wasn't worth going to bed."

I didn't know what to say. I felt I should offer condolences for her mother's poor health, or ask about her condition out of politeness. But something about the way Bonnie had narrated the whole situation warned me to keep out. She could have been reading out loud from a children's book called *The Time Mommy Went to the Hospital*, and maybe she needed to hold things that way in her own mind, in order to cope. She certainly looked exhausted.

"Yes, I hate it when you can't get a good night's sleep," I answered, for lack of a better idea.

I'd never seen so many people in the main room. Ali and Will sat at the kitchen island, poring over a binder of selections for their new home. Teri paced in tight circles in one corner of the living room, her cell phone to her ear. A man in navy blue work pants knelt on the brick hearth, his head and torso disappearing into the (thankfully unlit) fireplace, and a hand groping backward toward an open toolbox. At first, he looked like a workman called in specially for some repair work, but I spotted a telltale bandage on the hand reaching into the toolbox. Kevin, the landscaper I'd met the night before in the garage. Maybe he hadn't been exaggerating when he'd said he did everything around here.

Brett was there, too, and no one who'd seen how drunk he'd been the night before would have been surprised at his appearance. He looked like he regretted rolling out of bed. His baby face had the beginnings of stubble, and although not glaringly obvious, the shoulder seams on his dark green T-shirt betrayed the fact that it had been put on inside out. I was relieved to see he obviously hadn't driven home last night. He sat on the sofa, his eyes staring unfocused out the back windows. A mug of coffee sat untouched on the end table at his side. He looked like he needed it, but maybe an intravenous drip would have been the way to go.

Will looked up as we walked in and wordlessly stood to pour me a cup of coffee. He set it on the island and slid the carton of oat milk across to me. He'd asked how I liked my coffee the second time I'd come to the house, and now we had the routine down. Ali smiled warmly. These two seemed determined to make me feel at home, regardless of how Teri chose to behave.

"Do you know anything about shower heads?" Ali asked me, turning a page in the binder.

I shook my head. "I saw a thing online that a new shower head was an easy and cheap way to upgrade a crappy apartment bathroom. Maybe, that is, if you know what you're doing. I just made sure all the walls and the ceiling got a nice soaking." I smiled at her and then thought. "Have you ever stayed at a hotel where you noticed the shower being really awesome or really terrible?"

"Oh, that's a good way to think about it! What do you think, babe?" She elbowed Will, whose attention had drifted to his phone.

"As long as you put it high enough, I don't care. That's the only thing I notice in hotels—when they put it so low I have to bend over if I want to get my head wet."

You should have thought of that before being six four, is what I wanted to say. Instead, I nodded. I tried to keep from speculating at the costs associated with building a custom home like the one they were planning. Knowing the area where they were building, I assumed the empty lot alone probably cost them more than a renovated home near our place.

Ali shook her head. "I've already made the architect redo the plan three times. Do you think nesting by proxy is a thing?"

We both laughed. I sat with them for a few minutes, catching glimpses of glossy photos showing kitchen appliances, crown molding, and shutters. Bonnie had gone right to work, pulling out a stepladder and gathering dried leaves off a towering ficus tree that marked the midpoint of the huge room.

With her hands stuffed full of leaves, she stepped off the ladder, and I caught her eye.

"Do you know, is Reginald ready for me?"

Bonnie glanced around. "He's around here somewhere. Any of you seen Reginald?" she asked the others.

Teri covered her phone with one hand. "He's probably still in the study." She used her chin to point at the part of the house that lay beyond the kitchen.

I took a few hesitant steps in that direction, giving the others the chance to say, "Oh, wait! Sorry! Don't go wandering through a strange house with only the world's vaguest directions! I'll show you where the study is." But no one paid any attention to me. I passed a few rooms with open doors and resolved to someday go on one of the house tours I saw advertised now and then for swanky houses in swanky neighborhoods. I'd never felt the deficiency before, but it would be nice to be able to guess at the purpose of some of these rooms. A little way down the hallway, I came to a heavy paneled door, shut tight. This must be the study.

I pulled the door open and Reginald trotted past me, moving fast for such an elderly dog. I followed him back to the great room, where he weaved a path through everyone's legs and pushed through the dog door in the French window. In hindsight, I should have known something was wrong, but I still thought I was in for just another normal day.

Chapter Nine

Teri watched him go and then hung up her call. "Is Grandma not up yet?"

Everyone in the room looked at her, and then each other, shaking their heads.

"That's not like her at all," said Bonnie. No one else spoke.

Teri disappeared toward the opposite end of the house. We could just hear her tentative knock, and then her voice, made low and indistinct by distance. Silence. Then another knock. Then the opening of the bedroom door. Then silence.

I think we all knew at that point. A knot formed in the pit of my stomach. I shouldn't have been there. This was so intimate, so private. I wanted to bolt, but I couldn't move. I didn't have the courage to look directly at anyone else. They weren't moving either.

Kevin had extricated himself from the fireplace. He spoke to the room. "She seemed fine on Saturday." His words, not loud, were uncomfortably near as we all strained to catch the faintest sound from the direction Teri had gone, while simultaneously trying to block out any sound from the direction Teri had gone.

She came back into the room, her face ashen. She didn't say anything, didn't need to. She looked at us all, then retreated again. Beside me, Ali stood and rushed unsteadily forward. Will and Brett followed right behind her. Then Bonnie, and then Kevin. I didn't want to move, but somehow being left alone in that room right then seemed like the worst thing in the whole world. As I followed, I rationalized that maybe I could be helpful somehow, but really a powerful, primal fear of being left alone dragged me along.

For just an instant, all of them clustered at the open bedroom door, reluctant to advance any farther. Then Brett retched and stumbled forward. His momentum carried him across the room, where he fumbled at the handles of the tall French doors, flinging them open on his second attempt. He fell to his knees on the edge of the brick patio, dry heaving onto the manicured lawn.

Mrs. Van Meer lay in bed, with a cream-colored duvet pulled halfway up her chest, and her head turned ever so slightly to one side on a matching pillow. One of those clichés you hear over and over again is that a dead person looks like they're sleeping. Maybe if you'd shown me a photograph of the scene, I'd have guessed she was asleep, but something about the atmosphere in the room made that an impossibility. Maybe it was her utter stillness, despite the activity around her, or the uncanniness of the daylight streaming into the room, or some subtlety about the muscle slackness in her face.

The cold air streaming into the room served the same purpose as a slap in the face, spurring everyone into motion. Teri grabbed Ali, who looked like she might pass out at any second, and guided her to a chair. Will pulled out his phone, and I heard him talk in a low voice to a 911 dispatcher. Bonnie, bizarrely, went out onto the back lawn and laid a hand on Brett's back. Maybe she couldn't cope with the larger tragedy, so she wanted to address a smaller problem.

No one had approached Mrs. Van Meer. We all knew for certain that a body lay in front of us, but someone needed to verify that fact. As far as I knew, none of them had any medical training. It might be that I, with a few long-ago years' experience as a vet tech, was the most qualified to check vitals.

It took more nerve than I knew I had to approach the bed. My throat had gone dry, and I tried, unsuccessfully, to swallow. Mrs. Van Meer's mouth was ever so slightly open, her eyes closed, and her cheeks pink. I touched her neck, planning to press hard to search for even a very faint, thready pulse, but her skin had no warmth at all. I recoiled, disconcerted to touch another person and feel a surface at room temperature. After a deep breath, I tried again, this time keeping my fingers in place long enough to confirm the lack of any heartbeat, if only to demonstrate to the others in the room my reason for approaching the body.

Will, still on the phone with the dispatcher, wasn't paying attention to the call. I could tell he wanted to go and comfort Ali, who was crying into Teri's shoulder. I guessed the dispatcher wouldn't let people disconnect until the first responders made it to the scene. It made sense in an emergency, but the only emergency here had happened hours earlier. This was just the maddeningly slow aftermath of an emergency.

"Do you want me to take over the call?" I asked him, glancing toward Ali and Teri.

He nodded and passed me his phone, not saying anything to the dispatcher, whose tinny voice I could hear as soon as the phone came away from his ear.

"Sir? Sir? Could you tell me the victim's age? Sir? Are you there?"

I walked with the phone to the front of the house, planning to direct traffic when anyone showed up. "Hello? I'm so sorry, but I don't know much information about the victim. She's elderly. Maybe late eighties? I don't really know."

It took a few exchanges before the dispatcher would accept I didn't know anything helpful, and that I refused to reenter the house to pass the phone back to a grieving family member. She assured me help had been sent, and I assured her we had plenty of people on the scene who'd be able to supply any necessary information when asked in person. I felt sorry for her. She was just doing her job, and I was being an unhelpful stonewaller.

The few minutes before the police car and ambulance showed up dragged on and on, and I kept the phone to my ear the whole time. Both of us were relieved to end that call.

I showed one of the officers to Mrs. Van Meer's bedroom, the other hanging back while the paramedics unloaded some gear. He strode across the room without acknowledging any of the family members and checked again for a pulse. He was still for just a moment, his fingers pressed into Mrs. Van Meer's neck, his gaze focused on one spot of the duvet. Everyone else had frozen when he'd entered, and they remained as they had been. Brett still hunched on all fours just outside the French doors, with Bonnie tending to him. Teri and Will huddled with Ali, and Kevin stood in one corner, looking as out of place as I felt, standing outside the bedroom door and peering in.

I wished someone would tell me what to do. Was I supposed to stand here and wait, making myself available for the officer, or would it be more helpful to go and direct the first responders still outside? I really felt like I should just leave. I had no part in this. But Will's phone in my hand had me stuck. I couldn't take it with me, but this was not the right moment to give it back.

The police officer marched back out of the room, again without saying anything or even looking at anyone, going to get the others, which meant I really wasn't needed for anything. I tiptoed away from the bedroom and went back into the great room. Reginald had gone to his dog bed by the fireplace. He lifted his head when I walked in, and gave a tootling, old man version of a greeting. Poor Reggie.

I sat on the floor next to him and scratched his ears, using the other hand to scroll on my own phone, hoping to distract myself from thoughts of the room next door.

A notification chimed, and before I could stop myself, I glanced down at Will's phone, lying on the floor next to me. He'd gotten a text message, and a preview flashed on his screen. I felt bad for glancing that direction, but the impulse was automatic. I heard the sound, I turned my head, with no intention of snooping, or prying, or even curiosity. A Pavlovian reaction out of my control. In the instant before my civilized brain took over, I had already seen what popped up. A message from someone named MacKenzie, only one phrase registered before I turned the phone screen-side-down: "wrongful death."

"Hello?"

The tentative greeting came from a middle-aged woman poking her head into the room, having taken advantage of the still-open front door. I scrambled to my feet, without knowing exactly why, disrupting Reginald.

"Hello," the woman said again as if glad to have found someone. "I'm Debbie Schluester. I have an appointment with Ruth, but I'm a little early." Her voice started to trail off in reaction to the expression on my face. Dressed in all black and white, but with a tropical-print silk scarf arranged artfully around her neck, she clutched a binder to her chest, holding it a little higher than was natural, as if it might afford her some protection. "I saw the paramedics . . ."

It sounds stupid to say I hate delivering sad news. Everyone hates delivering sad news. I wished with all my might I could guess how close this woman was to Mrs. Van Meer. She'd called her "Ruth," but in the same breath said she was here for an appointment. She could be here to quote a piano-tuning job, or because she suspected Mrs. Van Meer might be the birth mother who gave her up for adoption in the early seventies.

"I . . . my name's Nikki." No, I don't know why that came out. There was absolutely no reason to assume this woman gave a flying flip who I was, but there it was, laying limply between us. Maybe I was buying some time. It worked.

"Hello, Nikki. I'm Debbie." She stepped forward and extended a hand to me. She had a good handshake and a warm smile. "I'm Mrs. Van Meer's realtor. We were supposed to meet last week, and we rescheduled to this morning."

Does awkwarding people into identifying themselves more fully count as a superpower?

Realtor. OK. Got it. So, mostly a professional relationship, but probably a long-established one, that may well have a more personal dimension.

"I'm sorry, Debbie. I don't know exactly how to tell you this, but Mrs. Van Meer . . . We think she must have passed sometime during the night."

One hand flew to her mouth, while the other hand tightened its grip on the binder so much that the knuckles turned bright white.

I nodded my head toward the east side of the house. "Teri and Ali are with her now. Her granddaughters, I'm sorry, I don't know if you know them."

She'd found her voice, but she spoke with effort. "I should go. I should offer my condolences. Of course, I know the girls. Do you know if they need anything? Oh, no, it's too soon. They'll need some time to themselves. I should go."

I really wanted to say, "Lady, I know exactly how you feel. You think you should go? I'm the fricking dog walker." But I didn't say that. Looking back now, I don't think it would have helped the situation in any way. I wanted to blabber about everything that had happened that morning, including taking Will's phone to be helpful, which had now trapped me in this big, impersonal house, because I couldn't very well interrupt the paramedics to give him his phone back. I wanted to tell her that what the poor girls really needed was for her, Debbie, to take this cell phone and sit here until it was socially acceptable to return it to Will, and that I was heading out, and that it was very nice to meet her, despite the horrible circumstances.

Instead, I did the world's most noncommittal shrug, combined with both a shake of the head and a nod, for maximum ambiguity.

"I think I'm going to go. I'll give them a few days and then reach out to Teri with my condolences." I don't know if Debbie always did her thinking out loud, or if this was a special occasion.

She gave me a sad smile and left, tiptoeing, which endeared her to me. I decided I could take my cue from her. I set Will's phone in the exact center of the massive kitchen island, still screen-side down, gave Reginald one last scratch under the chin, and left through the front door. I think I tiptoed, too.

Chapter Ten

Mrs. Van Meer and the others consumed my thoughts, so I forgot to evade our new downstairs neighbor. I only remembered she existed as I mounted the porch steps and saw that she'd set a giant stuffed cat in the front window. Its fluffy white fur shone in the sunlight as the toy stared stonily into the distance. Luckily, McKayla herself didn't emerge. I made it through the door without an encounter.

When I'd set out that morning, I'd had vague plans of a lazy afternoon. Jai had made it out of Kansas City safely and would be home in an hour or two. He'd have to catch up on work almost immediately, since he hadn't planned to take the morning off. I had several calligraphy jobs I could have worked on, but I wasn't relaxed enough for that. If my hands shook at all, or even if my shoulders were too tense, I wouldn't be happy with the finished product. I had orders of cat toys to fill, but I was temporarily out of catnip, with the next shipment not scheduled to arrive for a few days. I usually hate diving into a project I won't be able to finish, but I needed something non-death-related to focus on. Even if I couldn't stuff them and sew them closed, I could at least cut out the pattern pieces for the cat toys on order. I pulled out the right fabric (tie-dyed, with black paw prints) and started cutting out my medium-size kickers, long rectangular pillows that cats can hug with their front paws and kick with their back paws, as a healthy sublimation of their desire to murder smaller animals.

But the repetitive rectangles proved too simple to occupy my attention. My mind kept wandering back to Mrs. Van Meer, lying dead in her bed, with rosy cheeks and cold skin, like some horribly lifelike doll. I switched over to a pattern for a fish-shaped toy, hoping that cutting around the fins would be intricate enough for my current mental state. I didn't have any active orders for this style of toy, but it wouldn't hurt to have backstock.

I gave it my best shot. I forced myself to work with the small pieces of fabric for about twenty minutes. It turns out, you'll be shocked to hear, that cutting out fish shapes was not enough to take my mind off the dead body I'd seen that morning. I needed fresh air. Walking Reginald that morning hadn't been an option (see above: dead body), so I was dealing with some pent-up energy.

When I made it back out onto the porch, I glanced at McKayla's front window, with the stuffed cat, and did a double-take. The cat had shifted position. Now lying down, with the same stony expression in its unblinking eyes.

There was only one explanation, and it was obvious in hindsight. What I'd taken for a stuffed cat was a live cat. Obviously.

Sad to say, that thought didn't occur to me instantly. I can't emphasize enough how unreal this cat looked, both the first time I'd seen it and now. I looked around wildly with no idea what I was looking for. After an embarrassing delay, I realized the cat was real.

What should I do here? Our landlord didn't allow pets of any kind. Had McKayla worked out some special arrangement with him? I remembered her manner that morning and couldn't imagine her doing anything so practical. Although, to be fair, I couldn't really imagine her existing in the world at all, and she'd somehow made it this far.

I couldn't bring myself to knock on her door. Better to wait and mention the landlord's attitude toward pets the next time I ran into her. Dwayne didn't come around too often, so I had time before he noticed the massive, starkly white cat who'd taken up residence in one of the front windows of his pet-free building. Or with any luck, he'd be as dense as me and assume it was a toy cat.

Tower Grove Park has miles and miles of walking paths, and I knew them all. Enough trees make each route feel secluded, even though it's impossible to get more than a couple of hundred yards away from a busy city street. Even in winter, when the branches are bare of leaves, it's clear that you have left civilization and are now in nature. I say I know all the paths in the park, but I admit, I really hadn't spent very much time there at all without at least one dog on a leash. Let me tell you, the squirrels and rabbits are way more chill when you don't have a barking carnivore tethered to you.

The morning had been overcast, but the clouds had broken now and the sun shone. I wound my way through the park, taking turnings kind of at random, enjoying the fact that I didn't have a dog tugging at me if I decided to stop and watch the ducks on one of the ponds or a pair of squirrels chasing each other around a tree trunk. I settled down at a picnic table near the Turkish pavilion, enjoying the red-and-white striped domed roof, looking like a cross between an old-timey circus tent and St. Basil's Cathedral. Too cold to sit under the pavilion itself, out here in the sun felt comfortable.

My bag held five pens that day: the orange one for notes about my pet behaviorist clients, a navy one for dog-walking logistics, a purple one for personal to-do lists and grocery lists, a metallic red one for notes about the cat toys, and sky blue for my freelance calligraphy business. I dug around for the blue pen, pulled out my notebook, flipped to a clean page, just past my notes about Reginald, and tried drawing leaves. I suck at drawing. Like, a whole lot. But, logically, decorative, stylized vines and leaves aren't much more than the flourishes I already use in my calligraphy, just put together. If I could figure out the right combinations of swoops and swooshes to give the impression of foliage, I could start adding more artistic elements to my calligraphic work. The brush-tip pen wasn't behaving the way I wanted. Great for fine lines and writing, it wasn't transitioning to wider lines smoothly. Or it could have been my inability to relax and immerse myself in the work, but I chose to blame an inadequate pen. Of course, it wasn't a dip pen or fountain pen I'd use for a project, but those can't really be thrown in a bag and carried around.

I don't know how long I sat there, drawing disappointing leaf motifs, listening to the sounds of the park and the more distant sounds of the city, and watching the other Monday lunchtime visitors to the park. Long enough that I was able to drag my mind away from the tragedy of the morning and to stop picturing Mrs. Van Meer, and the shocked faces of all the others. To stop replaying the soundtrack of that morning:

Teri's knock, Ali's wail, Brett's retching, Will's 911 call. I sat there long enough that when I went back home, I was able to tell Jai what had happened without reliving it, without dredging up the emotions I had felt in the moment. There was no point in dwelling on it.

With Mrs. Van Meer gone, I would probably never see any of those people again.

Chapter Eleven

The next morning, Tuesday, was a brilliantly sunny day, but bone-chillingly cold. My schedule was different than normal, because Princess's owner had the day off work and didn't need me. I got to consolidate my morning walks by letting Freckles, a mutt who's built like a pit bull and has the energy of a retriever on Red Bull, join the group walk. She normally gets a solo walk, so she was ecstatic at the company, once she understood what was happening. Lady had a brand-new quilted jacket, and she threw in some fancy high-stepping to show it off. The fleece-lined hood did keep flopping and bouncing in a way that undercut her sense of dignity, but I didn't tell her that.

As we walked down a tree-lined block halfway between Freckles's house and the park, I spotted Dwayne, our landlord. He's hard to miss. He played defensive line in college and has the build and the knee braces to prove it. He stood pruning the hedges out front of one of his other properties. When within hailing distance, I waved and called out, "Hi, Dwayne! It's Nikki!" He's super friendly, but terrible with faces, so I always identify myself if I run into him away from my building. I have no reason to believe he knows anyone else likely to be found walking three mismatched dogs, but it feels polite.

When he spotted me, he gave me a huge grin and laid his hedge clippers down on the grass. "Hello, fellas!" he called, bending and extending his hands to the dogs.

None of the dogs kept their cool, but Freckles, in particular, lost her mind. This person had talked to her. This person was holding out his hands. This person would pet her. Never mind her leash clipped onto the belt of a human person, it was important to get over there. Right now.

I allowed myself to be dragged over, and Dwayne busied himself petting three incredibly happy dogs for the next few minutes. He even complimented Lady on her jacket. For someone so adamant about maintaining pet-free rental properties, Dwayne was a sucker for a good dog. I've toyed with the idea of getting a dog and then convincing him it's no big deal. Kind of an "ask for forgiveness, rather than permission" thing. Surely if faced with an actual cute dog, rather than a hypothetical, he couldn't say no, could he? He's always going on about ours being a historic building, but he just means historic as in "old," not historic as in "historically significant." Well, pretty soon I'd be able to stop speculating about his reaction to a secret pet on his precious hardwood floors. I'd just have to wait for the situation with McKayla and her giant cat to play out. If he evicted her in a rage, I'd know to stay pet-free. But if he let it slide . . .

The daydream of all the animals I would adopt once Dwayne relaxed his pet policy occupied my thoughts for the rest of the walk. Despite the temperature, I managed to work up a sweat, and the damp underlayers made me even colder.

As soon as I got home, I put on sweatpants and an oversized sweatshirt and settled down at my desk with a blanket over my lap. I was just summoning the energy to work on an order of hand-written place cards for a wedding when I got a text from an unknown number.

You're late. You were supposed to walk Reginald.

After a slight pause another message popped up. *This is Teri.*

I stared at my phone. Of course, Reginald would still need to be walked. Of course, the other members of the family weren't any more willing to step up and do it than they had been before. Who knew Teri could even think of the dog's needs while she dealt with both the grief and the bureaucracy that accompanies a death in the family? I guess I'd shamed her pretty effectively when we'd talked Sunday night.

Was this a simple request for a walk? If I could sneak in, grab Reginald, and get him back home without too much human interaction, I could cope. But what was I supposed to say to any of the humans at that house? Mrs. Van Meer had died just the day before.

And polite condolences would be awkward enough. What if they were looking for another pet behaviorist consultation to help Reginald deal with Mrs. Van Meer's death? Teri had been hostile to the whole idea, initially. Maybe she'd changed her mind. Or maybe Ali wanted me to come and talked Teri into it. I really hoped they just wanted me to walk the dog. There's no way any kind of consultation could be productive while they were all dealing with such a fresh loss.

I replied that I'd be happy to come by, adding that I'd been trying to give them some space, but that I could be there in half an hour, if I wouldn't be intruding.

Her reply was an unpunctuated, *let yourself in.*

Walking up the driveway, I had a hard time believing only one day had passed since my last visit. The morning before had been gloomy and overcast, with the temperatures hovering around freezing as the tail end of the weather system that had hit Kansas City passed over. Today, the cold had hung around, but the sun shone enough to make you forget about it for a second or two. Maybe it was this difference in atmosphere that allowed me to compartmentalize so well. If you'd stopped me right then and asked me how long it had been since we'd found Mrs. Van Meer's body, I might have guessed a couple of weeks before remembering the tragedy had happened only yesterday.

My distorted sense of time passing was flipped upside down when I walked into the great room. My first impression was that the family had intentionally staged a reenactment of the day before, like in some melodramatic psychological thriller. I snapped from feeling a strange time dilation into the strongest sense of déjà vu I'd ever felt.

Teri occupied her place in the corner, again pacing with her cell phone to her ear. Brett was on the couch, head in his hands, with what must have been a fresh hangover, but which looked identical to the one from the day before. Ali and Will sat together at the kitchen island, until Will noticed my entrance and stood to pour me a cup of coffee.

After my initial disorientation, I noticed enough small differences in the scene to reground myself in the present. Kevin was absent. Bonnie, instead of pruning the ficus, sorted the mail. The binders of house selections that lay in front of Ali and Will were closed. Brett's shirt was right-side-out. And Reginald wasn't shut up in the office this morning. He lay curled up in his bed next to the hearth, watching me, in case I'd come to take him for a walk.

I interpreted the coffee Will passed me as an invitation to join them at the island. I perched on a stool and sipped the coffee, after blowing on it to buy myself some time. I didn't know what to say to any of them.

"I'm so sorry about your grandmother," I said, directing my words toward Ali.

"Thanks." She smiled, eyes vacant, and rubbed her hand over a brocade fabric swatch sticking out of one of the binders. "It just sucks losing both of them, you know, one right after the other."

"Yeah, I bet. Your grandfather was what, just a month ago? That sucks." I knew I was echoing her, but I couldn't think of anything to add.

I gulped the coffee and stood to set the mug in the sink. Since my first visit to the house, when Will and I had hunted around for a leash for Reginald, the fluorescent blue strap had found a permanent home on a hook by the refrigerator. As my hand lifted toward it, Reginald got to his feet. This visit was going well, he was probably thinking. She's not wasting too much time chattering with these people. The others had noticed his excitement, too. I saw smiles across the room, not joyful smiles, but smiles recognizing the existence of joy. But Ali, who'd been dry-eyed when we'd exchanged our very few words, began to cry.

Reginald led me along the same path every single day. The only variation in our daily routine was how long he spent sniffing any given landmark. He stopped at them all, but it remained a mystery to me which would only warrant a quick scan one day versus an in-depth investigation on another. We had encountered other people, either jogging or walking, with dogs and without, with strollers and without, on previous days. These had invariably consisted of nodding from a distance, and a tight smile if we passed face to face.

Today, however, those who recognized Reginald were angling for gossip. They must have seen the ambulance and police car at the Van Meers' house the day before. I had no idea how news spread in a neighborhood like this. In the kind of suburban neighborhood Jai came from, word would be spread from neighbor to neighbor as people went outside to rake leaves, or collect the mail, or supervise their children's games. In the neighborhood I'd grown up in, the adults would swap news when they ducked outside to smoke, or ran into each other at the laundromat or the gas station on the corner. In our current neighborhood? I doubt news would be spread at all. If you showed me a line-up of people and asked me to pick out which ones lived on our street, the results would be pitiful. If a hypothetical elderly lady down the street passed away in her sleep, I'd never hear about it, unless I chanced to walk by while she was being carried into the ambulance.

But apparently the people in this neighborhood knew each other. Wasn't that evidenced by the loosely organized football watch party that past weekend? Yeah, there'd been a lot of cars, but surely some percentage of the attendees were neighbors, if only because otherwise wouldn't there have been a noise complaint?

We made it around the first bend, just out of sight of the house, when a woman came out of her house waving and calling to me. Like, literally calling "Yoo-hoo, yoo-hoo," which wasn't a call I'd experienced before. She only stopped her ridiculous shouting when Reginald and I stopped walking. We stood still and waited for her to make her way to the end of her driveway and join us.

"Do you know this one?" I muttered to Reginald. "She seems a little . . ." but there was a slight chance she was within earshot, so I didn't finish the sentence.

"You're walking Ruthie and Frank's dog, aren't you?" she asked, without glancing down at Reginald. "Poor Frank, but I guess you never met him. I'm so afraid to ask, but is it true about Ruthie?"

She was middle aged, I don't know, late fifties or early sixties? Almost as tall as me, but with much more pronounced curves. Her chest was barely contained by a zip-up velour jacket, and I found myself staring at the zipper pull, wondering how exactly it was defying gravity so effectively. She blinked at me, almost like she thought this might be a topic she should feel tearful about, so she wanted to get ready physiologically, just in case the emotions weren't there.

I nodded. I had no idea what kind of details to give. This wasn't my news. This was Ali and Teri's news. But maybe it was better if everyone just knew, without them having to go through the ordeal of spreading the news themselves?

"The poor dear! Was it her heart? Ever since Frank went, we knew it was a matter of time for old Ruthie, Henry and me." She stuck out a hand. "I'm Jackie, by the way."

"Nikki."

"So pleased to meet you, Nikki," she replied. "Henry and me, we've seen you come by. 'She's walking Ruthie and Frank's dog,' I said. 'Shame about old Frank,' I said, and now it's 'Shame about old Ruthie,' isn't it? Terrible, terrible."

I smiled politely. I felt like I was supposed to say something, but none of her statements invited reply. "Teri and Ali are heartbroken to lose her."

Jackie waved a hand. "Teri and Ali? Naw, they're sad now, but they won't miss a beat. If you believe what Bonnie says, there's no love lost there. Bonnie, now, she's the one. Bonnie'll be heartbroken. She lived for old Ruthie. I don't think she had any kind of life outside of taking care of the old dear, and taking care of her mother, of course. I bet you she never expected Ruthie to go while her poor mother, Bonnie's mother I mean, is still clinging to life."

The way Jackie kept referring to Mrs. Van Meer as "old dear" made me picture an almost-completely catatonic elderly woman in a nursing home, being spoon-fed applesauce, not the take-charge head of household I'd met.

"Oh, you know Bonnie pretty well?" I asked, not caring at all, but happy to take any conversational path that led us away from Mrs. Van Meer's death.

"Of course, of course. We're always running into Bonnie, Henry and me, and she's such a talkative old thing, isn't she? Really easy to get to know. She's always got Ruth on her mind, doesn't she? She's always 'Ruth this' and 'Ruth that' and I just can't imagine what she's going to do now that old Ruthie's gone."

If Reginald were an impatient dog, ending this conversation would have been easier. I've walked dogs before who would barely allow a sentence to be exchanged before they pulled you away. I won't name and shame, but there's a particular husky who leaps to mind. And leaps to everything else, for that matter. But Reginald stood still, watching us, waiting to see what would happen next, equally content to stand here and talk for the next hour or set off immediately for the rest of the walk.

I'm afraid I engineered a tug. I choked up on the leash at the same moment I lunged toward Reginald. I have no idea whether it looked convincing, but he followed my lead and trotted away.

"Oof, looks like Reginald's tired of standing still," I said, holding the shortened leash with an outstretched arm, to really sell the effect. "So nice to meet you," I called back over my shoulder.

Jackie wasn't the only neighbor who approached us during the walk. One man patted Reginald on the head and asked if I would please give his condolences to the family. Him I didn't mind so much. But the rest tried to pump me for information, some couching their questions between statements of sympathy, and others just asking for details with no attempt to camouflage their gossip. Bunch of vultures.

Chapter Twelve

When we got back to the house, Brett was waiting outside on the patio, standing with his hands clasped behind him and his shoulders pulled back. I couldn't read any expression on his face, and I felt disconcerted by the way he watched me steadily from the time I rounded the corner of the house, all the way until I made it onto the patio.

"Nikki. We need to talk."

I bent down to unclip Reginald's leash and gave him a prolonged scratch around the ears. He waited for me to be done with him and then bounded through the dog door and his food bowl. The walks really were doing him a world of good.

I looked back to Brett, winding the blue leash around one hand. He hadn't moved a muscle. I wished I had even a guess as to what we needed to talk about. I also had no idea what tone I should reply with. My instinct was to try to keep things light, just a form of rebellion against his almost comically serious tone. But I couldn't forget that someone had died here yesterday.

"What's up?" I asked.

He reached forward, and I flinched away. A second too late, I realized he'd been trying to take my elbow in a gentlemanly and misguided attempt to lead me to wherever he wanted to go. He gave a slight shrug and started walking back the way I'd come. I trailed after him, and he opened a set of French doors, then stood aside and allowed me to enter first. Heavy green curtains blocked the room beyond, but I figured, from my understanding of the house's layout, this had to be Mr. Van Meer's study.

When I'd let Reginald out of the study the morning before, I hadn't paid any attention to the interior of the room, but the dark wood paneled door matched the decor I saw once I windmilled my way through the curtains. Although the dimensions of the study matched the rest of the house—high ceilings, large rooms—the decor gave it a different feel. Everywhere else was light and airy, with windows open to the outside and white furnishings dominating, with a few pops of bright colors to wake things up. Here, the furniture was dark wood, with dark leather, and the walls were covered with so many heavy, layered treatments that they closed in on me. Dark, carved wainscoting, with a dark, carved chair rail, below dark, thick wallpaper, with dark, carved moldings. Just like in the rest of the house, there was artwork on the walls. But where the great room had bright, abstract canvases, here I saw smaller, more representational prints in muted colors. They were in nice frames but otherwise reminded me of the kind of art we had on the walls when I was a kid, which had largely been sourced from old calendars.

Brett followed me into the room, cutting a path through the choking curtains with much more dignity than I had managed. He thought about taking a seat behind the giant wood desk, then chickened out and guided me toward a smaller, round table in one corner, with four matching leather and wood chairs clustered around it. I waited until he chose a seat and settled in and then sat on a chair across from him.

He seemed to be waiting for me to say something, but he had called this meeting. I sat tight, letting my gaze wander across the three small pictures on the nearest wall. They wouldn't have looked out of place on the walls of the Catholic schools in which I'd spent a depressingly large amount of my childhood. The one on the far right showed a mother and child, presumably Mary and Jesus, in a cozy, rural setting, with a rooster walking by providing the only excuse to use a color that wasn't a shade of brown. On the left hung a portrait of a saint I'd learned about, but whose name I couldn't for the life of me come up with right then, wearing a long, brown robe and surrounded by woodland creatures like some kind of Disney princess. The smallest, in the middle, showed a peasant couple standing in a field, heads bowed, praying over a small basket on the ground between them. These pictures seemed so different from the ones elsewhere in the house, it was easy to imagine I was in a different building altogether. I wondered if Frank Van Meer hadn't cared about the decor in the rest of the house, or if he'd had his wishes ignored.

Finally, Brett got tired of waiting for me. "We need to talk," he said again.

"What's up?" This would be easy, if somewhat unproductive. We'd just keep repeating the same lines over and over until one of us gave up.

He sighed. "We need to talk about the trust. Reginald's trust. I had to tell Teri and Ali. They're likely to contest it, but

I had to tell them. But I want you to know I'm fully aware of Mrs. Van Meer's wishes. They won't have a leg to stand on with a judge."

"What are you talking about?"

"The trust for Reginald's care. In Mrs. Van Meer's will. The three hundred thousand dollars."

Surely this guy could explain things better, if he tried. "Why don't you start at the beginning, and use full sentences, and tell me what you're talking about?"

He ran a hand through his hair and leaned back in the chair. He gave a low whistle. "You don't know anything about it." His tone was one of wonder, as if I'd just asked him how the tooth fairy figures out which houses will have teeth under pillows on any given night. "She said she'd told you."

I stared at him. When he was ready to talk, he would talk.

And, after another second or two of rearranging his thoughts, he did. "Since her husband's death, Mrs. Van Meer's will has included a provision for Reginald's care. It's called a 'pet trust,' and it's not unusual. It's a portion of her estate set aside for the care and maintenance of a companion animal. After meeting with you last week, she directed me to name you the executor of that trust."

I felt a quick surge of warmth toward Mrs. Van Meer, in whose company I'd been for a total of, what, an hour? An hour and a half? But who'd trusted me with her beloved pet. These feelings were immediately swamped by practical concerns. I couldn't take in a dog right now.

"She willed Reginald to me?"

"Strictly speaking, no. She willed money for the care of Reginald and chose you to manage and oversee the funds."

"Because my building doesn't allow pets."

"That's not a problem. Ideally, Reginald would continue to live here. You would pay for his food, veterinary care, or whatever is needed, not out of your own pocket, of course, but out of the trust funds. Since you were employed as a dog walker prior to Mrs. Van Meer's death, I'm sure we could justify to the courts if you chose to continue walking Reginald at the same rate of pay. Your charge is to ensure Reginald's quality of life is maintained."

I nodded, overwhelmed. It sounded like all the stresses of owning a dog, and none of the positive companionship. I thought back to how he'd opened the conversation.

"Did you say something about Teri and Ali?"

He shook his head. "Don't worry about that right now. That'll all turn out fine."

I couldn't imagine Teri would react well to the news that her grandmother had written me into her will. I'd only just gotten her to believe I wasn't selling Mrs. Van Meer unnecessary services. Now it was going to look like I'd insinuated myself into the affections of a dying old lady with the hope of inheriting. "Are you sure?"

"Three hundred thousand dollars is a small enough portion of the estate. They won't lose too much sleep over it."

He'd mentioned that figure earlier, although my brain hadn't registered it. I can't really say my brain registered it then either. "Three hundred thousand dollars?" I parroted. As soon as the words left my mouth, I worried I'd sounded either greedy or like a Dickensian orphan, who'd never even contemplated so large a sum before.

He apparently hadn't heard either of those things in my tone, because he answered as if I'd asked an articulate question about the process used to arrive at such a sum.

"I think Mrs. Van Meer's idea was that three hundred thousand is a safe amount, in that the funds run no risk of being depleted in Reginald's lifetime, if responsibly managed, without being so great an amount that to tie it up away from her heirs would pose an undue hardship. Any remaining funds at the end of the duration of the trust, that is, at the end of Reginald's life span, would revert to the estate. Less your executor's fee, of course." He tossed this last sentence in hurriedly, as though embarrassed he hadn't mentioned it earlier.

"Teri's motives worry me, I have to say. I can understand her objection, but not the strength of it, if you know what I mean." He started to speak and then stopped. He scooted his chair closer to the table, leaning forward with an air of confidentiality. "Pet trusts are vulnerable to misuse, without proper oversight. Some people, given access to a pet trust, have been known to treat it as their own personal checking account, and just make up whatever nonsense is necessary to justify the expenses after the fact, if they're ever even asked to account for their spending. And Mrs. Van Meer's estate is largely bound up in various investment accounts, and in the property she owns. The three hundred thousand dollars, though a relatively small amount, represents a disproportionately large amount of the liquid assets." He lowered his voice even more, forcing me to lean in. "There's a chance Teri or Ali was counting on that money for some immediate expense and was then planning on reimbursing the pet fund once Mrs. Van Meer's estate is liquidated."

Maybe it looked like I was listening. I think I have a pretty good poker face. But I didn't hear anything after he called three hundred thousand dollars "a relatively small amount." Three hundred thousand dollars would pay off all Jai's student loans and allow us to pay cash for a two-bedroom fixer-upper in our neighborhood, or put down a deposit on a specific refinished four-bedroom beauty on our block I'd been drooling over ever since it went on the market the month before. Three hundred thousand dollars was a life-changing amount of money. And to these people it was "a relatively small amount."

I toyed with the idea of asking Brett whether buying a house with a fenced-in backyard for Reginald would be a legitimate expense under the terms of the pet trust. But I already felt icky about his suggestion of paying myself to walk Reginald, and I didn't relish the idea of doing anything to further anger Teri.

When he'd said all he wanted to say, Brett led me out of the study, not back outside toward the patio, where I could have made a stealthy exit, but through the house, where the hallway dumped us out in the great room. Teri was waiting for us, arms crossed in front of her. She obviously knew the subject of our conference. I stayed a few steps behind Brett, using him as a human shield. He crossed to Teri and spread his hands wide.

"She claims she didn't know anything about the pet trust," he told her, with a note of pleading in his voice. "She's either telling the truth or she's a really good actress."

"Of course she's a really good actress," Teri spat. "She's a fucking scam artist."

She and Brett completely ignored me, standing in the room. I wanted to turn and walk out, but I couldn't leave things like this. Should I wait until the family settled all their squabbles and called me back to walk Reginald, if and when that ever happened? Or did I have a legal obligation now, and I'd just have to show up, day in and day out, to check on Reginald?

I didn't have Brett's number or even know his last name. I wondered if Jai could look him up by knowing he was the Van Meers' family lawyer. There might be some lawyer database out there, but it didn't seem like a lot to go on. Why hadn't I asked more practical questions?

Ali had been sitting at the kitchen island, her forehead scrunched with worry and concentration. She spoke up now, with a conciliatory tone. "Teri, calm down."

Teri whirled on her. "I will not calm down. She's trying to steal our money!"

"Sure, but . . ." Ali winced, remembering I was in the room. She started to look toward me but stopped herself before our eyes met. "We can't fight it this way. There's a process. Brett explained—"

"Brett! Oh, of course you'd take Brett's side! You two probably have this whole thing worked out without me, right?" Teri's voice sounded hysterical.

Brett took a hesitant step forward and held out a hand. He spoke soothingly. "It's your grandmother's will. Don't you respect her wishes?"

"Of course I respect my grandmother's wishes," Teri snapped back. "That's about all I respect. I don't respect this piece of trash, worming her way into my grandmother's will. I don't respect you, with your slimy, schmoozy, stupid face." She turned her back on me and Brett, facing her sister instead. "And I sure as hell don't respect you, with your lying, cheating, wide-eyed innocent act. You're both lucky I don't tell Will what you're up to."

I left then. Whatever my obligation to Reginald, I could at least give Teri a chance to cool off. I couldn't really blame her, even. She was dealing with grief and anger, and she'd already suspected me of scamming her grandmother.

This whole pet trust provision in Mrs. Van Meer's will was the worst thing that could have happened. It seemed to prove all Teri's worst assumptions about me and my motives. Besides, based on how readily she'd turned on her sister and Brett, she was ready to lash out at anyone in front of her. Unfortunately, I didn't think untangling myself from these people was going to be as easy as walking out of their house.

Chapter Thirteen

Jai must have been having a slow day at work, because he was sitting on the couch reading a book when I came in, slamming the door behind me. Some kind of video conference was happening on the computer behind him, so I winced in apology for the noise.

"Don't worry. I muted myself. They've been going on for an hour and a half about something that doesn't concern my department at all." He stood up and turned down the volume, turning the meeting into a white noise machine. "What's the matter?"

I groaned and flopped sideways onto the couch. "Those people are all crazy. It's like a soap opera. Brett, he's the lawyer, told me Mrs. Van Meer added me to her will right before she died. I'm in charge of something called a pet trust. The two granddaughters are pissed, rightfully so, in my opinion." I sat back up to make room for Jai, who joined me.

"Are you serious?"

"Three hundred thousand dollars! For a dog! They're all crazy. Bonnie, the housekeeper, apparently gossips to the neighbors that nobody in the family gets along. Kevin, the handyman, he seems OK. He just sits in the garage, smoking pot and playing video games. Will, he's the one engaged to the one granddaughter, the pregnant one, he seems like the most down-to-earth of all them, but did I tell you what I saw on his phone yesterday? I don't think I did."

Jai shook his head.

I had forgotten about it myself. "While the paramedics and everyone else were back in the bedroom checking on Mrs. Van Meer, I noticed a text pop up on his phone about a 'wrongful death,' so who knows what kind of stuff he's mixed up in?"

"Well, if that's bugging you, why don't you look it up? It's probably something innocuous, and you can stop worrying about it." Jai was almost maddeningly calm. He seemed more amused by how worked up I was than concerned. That fact, shockingly, did not help to calm me down.

"'Look it up?' What the hell are you talking about? You want me to look up the context for a text I glanced at? It's Google, not a crystal ball."

"'Wrongful death' is a legal phrase," Jai said, with studied patience. "There's no reason I can think of someone would bother to type that specific phrase into a message unless they're referencing a lawsuit. You want to know what kind of stuff he's mixed up in? See if you can find whether this guy is a party in any current wrongful death suits."

"I don't even know his last name." As grating as his patient, almost parental, tone had been, I was equally disgusted with the note of whininess creeping into my own voice.

Jai detected my mood, and decided nothing good could come from continuing the conversation. Either that, or he sensed something important happening in the work meeting he'd been ignoring, because he went back to his computer and put on headphones.

I sighed loudly and flopped back down on the couch. After staring at the ceiling for a few seconds, I sat back up and opened my laptop. While fully prepared for my search to come up empty, I had to give it a try, or I'd never hear the end of it from Jai. His main takeaway from law school was "when in doubt, research."

The fact remained that I didn't know Will's last name. I tried "william" and "van meer." Predictably, that got me nothing useful, although I did learn a Willem Van Meer had lived in Rotterdam from 1881 to 1965. I stared at the screen, my eyes unfocused. I needed to be more methodical.

Mrs. Van Meer was Teri and Ali's maternal grandmother. So their last name probably wasn't Van Meer. I needed to focus on the grandmother first, which would lead me to Teri and Ali. From Ali, I could get to Will.

I searched "van meer" "st louis", and wouldn't you know? The very first result was an obituary for Frank Van Meer. I felt a qualm of conscience in the instant before I clicked the link. Was this icky? Checking the obit of someone's grandfather to dig up dirt on their fiancé? I shrugged and clicked. In the end, it was public information, and I am a member of the public. It's probably fine.

Frank Van Meer was survived by his wife, Ruth Van Meer, or at least he had been as of the date of publication, about a month ago. His granddaughters were mentioned, Theresa and Alison Corcoran. I don't know why, but it flabbergasted me to see Frank's daughter, Abigail Corcoran, also listed as a survivor.

Why had I been so certain Teri and Ali's mother had passed away? No doubt an assumption based on nothing more than the fact that they lived with their grandmother. I thought back to the party Sunday night. Teri had talked about her mother. Had she said her mother was dead? I'd gotten that impression, but maybe it was just because of Teri's emphatic use of the past tense.

When Mrs. Van Meer had been found dead, no one said, "Oh, we'll need to notify her daughter." I shook my head. I couldn't stop my brain from making all these baseless assumptions. All I knew for sure is that no one had said anything about notifying Teri and Ali's mother in front of me.

Me.

The random dog walker who'd happened to be there when they found their grandmother dead. I'd been kept out of the loop on this one point. Shocking. I must confront them at the first opportunity about their audacity.

This new information distracted me from my original intention of cyber-stalking Will. I wanted to learn anything I could about Teri and Ali's mother. She'd suddenly gone from a complete nonentity to the most fascinating character of the whole bunch.

I spent the next ten minutes reading everything I could find about Abigail Corcoran, who had a successful career with the foreign service. I noticed whenever she appeared, it was in the past tense, about a posting she'd just left. Maybe that was the convention for that kind of job, for security reasons. It could be where Teri picked up the habit.

None of the profiles mentioned anything about her children or family, or in fact anything more personal than which local dish had been her favorite. The whole thing made me suspect she was actually a CIA spy, or something equally hush-hush. For the record, this is the moment I first suspected Teri had told me a real anecdote about meeting the King of Norway.

"Find what you were looking for?" asked Jai, making me jump. He'd given up on his meeting again to lean over the back of the couch and read over my shoulder.

I shook my head and closed the current tab. I felt like I'd been caught reading a novel during math class. "No, not yet. I got distracted reading about Teri and Ali's mother. She might be an international ninja assassin for the CIA."

He cocked an eyebrow at me but didn't ask any follow-up questions. Jai can be remarkably single-minded sometimes. If I were wondering about a dry legal term and someone raised the possibility of an international ninja assassin, you can bet money where my attention would shift. But not Jai. Oh, no. He expected me to research the answer to one question, and he wasn't going to engage on any other topic until I had a result. He sat next to me on the couch and opened his book.

I sighed again, less dramatically than before, and turned back to the laptop. A quick search for "alison corcoran" pulled up a page for her wedding, from which I learned Will was William Henry Forester, and they were registered at Pottery Barn and three other places. The search results also included tons of pictures of the two of them at various galas and fundraisers in the society pages.

With Will's full name, I could look him up directly. I wasn't sure exactly how I would narrow the search, but it turns out I didn't need to. The very first page of results had news stories from several different outlets, with near-identical headlines about a death. I sucked in my breath.

"You found it?"

I nodded without looking up, scanning the first story quickly, remembering this happening. It was horrible.

"Do you remember that busboy who died at a bar last spring? The seals on the carbon dioxide tank failed as it was being filled, and the gas flooded the basement without anyone noticing, and he went down there, and it suffocated him?"

Jai squinted, clearly not remembering. "Maybe? Sounds familiar. Is there some connection to this guy?"

I didn't answer at once. I'd found an article with all the details. How a twenty-year-old busboy, they later figured out, was upset after a table yelled at him, and had snuck down into the basement to steal a few minutes alone. The busboy, Jake Hernandez, had made it all the way to a disused storage area when he succumbed to the poisonous gas, and no one noticed that he was missing until the next day. I shivered. The idea of suffocating to death alone in the basement of a crowded bar . . . well, I could already tell it was a scenario my brain would dwell on at three in the morning for the foreseeable future.

When I'd read through the article, I related the gist of the story to Jai. "And the bar, Afterhours, is one of the places Will owns. He's quoted in all the news stories, offering condolences to the family, and condemning the state of the building and its equipment."

"There's your wrongful death suit," Jai said. "Something like that, they'd investigate for criminal negligence or code violations or whatever, but it'd have to be pretty egregious to end up as anything more than a slap on the wrist for the owner of the building. Sometimes freak accidents just happen, and there's no fault to be found. But the family might think the restaurant itself or its management needs to be held responsible, so they might sue in civil court."

I nodded, unsure of how to feel. The mental image of the dying busboy gave me chills. But I liked Will. The few interactions we'd had gave me the impression of a trustworthy, upstanding guy. That tiny snippet of a text had grown to outside proportions in my mind, hinting at a sinister backstory lurking behind the facade of kindness. Maybe I should be relieved. A horrible accident, but that was it. An accident. I don't know exactly what I had been expecting, but plenty of other possibilities would have ruined my opinion of him. This wasn't a drunken hit-and-run or a toddler left in a hot car or anything else to trigger my sense of moral outrage.

A tiny, tiny bit of me felt disappointed it wasn't worse. I'm not proud of this or anything, but there's something exciting about the prospect of uncovering a skeleton in someone's closet. If I were a heroine in a gothic novel, and I'd seen the words "wrongful death" inscribed on a scrap of parchment in the estate of the wealthy landowner, you can bet he'd have the virtuous father of a beautiful peasant girl locked in the dungeon, or something. My idea of "gothic literature" is more heavily informed by *Beauty and the Beast* than it should be, but I can't really help that, can I?

I was also a little cocky about my Googling skills at this point. Ignoring the fact that I'd been utterly lost when I started, I had now decided no information could elude me. I turned my attention to the other people at Mrs. Van Meer's house.

I failed completely. Other than the fact that Ali really liked attending charity events, and that Teri ran a commercial real estate firm, and that the late Frank Van Meer had been an investment banker with a firm I was too poor to have heard of, I struck out. Maybe I could find Brett's full name somewhere on the corporate website for Teri's firm, since he seemed to be involved, but it was a pretty minimalist site. I tried "van meer" and "bonnie," and got nothing relevant. I couldn't even imagine a starting point for tracking down Kevin, since literally all I knew about him was his first name and the fact that he often worked there. He could be a full-time employee, or some kind of self-employed handyman/landscaper who just happened to do work for Mrs. Van Meer.

My only consolation was that Jai failed, too. He found my Google search way more interesting than whatever he was supposed to be doing for work, and joined in. I'd found the perfect combination of his love for research and his stupidly competitive nature. He wanted to find facts, and specifically, to find facts that I hadn't found. The one thing he tracked down that I thought was truly impressive was Mrs. Van Meer's maiden name. Given that she'd probably been married for fifty years, and that it was probably the answer to a security question somewhere, I'd call that an impressive find. We kept at it, off and on, until it was time to leave for Dicey's for our regularly scheduled Tuesday dinner and game night with Ruby and AJ, a married couple we're good friends with. They'd always been very supportive of my pet behaviorist venture, offering advice and encouragement, so this whole mess was basically their fault.

Chapter Fourteen

AJ and Ruby waited for us, heads together, checking out something on Ruby's phone. AJ looked up first, tilting her head to let her maroon hair slide away from her eyes. Ruby barely waited for us to sit down before she slid the phone across to our side of the table.

"Mock-ups for new merchandise! The printer just emailed me the proofs ten minutes ago." Ruby bounced in her chair, her poofy ponytail bouncing even more enthusiastically.

I swiped through the dozen or so brightly colored pictures, all featuring the characters from Ruby's webcomic: *The Adventures of Pete and Fred* by Ruby Burton-Flores. "Oh my gosh! These are great! I want a tote bag with Space Fred. Oh, and the one with Fred and Pete as trapeze artists. And Vampire Pete. Let me know the instant these go live, and I'll buy you out."

Ruby laughed and took her phone back. "It'll be a couple weeks. I'll let you know." She set the phone down on the table beside her, but it took some effort for her to drag her eyes away from the artwork.

I read through the menu, just like always, and then ordered their tonkatsu ramen and a bottle of cider, just like always. I caught Jai looking wistfully at the breakfast side of the menu, but he flipped it over and settled for nachos. Our waitress left, we started setting up the pieces for the night's game, and I got around to mentioning Mrs. Van Meer's death. I didn't go into a lot of detail but made it clear to my friends that I'd been there when the body had been found. Then I told them about the news Brett had given me that morning, about Mrs. Van Meer's will and the pet trust, and about Teri and Ali's reactions.

I told the story off-handedly, like relating an interesting anecdote. I don't think any of the anxiety I felt came across. But if I'm honest with myself, I'd been waiting all day to hear AJ's reaction. She had been in Jai's class in law school, and unlike him, became a practicing attorney in criminal law. In court she goes by her full name, Amira Jasarevic, but I've never personally heard anyone call her anything other than AJ.

The second I finished talking, she leaned forward. "I don't think they'd have reasonable grounds to contest that provision of the will. I'm not an expert in probate law, but I don't think they'd have any way to demonstrate that you'd been in a position to exert undue influence after such a short acquaintance." She squinted into the distance, accessing some underutilized corner of her mental legal library. "Did you have any conversations that could be interpreted as threatening or coercive?"

"Of course not!" said Ruby, jumping in to defend me. "Can you imagine Nikki trying to threaten someone, even a little old lady?"

AJ leaned back in her chair and shook her head. We all grinned at her characteristic mannerism, a dead giveaway of a forthcoming lecture.

"You're conflating impropriety with the appearance of impropriety."

"I do beg your pardon," Ruby said, putting a hand to her chest. "Can you find it in your heart to forgive me?"

AJ made a halfhearted stab at continuing her lecture on legal distinctions and varying burdens of proof, but Ruby had successfully interrupted her train of thought before she'd really gotten warmed up.

The subject dropped through the next three turns of the game, an intricate one in which I couldn't seem to keep track of all the rules. The others seemed to pick it up quickly, while I felt like my brain was melting. But the artwork on the cards was pretty.

"So, you can spend the three hundred thousand dollars however you want, as long as you can make some kind of argument that it's in the best interest of this dog?" Ruby tapped a card with an anthropomorphic radish against her chin thoughtfully. "That's a situation that might inspire some . . . creative thinking."

"Hypothetically," said Jai, matching Ruby's tone, "it just has to be something that you could have reasonably thought would be in the dog's best interest. The court wouldn't even have to agree that it was, just that you could have thought that it was."

AJ had been focused on the cards in front of her, brow furrowed, but Jai had said her favorite word—"hypothetically." "I'd have to read the actual terms of the trust, but from how you've explained it, I'd bet the only oversight is set up to prevent truly egregious abuses."

"You can't have a dog in that tiny apartment," said Ruby. She was going to say more, but I interrupted her.

"Oh, no. I don't have to take in the dog. I'm just in charge of his welfare."

"Like I was saying," Ruby continued, ignoring me, "you can't have a dog in that tiny apartment. You'll need a bigger house, with a yard. Something in the range of three hundred thousand dollars might do nicely. It'd be in the dog's best interest."

We all laughed, and my cheeks burned.

"I'm so ashamed to admit it, but that thought did occur to me when the lawyer was explaining it all."

A fresh burst of laughter followed.

"I don't think you could get away with that," said AJ, still grinning. "But you'd be completely justified in continuing to pay yourself for walking the dog."

I shuddered. "That's exactly what he said. It feels so gross."

"Look at it this way," she said, "you know for a fact the old woman saw that as an acceptable expense for the dog's well-being. Her beneficiaries and the executors of her estate don't get to suddenly decide it's an extravagance, just because she passed away. The courts know that inheritors tend to get stingy with money that might end up in their pockets. That's kind of the whole thought process behind making a pet trust that's separate from the rest of the assets."

AJ's matter-of-tone should have been reassuring—was reassuring—but this conversation also made the whole messy situation feel more real. The fact that I could actually end up in a courtroom, in front of a judge, having to account for my actions made me feel queasy. I could always refuse, I guess. But could I count on any of the others to take care of

Reginald? Mrs. Van Meer hadn't trusted them, and had instead turned to me. I couldn't turn my back on Reginald and just hope that one of the others would step up.

I forced a laugh, conscious that the others were waiting for some kind of reply. "Well, you little poor people better hope I remember you when my ship comes in. Now, enough about wills and dogs. I've lost track of whose turn it is, but no matter what anyone else does, I'm going roller-skating." I slammed down the last card in my hand, a duck in bell-bottoms, zigzagging under a disco ball, and looked expectantly at the rest of them.

As it turns out, I didn't get to go roller-skating that turn, or for the rest of the game. As the others laid down their cards, it became clear that, instead of boogying the night away at the roller rink, my in-game character loaned her skates to a pitiful-looking child and ate nachos alone at the rink's concession stand. Not the outcome I'd wanted, but I had successfully ended the conversation about milking the estate of a dead woman.

Chapter Fifteen

The next morning, I got up bright and early and felt optimistic about starting the day. At some point during the night, I'd decided to recuse myself from walking Reginald. I'd tell Teri and Ali it would be in their best interest to find a teenager in the neighborhood who would walk Reginald for a fraction of my rate. Then they wouldn't believe I was a scamming them—not if I passed up such a lucrative gig. It should have given me a slight pang to turn my back on a source of income while we were trying so hard to save for a house, but I just wanted to be done with these people. And then, once everyone had calmed down, I could talk to Brett. There must be a way to transfer the pet trust to someone else while still ensuring Reginald's best interests were being looked after.

Nobody was around when I picked up Reginald, which meant they were avoiding me. Fine. So much the better. As Reginald and I traced his favorite route, I used the time to rehearse my speech.

"Teri, your grandmother was paying above market value to get me to drive out here every day to walk Reginald. I'm sure someone in the neighborhood is looking to pick up some extra cash."

Reginald, who had been sniffing a tuft of crab grass growing out from under a decorative boulder on the edge of someone's property, looked up at me.

"No, not the right tone for her? Maybe I should start with Ali. Ali, I've really enjoyed my time with Reginald, and getting the chance to help him out, but at this point, you really only need a dog walker, not an animal behaviorist. You're on the right track with him."

Reginald flopped his butt to the ground and watched me, twitching his ears when a siren wailed in the distance.

"Oh, you good little man! Did you hear me say your name? I'm going to sneak into the garage when we get back and find you a treat."

He stood back up, ready to resume his walk, now with a promise of treats. I kept at it, trying to figure out wording that would explain why I couldn't keep charging Mrs. Van Meer's estate for these walks, without suggesting I'd been taking advantage of her while she was alive. A difficult line to toe, especially because at least some part of me believed I had been taking advantage of her. Sure, I'd been steamrolled into the dog walking, but I could have put my foot down.

As we approached the Van Meer house, I wasn't any closer to a final draft of my speech, so I slowed our pace, hoping to delay the moment of confrontation. But as we rounded the last bend, flashing lights greeted us. I'd found the source of the sirens. Half of me wanted to slow down even further to put off finding out what terrible thing had happened, and half of me wanted to rush forward. I forced myself to keep the pace steady, to avoid alarming Reginald. I kept up my steady stream of chatter with him.

"Well, it looks like your house had some visitors. I wonder who they could be. Were you expecting guests, Reggie? All those red and blue lights make it look like they're ready for a party!"

A fire truck, two police cars, and a white utility van filled the circular drive. As we got closer, I saw that the van bore the logo of the gas company. At the curb, a uniformed police officer stood with a group of firefighters, who, to my relief, looked relaxed. Nothing in their stances suggested they expected to run into a burning building. Every member of the household also stood by the curb, in a small cluster a little way from the officers. They stood together, but each one of them looked drawn into themselves, arms crossed, not speaking to each other. As I approached, they widened the circle to make a spot for me, but still no one said anything.

Reginald gave a low whine and then a short bark. He could tell something serious was going on. Still, no one spoke.

"What's going on?" I asked.

Bonnie shook her head but didn't say anything.

"We don't know," Teri said. Then she seemed to realize how incredibly inadequate that response was to someone who knew even less than she did. "They won't really tell us anything. They ran up and said we needed to evacuate immediately. Something about a report of a gas leak. But they haven't said anything since then, and none of us smelled gas at all."

A pause, and then Ali offered, "Well, they did ask me where Grandma's room was."

"What?!" Teri rounded on her. "You said they were asking if there was anyone else in the house."

Ali crossed her arms. "That's what I thought they meant at first. Like maybe they had a list of the people who live here, or they got her name off the tax records, or something. Then I realized how weird it was, and I wanted a chance to figure it out myself, but then you asked, and I just said . . . that. I wanted to think about it."

Will put an arm around her shoulder, and she leaned into him. Teri glared at her and then looked around the circle, either looking for someone to help her gang up on Ali, or looking for another target for her impotent fury. I avoided her gaze, and I think most of the others did, too.

It seemed that they'd told me all they knew, since none of the others chimed in with further information. Of course, if there was something else, and they hadn't mentioned it before, they'd have to be brave to bring it up now and incur the wrath of Teri. I wanted to just go, but I'd left my purse in the house, and the plastic bag of dog poop I clutched made a poor substitute. Instead, I resigned myself to wait it out with the rest of them. Reginald sensed we were in for the long haul and lay down at my feet.

After another ten minutes or so, we all turned at the sound of the front door opening. Two police officers came out, followed closely by two workers wearing fluorescent vests with the gas company logo. The gas workers went to their van, while the officers joined the cluster of firefighters, reporting their findings to the others. The officer who'd been outside the whole time stepped a little away from the others and spoke into his shoulder radio.

Then, absolutely nothing happened. The gas van didn't leave, although the two workers sat in the cab. The fire truck didn't leave, even though we could hear their radios squawking with what might have been other emergencies. As far as we could tell, this was a grand old reunion of the police and fire departments, and they were just taking some time to catch up on each other's lives.

Teri nudged Brett. "You should go find out what's going on. I bet they won't flat-out refuse to answer a direct question."

He shook his head. "They're clearly waiting for something. Maybe the gas guys are filling out paperwork saying there's no danger, but the police and firefighters can't leave until they have that in writing. Or maybe they're waiting for a crew to come out with more sensitive equipment. I have no idea. But there's nothing to gain by rushing them and risking antagonizing them. We just have to wait until they're ready to deal with us."

The group dynamics changed as time passed. Ali started shifting from one foot to another, before sitting down on the curb with Will's help. I didn't envy her having to be on her feet so long at seven months pregnant. Then Bonnie stepped a little apart from the group and lit a cigarette. A flicker of envy passed over Kevin's face. I sat on the grass with Reginald.

We'd been there for a little more than half an hour when a silver car pulled into the driveway. The extra mirrors on the side and lightbar mounted above the driver's head gave it away as an unmarked police car. The woman who got out of the driver's side was short, with glossy black hair collected in a bun. She wore pressed khaki slacks and a pale blue button-down shirt that set off her dark, olive skin. I couldn't see much about her face because she wore sunglasses, though not the reflective aviators police detectives always seem to wear on TV.

She approached the cluster of police officers and firefighters first, talking at length with the one who'd evidently radioed for her. His conversation with her involved a lot of pointing: at us, at the house, at the gas company van, at the house again, at the fire truck (which he may have thought was feeling left out), and back at us again. I had no idea what the etiquette here was supposed to be. On the one hand, it felt OK to watch them, since we were obviously the subject of the discussion. But on the other hand, some part of me desperately wanted to "act natural" in the sense of putting on a great show of aloofness, until something was said directly to me. I don't know if the others struggled with the same feelings, but I can tell you we all ended up watching the new arrival, either like a cat watching a mouse or a mouse watching a cat. I'm not sure which.

Next, she hiked up the driveway to the gas company van, which the firefighters took as their cue to leave. They piled into the fire truck and pulled away, leaving the uniformed police officers standing around as awkwardly as us. Now everyone watched the plainclothes officer talk to the workmen from the gas company who still sat inside their van. She leaned against the driver's side door, an elbow resting on the open window. No sound from their conversation reached us.

I heard Brett mutter, "Anybody read lips?" but so quietly I'm not sure who else heard him. If he'd really sold it, he could have lightened the mood. The mood could have used some lightening.

Finally, it was our turn. When I'd joined, the circle had widened to receive me but had maintained its shape. During the long wait, the circle had broken up, but reformed when the silver car pulled up. Now we fanned out to present ourselves to the officer, with a tacit understanding that, instead of joining us, she was confronting us. I wondered if this was in any way similar to the instinct that allows flocks of birds to react to obstacles and predators.

"I'm Detective Maria Tanghal, St. Louis County Police." She tilted her head down, toward the badge clipped to her belt, right in front of her holster. "Could you tell me your full names, and your relationship to Ruth Van Meer, please?"

My relationship to Ruth Van Meer? Oof. I'd better make sure I answered for myself. Who knows what Teri might say.

Chapter Sixteen

"What's all this about?" Teri obviously intended to sound self-assured, but a waver in her voice gave away her nervousness.

Detective Tanghal wasn't fazed by the question. "I'll explain in a minute. Your name, please?" One of the uniformed officers had come up behind her and held a notebook ready.

Teri scuffed one shoe on the ground in front of her and gave her name, sounding a little like a sulky child. She liked to be in control of the situation, and Detective Tanghal wasn't going to allow her to be.

The officer went around our semi-circle and collected names. You remember how just the day before, I'd been kicking myself for not knowing everyone's full names? You'd think my Googling adventures would have made me pay attention at this point. Instead, I used those few seconds to rehearse what I would say when my turn came, and let everyone else's answers drift in one ear and out the other.

"Nikki. Nicole Jackson-Ramanathan." As expected, the officer had no problem with the first part of my name but politely asked me to spell "Ramanathan." For the first year or so after marrying Jai, I would always tell people to spell it like it sounds, because . . . you spell it like it sounds, but now I just spell it for them. When I was asked for my connection with Mrs. Van Meer, I gestured at Reginald and said she'd hired me to walk the dog. As much as I wanted to get in front of what accusations Teri might start flinging, this didn't seem to be the time or the place to bring up Mrs. Van Meer's will. Thankfully, none of the others jumped in with more information.

"Preliminary indications from the office of the County Coroner are that Ruth Van Meer had elevated levels of carbon monoxide in her system. The levels are high enough that carbon monoxide poisoning is being treated as the probable cause of death at this time." Detective Tanghal glanced around the circle. The sunglasses made it impossible to tell exactly when she was looking right at you.

The instant I could be sure the detective was looking elsewhere, my eyes snapped to Will, who had an arm around Ali's shoulders. I'd spent more than an hour yesterday reading about someone dying of gas exposure in his restaurant, and now someone in his own family had died of something similar. This must be his worst nightmare. His face remained almost eerily blank. His eyes met mine, just for a second, and I looked away. I didn't want him to think I was staring.

And, after all, I had no excuse for knowing what I did about him. There's no graceful way to say, "Using your fiancée's grandfather's obituary and your wedding registry, I found out about the time one of your employees died a horrific death on the job." If it came out, I'd have to claim I put two and two together since Ali told me he owned Afterhours. Was it plausible for me to have remembered the original news stories from last spring? I bet the full-time employees at the neighboring bars remembered all right, but I just picked up the occasional shift.

Detective Tanghal continued, "It's too early for a conclusive determination as to the cause of death. The initial indications triggered concern for the other occupants of the house. It's not uncommon for a carbon monoxide leak to go undetected, even after the most vulnerable members of the household suffer the effects of exposure. A search has been performed throughout the house, and the technicians were unable to find elevated levels of carbon monoxide, or to identify a specific malfunctioning appliance that could account for the presence of the gas in the victim's body. Have any gas appliances been serviced in the time since Ruth Van Meer's death?"

Teri shook her head.

Ali looked at Kevin. "Weren't you working on the fireplace yesterday?"

He shook his head. "I mean, yes, but it wasn't anything to do with this." He scratched his head and looked around the circle. After a few seconds he realized that wasn't good enough. "The remote stopped working last week, so Bonnie switched out the batteries. She just told me about it, so I switched out the receiver batteries, too. He frowned at the officer behind Detective Tanghal, who was writing furiously. "You wanna keep them on the same schedule."

"That's true!" Bonnie jumped in. "I told him about it, and he said he'd take care of it."

"Thank you," said Detective Tanghal. "Other than that?"

Ali shook her head.

"Then, we have no evidence to support a theory of accidental carbon monoxide poisoning. Until we receive further information from the coroner's office, we will be investigating the possibility of intentional administration."

"Suicide?!" Brett ran a hand through his hair, then laid it on Teri's shoulder. "Oh, my god. I'm here for whatever you need." He looked at Ali. "For both of you."

Teri glared at Brett, and Ali offered him a weak smile. I grimaced and looked down at the ground, embarrassed. At Detective Tanghal's words, my mind had jumped to murder, not suicide. Clearly, I'd been watching too much TV. Of course, suicide was the more likely alternative, and I'd let my imagination run away with me.

"I understand from the reports that Ruth Van Meer's body was discovered Monday morning. You were all there?" She glanced around, satisfied with our nods. "Who was the last to see her alive? Was it one of you?"

Well, there's a point. I felt vindicated. Suicide didn't make any sense, after all. We hadn't found her slumped over the wheel of a car running in a closed garage. She'd been tucked into bed, looking for all the world like she'd gone to sleep and just never woken up. And if it wasn't suicide, and it wasn't an accident, then my instinct had been correct. It must have been murder.

I'd had another instinct. Was there any chance it was right, too? Maybe my gut was more accurate than my brain. I'd thought I caught a deep emotion behind the blank look on Will's face when our eyes met. Could it have been guilt? The accident at his restaurant had been carbon dioxide and this carbon monoxide, but the accident might have given him the idea for the murder.

Teri answered Detective Tanghal's question. "I think we all, or most of us, saw her Sunday night, when she came out to say goodnight. We had some people over, and she always put in an appearance."

"What time was that?"

Again, the group looked around at each other. No one looked certain.

"Nine-thirty?" Teri volunteered. "But just because that's when she normally went to bed. I don't know for sure." She shrugged, and I could see her frustration at not really being able to contribute anything helpful. I'm sure she wanted to say, "I happened to glance at my watch, and it was exactly nine-twenty-seven."

I could do that, kind of. Of all the people at the party, I'd been the one most focused on the game, as opposed to socializing and catching up.

"Um," I began, forgetting how to string words together. I'd planned what to say, but, somehow, I hadn't thought far enough ahead to realize everyone would turn their attention to me. I ignored everyone else and focused on Detective Tanghal. "I don't know if you have a way to look it up or anything, but it was late in the third quarter of the Chiefs-Chargers game. The Chiefs were either third-and-seven or third-and-eight and they completed for eleven. It was the longest pass of the quarter." My cheeks burned. I sounded like some kind of football savant, but that pass had been one of the few offensive bright spots in an otherwise terrible game. If the police needed to pinpoint the time Mrs. Van Meer had gone to bed, that was a surefire way to do it.

Detective Tanghal stared at me without saying anything, for just a tiny bit longer than was comfortable. I don't know if she was pressuring me to say more or just giving her fellow officer time to finish writing down what I'd said. I glanced at

Teri, who was, predictably, also staring at me. She wouldn't see this as a collaborative effort to get the police the information they needed. Oh, no. I'd one-upped her in front of the cops.

"Thank you. Can anyone else corroborate the timing?" No one spoke up, so she continued. "I'll need a list of everyone who was at the party. Then, those of you who don't live here are free to go. Make sure you give Sergeant Townsend your contact information. Those of you who live here are going to be displaced for a few hours, I'm afraid. I have a forensic team on the way."

After giving the sergeant my address and phone number, I described my purse, and he had one of the other officers fetch it for me. I passed Reginald's leash to Will and headed toward my car. Kevin had been the first to leave, followed by Bonnie, which surprised me. Somehow, once I'd gotten used to the idea of a personal assistant/house manager, I couldn't imagine Mrs. Van Meer being forced to survive without her for even a few hours. I imagined her like a housekeeper or butler from an old movie, always around whenever needed.

It surprised me even more when Brett peeled off from the group. He'd been there every time I'd been to the house, so I assumed he lived there. I don't know exactly why I thought that. No part of my brain thought that "family attorney" was a live-in position, but I was stupefied by the entire lifestyle of this family, and ready to believe anything.

Brett fell into step beside me, and I said what I was thinking, for no other reason than to fill the silence.

"Don't you live here?"

He looked at me with an eyebrow raised. "No, of course not."

Of course not. Why in the world would he? I had just come to that conclusion on my own. Why did I say the thing out loud?

"I mean, I do end up spending a lot of nights here," he continued. "Will and I have a few drinks, and I crash in the carriage house instead of driving back to my own place. Not every night," he hastened to add, apparently worried I might judge him.

Little did he know I was over here celebrating the fact that I hadn't been so far off, after all. He did basically live with the Van Meers, more or less. And my assumption wasn't based on nothing. Everything about his demeanor Monday morning had said that he'd just rolled out of bed, and turns out I'd been right about that, after all. Who knew that kind of couch-surfing perpetual guest existed in this socioeconomic class, too?

Something about my vibe must have still read as judgmental to him, though, because he kept talking. "They've got the carriage house set up real nice for guests, but they never have anyone over, and I live on my own, so it's not like someone's sitting up at home waiting for me. It's no big deal."

We'd reached my car. I flashed him a small smile. "See you later."

He nodded. "You'll be back tomorrow? To walk Reginald?"

How did I get mixed up with these people? Normally, you hire a dog walker because you work long hours. These people seemed to be sitting around the house all the time, but for some reason they needed to outsource their dog-walking needs. But I just smiled again and said, "See you then."

I thought I'd made a pretty cool exit in the face of the bombshell Detective Tanghal had dropped on us. It's how I imagined Audrey Hepburn would have left the scene. Only when I leaned over to set my purse in the passenger seat did I discover the bag of dog poop had come along for the ride.

I froze for a second, unsure of what to do. Then I set the bag on the floor, as far away from me as I could reach, and pulled away, wondering how many of those people had noticed the bright green bag in my hand.

On my way home, I turned into the parking lot of a park with trash cans at the entrance. For some reason, I checked to make sure no one was watching before I threw the bag away. If I could explain why I did that, I'd owe myself a cookie.

Chapter Seventeen

I opened our front door quietly. On Wednesdays, Jai has a departmental meeting, which is smaller and more relevant to him than the company-wide meeting he'd blown off the day before. As I entered, he swiveled around to give me a small wave and mouth "Hi." I tried my best not to interrupt, but he must have seen something in my expression because his face changed. He turned back to his screen, typed something, and then shut the laptop and pulled out his headphones.

"What's wrong?"

I couldn't answer at first. Something about the concern in his tone brought everything home to me. I slid off my shoes, put down my purse, pulled off my jacket, and sat down on the couch. He joined me and gave me a quick kiss on the cheek. I wanted to lay my head on his shoulder and stay there for the next four or five hours, not thinking about murder or death or the Van Meers. But that might make it a teensy bit hard for him to finish out his workday, so I settled for a quick embrace.

"The police were there. Mrs. Van Meer's death wasn't an accident."

"An accident? What do you mean? I thought you said she died in her sleep."

I shook my head, more to clear it than to answer him. Having trouble remembering what information I had that Jai didn't. I shook my head again.

"Yes, sorry. I'm a little shaken up. Let me start over." I took a deep breath, and Jai laid a reassuring hand on my leg. "They found out that she died of carbon monoxide poisoning. The fire department came to the house assuming there was a leak somewhere. But they couldn't find anything, so now the police are investigating. They think it was either murder or suicide."

"Oh, wow." He grimaced. "I'm sorry. I don't know what else to say. Are you OK?"

I nodded automatically, then shook my head and leaned into him again. "I guess. I can't imagine what the family's going through. Murder." I looked away from Jai. "And here I am, worrying about myself. Teri hates me. You should have heard the horrible things she said when she found out about the will. If there's going to be a police investigation, who knows what kind of accusations she'll start flinging around."

"Did you already tell the police about the money the old woman left you in her will?"

"She didn't leave it to me!" My voice rose, sharp and defensive. "She named me the custodian of it, remember? Last night, you and AJ were perfectly clear on the distinction."

He waited. Jai had never been someone who would move on with an unanswered question hanging in the air.

"No, I haven't told the police about it. Yet. I haven't really told them anything. They only asked us, all of us, all together, a couple of questions, trying to figure out when Mrs. Van Meer had last been seen alive. Then they sent away everyone who didn't live there."

"Should we call AJ?"

Jai's tone and face were too serious for me to deal with right then, so I forced a laugh. I needed him to tell me that this was no big deal, and instead he suggested I line up legal representation. Admitting the situation was too serious for him. Despite his law degree, he wasn't a practicing attorney.

"I'm not joking," he said. "You should get her advice before you talk to the police any more than you already have."

I shook my head, hoping the smile I plastered across my face concealed the nausea roiling my stomach.

"Listen, Nikki. You've heard her talk about all the cases she's worked on. What do most of them have in common? The police find one little incriminating thing, and from that point on, they never even look at any other suspects. Once they focus on somebody, they'll see all the evidence through the lens of their conclusion, and the jury will, too."

I didn't say anything. I couldn't say anything. How many times had we heard the same story from AJ, who worked to overturn wrongful convictions? She'd take on a case and start looking for alternate theories, only to find law enforcement had never investigated any other suspects.

Jai took a deep breath. I think he wanted to stop himself from scaring me. "Maybe they'll find clear forensic evidence and wrap the case up in the next day or two. But if this thing drags on, and they need to find a solution . . . I'm sure the family would rather point the finger at you than entertain the idea that any of them is involved. You've only known these people a week. They have no loyalty to you. Promise me you won't wait too long to talk to AJ."

I nodded, trying to smile again. Tears were imminent, and I needed this conversation to end before they came. I waved a hand toward Jai's desk. "Sorry I interrupted your meeting. You get back to that. I'm going for a walk."

Jai's face lightened as he rolled his eyes. "They're using our departmental meeting slot for mandatory training. It's been two and a half hours already, with no end in sight. Did you have any idea it's important to make clients happy with the work we're doing, while still being sure to adhere to internal policy?"

"Stop! Stop!" I grinned and slapped my hands over my ears. "You're giving away confidential corporate strategy!"

I closed the apartment door behind me. The instant I headed out, the tears started spilling. I sank onto the top step and let them fall. The tears came from feeling overwhelmed. If I didn't know exactly how to feel or what to do, I'd have a good cry and then move on. There was no point in trying not to cry. I'd learned that from experience. After a minute or two, the tears stopped, as I'd known they would. I wiped my face and then sat for a few more minutes, playing a distracting game on my phone, to give the redness time to leave my eyes. I'd told Jai I needed to take a walk, so a walk it was. Two blocks up to the park, and then along one of the winding paths until my head cleared.

I'd made a plan. No sitting helplessly and waiting for the police to investigate. I knew these people, and maybe I was even there when the murder happened. If the police didn't figure it out from whatever conclusive forensic evidence they collected, maybe I could beat them to the solution.

When I've made a new plan, step one is always the same. Whether it's studying for the bartender's exam or planning my wedding or starting a pet behaviorist business or investigating a murder, my first stop was Crosshatch, an independent art supply store on the opposite end of the park. I'm a visual thinker and a verbal processor, and unless I get my thoughts down on paper, nothing productive ever happens. Already my brain swirled with facts and theories about the people in Mrs. Van Meer's life, but it would all disintegrate into mush soon. I needed a new pen.

Crosshatch was a small-looking corner storefront with a picture window, a striped awning, a welcome mat, and a bell above the door. From the outside, it looked like the kind of niche shop where you can walk to the center, sweep your gaze across the contents in ten or fifteen seconds, and know immediately whether anything has caught your interest, or whether it's your kind of shop. But the inside was a rabbit warren of tiny rooms, each devoted to a discipline of visual arts to a, frankly, unwieldy depth. The building dated from the late eighteen hundreds, with all kinds of ornate detailing layered on top of the orange-red brick of this vintage of building. Originally, the first floor housed a large dry goods store, and the second and third floors were a single residence, probably occupied by the owner of the store. Sometime in the twentieth century, with space at a premium, the building had been partitioned into offices below and apartments above, with an unassuming art supply store occupying the southeast corner. Over the years, as tenants moved out, Crosshatch expanded to fill all the available space, in such a piecemeal fashion that all the partitions remained in place, with doorways knocked through wherever needed. At the cash register by the front door, newer visitors could pick up a photocopied map drawn by a local cartoonist, although the one being handed out currently was at least three years out of date and made no reference to the shibori closet on the third floor, off the general textile room.

I, like most of the freelance artists and hobbyists living in this part of town, knew my way around. I waved at Alex, up a ladder restocking a shelf with prestretched canvases, and headed toward the second of the four staircases at the back of building. I skirted a freestanding display of polymer clay and ducked into the well-lit ink room. I forced myself to turn my back on the glittering south wall, where plain wooden shelves held glass jars of ink in hundreds of colors. I had a calligraphy job coming up, and the bride wanted "mermaid-ombre," as she described it. I was looking forward to shopping for that ink, but this was not the time. As much as I love the effects dip pens could create, they were too impractical for what I needed today. I wanted a pen handy to grab when a thought struck me. But it needed to be an exciting color.

I pulled out pens almost at random, letting colors and styles catch my eye. If they felt right in my hand, I'd doodle with them on the pads of scratch paper that hung from every shelf. Apparently, greens called to me today. I tried out a mossy green, a smooth mint green, and a shockingly neon green, before settling on a deep blue-green with a metallic sheen. I mentally named the color "dragon green" and left the room clutching my single new pen, congratulating myself on my restraint.

Once I checked out, I headed back into the park. I passed up several benches in a thickly wooded area where it was too cold to sit in the shade. Toward the center of the park, the trees thinned out and created more open spaces. The park wasn't anywhere near as crowded as first thing in the morning, or after school let out, but it wasn't deserted. I avoided a couple of parents with very young toddlers, and an elderly couple with a pair of rambunctious Pomeranians who got their leashes tangled up every few steps, then chose a bench and sat down to work.

I turned to the first blank page in my notebook, skipping past various notes and lists and doodles, all in their assigned colors. With my brand-new pen, I needed to make a chart. Means, motive, and opportunity. The necessary elements for a good suspect, right? If one of the people from the Van Meer household was missing one of those elements, I could eliminate them as a suspect. If just one of them had all three, I could call Detective Tanghal and be done with the whole thing. I wrote everyone's name down the left side of the page, and used another page, folded back, as a ruler to draw perfect gridlines for three columns. You might accuse me of stalling, but there's always time to make your notes look nice.

That much done, I stared at the chart, then flipped to the next page and sketched Reginald. It looked terrible—like a kind of dog/duck/giraffe hybrid. I squinted. Maybe I was being charitable by including "dog" in that mix. I added more lines. If it couldn't look good, it could at least look artistic.

Maybe later I'd look up some hound dog reference photos and try again.

Now I really was stalling.

I flipped back to the chart and forced myself to focus. I hadn't murdered Mrs. Van Meer, but somebody had.

Chapter Eighteen

Motive was the easy one. Teri and Ali, and by extension, Will, could have killed Mrs. Van Meer for the inheritance. They all seemed like they had plenty of money, but you can never really know anyone's financial position from the outside. Kevin had been angry about Mrs. Van Meer's intention to sell the house, which would have cost him his job. Bonnie might lose her job, too. You didn't need a landscaper in a condo, but did you need a personal assistant or house manager, or whatever her job actually was? I dug around in my bag for a pencil to add Bonnie's motive. It didn't feel as solid as the others. I couldn't see a clear motive for Brett, which either meant he didn't have one and was in the clear, or I hadn't discovered it yet.

Messiness surrounded Brett, though. Like the fight after Brett had revealed the details of the pet trust. I thought Teri had implied Brett and Ali were having an affair. She'd made some hints during the football game about a complication around Ali and Will's relationship. Could that be what she meant? If Brett and Ali were having an affair, and Mrs. Van

Meer had found out, what would she have done? Fire Brett as the family's attorney? Disinherit Ali? Tell Will?

They added up to strong motives for Ali, and potential motives for Brett. Maybe Brett was in the same boat as Kevin, fearing for his job. As far as I'd been able to tell, the Van Meer family accounted for 100 percent of his business as an attorney. I stuck with the pencil and wrote it down, writing a little more faintly than I had for Bonnie, so it'd be easier to erase.

Fuzzy on the means, I skipped it for now.

Opportunity headed up my third column. A complete waste of time as everyone except Bonnie had been there Sunday night. Any one of them could have done it. I put an "X" next to Bonnie's name, still in pencil. It's not like I really knew where she'd been, so she could have been lurking upstairs while we partied out on the patio. That still left a ridiculous number of people who could have done it.

"It?"

The absurdity of me solving a crime hit all of a sudden. I didn't have any idea what had happened. How in the world could I figure out who had killed Mrs. Van Meer, when I had no idea how Mrs. Van Meer had been killed. Carbon monoxide? People died of carbon monoxide by accident, when furnaces malfunctioned, or by suicide, when they inhaled car exhaust. How did you murder someone with carbon monoxide?

I set the notebook on the bench beside me and switched to my phone to look up "sources of carbon monoxide."

Oh my god.

There were so many things that could produce carbon monoxide and kill you. Why did Jai and I not have a carbon monoxide detector for every room? The question was no longer "How had Mrs. Van Meer died?" It was, "How had any of us survived this long?" I turned to a clean page in my notebook and started copying out a list of potential sources.

Clothes dryer. I'd only seen a tiny portion of the house, and not the laundry room. Was the dryer in the basement, directly below Mrs. Van Meer's bedroom?

Gas furnace. I had no idea what kind of heating they had, but most people have gas, right? Probably the first thing the gas company had checked that morning, though.

Car. Preferably old enough not to have a catalytic converter. I will not claim to know anything about cars, but the two in the smaller garage Sunday night were about as old as I'd ever seen.

Space heater. I frowned at that one. Not likely. I associated space heaters with drafty old houses and absentee landlords who didn't fix furnaces. I couldn't picture a space heater in the comfortable Van Meer home. Even the garages seemed climate-controlled.

Fireplace. There was one in Mrs. Van Meer's bedroom. I'd seen it Monday morning when we'd found her body. I put a star next to that one.

Gas stove. Yes, one in the main kitchen, and one in the outdoor kitchen.

Gas grill. Yes, on the back patio. And in use Sunday night. I almost starred that entry, too, unsure whether the grill being in use made it more or less likely to be the source of the deadly gas.

Propane heater. I almost skipped that one, thinking along the same lines as space heaters, picturing the porous walls of a rural cabin somewhere. But they did have propane heaters! Surely the tall, chrome heaters used to make the outdoor patio comfortable for the NFL watch party had been propane-powered.

I looked at my list, amazed people weren't dropping like flies. I needed to stock up on carbon monoxide detectors soon, or surely everyone I loved would be dead within a day or two. I didn't see how any of these sources could be weaponized, but it no longer seemed impossible.

Chewing my lip, I flipped back to my chart. That morning, the gas company had checked the whole house for carbon monoxide without finding an obvious source for the gas. Hence the whole police investigation. That meant that whoever had done this hadn't just set everything up on Sunday night.

They must also have had the opportunity to clean up after themselves, and undo whatever they had done. Otherwise, other members of the household would have gotten sick from exposure, and the gas company would have found the source of the leak.

I subdivided my "opportunity" column. I labeled one half "set up" and one half "clean up." If anyone hadn't had a chance to do both, I could cross them off my list.

That didn't really narrow things down, though. Everyone had been at the house at some point between Sunday night and this morning, Wednesday, when the house was checked. Would they have risked leaving things as they were for so long?

Until I knew what exactly had been done, it was impossible to say for sure. But to imagine someone deliberately rigging an appliance to leak CO into Mrs. Van Meer's bedroom, and then leave it like that, for anyone to stumble onto? It would take someone with ice water in their veins. Surely, they would have undone their tampering as soon as possible, maybe even before the party broke up, depending on how quickly Mrs. Van Meer died.

I tried Googling for that answer but gave up after checking two different pages. If I knew the cubic volume of the room, the rate of the gas flow, and was prepared to do some math in the form of simple algebra that might as well have been differential calculus, I could find out how long it would have taken for the gas concentration in the room to reach fatal levels.

I chewed on the end of my brand-new pen and stared into space. The complexity of the math had disconcerted me. It reminded me how utterly unequipped I was for the task I had set myself. The police had a whole forensics lab working on this. They probably had a gas diffusion expert who had already modeled various scenarios and done 3D renderings to explain the concepts to the team of detectives assigned to the case. Their pathologist would have already given them all the data they'd need about Mrs. Van Meer's relative state of health and estimated her sleeping respiration rate to further refine the scenario.

They might have already pinpointed the source of the gas, by the chemical composition of the air in Mrs. Van Meer's lungs. The phrase "mass spectrometry" floated through my brain, probably from one of the web pages I'd just scanned. Whatever that was, they probably had an expert working on it. Then they'd check the appliance for DNA traces, plug that into their database, and arrest the murderer.

I almost threw my pen in disgust at how much time I had wasted. Sitting on a park bench with a sketchbook, imagining I could solve a murder somehow. Look at the pathetic chart

I'd made! I could come up with some motives for people! Big whopping deal.

No, I told myself. Maybe there was some worth in this. I did know about people's motives. I knew about them because I'd interacted with them before Mrs. Van Meer's death. Now all these people, especially the murderer, would be on their guard in police interviews. I couldn't imagine any of them telling Detective Tanghal, "Yes, I wanted her dead, but I didn't do it." They'd lie, or minimize, or rationalize, with her death hanging over their heads and coloring everything they told the police.

I could never tell whether the part of my brain doing the pep talk was the more rational half, trying to bolster the overly pessimistic half. Equally likely that pessimism was the reasonable position here, and the pep talk sprang from a stupidly Pollyanna-ish part of my psyche.

I shrugged at that impossible question and focused my attention back on my chart.

Maybe I could fill in some of the blanks in my motive column without resorting to direct questions that would give away my goal. I could make small talk with Ali about the sale of Mrs. Van Meer's house, to get a sense of how the sale would have affected Bonnie and Kevin. Teri worked in real estate. I could make small talk with her about the new house Ali and Will were having built. I could tell her that Jai and I were thinking of building but weren't sure we were financially stable enough to withstand all the unexpected expenses. Maybe I could coax her into talking about Ali and Will's finances. Would Brett know if Teri was having money problems? I was chewing on my new pen again and forced myself to stop.

The "means" column remained a sparkling, pristine white. If Mrs. Van Meer had been shot, this would be the easiest to fill. Who had a gun, or access to a gun? Instead, the question, apparently, was "Who had a clothes dryer, or access to one?" Did any of them have a concealed carry permit for a furnace? No, "means" meant something different with this kind of murder. Who could have pulled this off?

As a handyman, Kevin, surely, was familiar with the house's appliances. Possibly any of them knew enough to make this happen. People pick up information in unpredictable places all the time. But one name on my list understood how deadly gas leaks could be. Was it possible the accident at Will's restaurant had given him the idea for how to bump off his future grandmother-in-law?

Before I could change my mind, I grabbed my phone and texted a friend of mine, Sasha.

Hey. I've got to get out of the house. Do you have any shifts I could pick up?

Sasha Obiaka, a friend from high school, managed a bar called Franklin's Tower that is not actually in a tower. Every couple of weeks or so, she asked me to cover a shift when a bartender called off sick. I could get steady work there if I wanted it, but the shine would wear off after a second consecutive night of dealing with drunks. As it is, it's a fun adventure, and she pays me in cash at the end of the night. That said, I'd never asked her for a shift before. She'd assume I was broke and desperate, but I was OK with that.

Always. 6 to close tonight, if you want, she answered. *Everything ok?*

Fine. Just feeling restless. See you then.

Six to close worked for me. Jai was running a mock trial practice that evening, so he wouldn't be home anyway. Starting at six would give me plenty of time to poke around the neighborhood, maybe get a bite to eat. You know, innocent stuff like that. Definitely not investigating the murder. That would be foolish and dangerous.

Chapter Nineteen

Back at the apartment, Jai's meeting had finished, and he was packing his things to head over to his practice. I kissed him lightly, assured him I felt better now that I'd calmed down, and told him I had a shift to help Sasha out that night.

"Have fun and drive safe!" we both said, almost in unison, as he left.

I glanced in the mirror to make sure my hair wasn't doing anything maniacal after sitting in the windy park, and went right back out, this time getting in my car and heading for The Grove.

The Grove is a couple of blocks of nightlife and restaurants and shops and a microbrewery, all shoved together in a random part of St. Louis. Not downtown or next to any landmark that would draw crowds. You're driving along a perfectly normal street lined with run-down industrial buildings, and then, all of a sudden, for two blocks, it shifts to neon signs and crosswalks and blaring music and parking meters, before it all fades back into generic rust belt scenery again.

In addition to Franklin's Tower, my place of temporary employment for the evening, The Grove was also home to Afterhours, where, apparently, one of Will's employees had died in a horrific accident. I'd never been inside Afterhours, although I'd been aware of its presence, on the same block as Franklin's Tower, on the same side of the street, about three storefronts down. The time had come to patronize this establishment. I'd get an early supper, and, if I happened to glean some information from a talkative member of the waitstaff, so be it.

The sign outside, black with gold, cursive lettering, made it perfectly obvious this place was fancier than Franklin's Tower. The inside matched the outside. Black everywhere with gold and mirrored accents. It should have been empty at this time of day, but they must cater to the happy-hour crowd, because men and women in business attire started to fill up the standing room in front of the bar.

Fully aware that I stuck out like a sore thumb in the tie-dyed T-shirt that would serve as my uniform for the night, I found an empty seat at the bar, and a bartender confirmed my instincts.

"First time?" he asked. "What'll you have?"

He had longish curly hair and a pale complexion, with dark brown eyes under thick, dark brows. His chrome-plated nametag read Elliot. I looked over his shoulder at the offerings, written in gold cursive on the mirror behind the bar. No prices. Always a bad sign. I ordered a raspberry beer from a local brewery. He'd asked if it was my first time here. Did I need to justify my presence?

"I've got some time to kill before my shift at Franklin's Tower." I jerked a thumb over my shoulder, in what I later worked out was the wrong direction. Why hadn't I just gone there? Obviously, that would be the next question. I thought rapidly. "I don't love spending time with the guy working now. Gives me the creeps."

For a split second, I basked in my quick thinking. But Elliot frowned, deep in thought.

"Tim?"

Why did I try to get fancy? Especially when I was so bad at lying. Now that it was too late, a million better explanations came to mind, up to and including, "I wanted to check this place out." Of course, the bar staff at the places on this block all knew each other. They probably all hung out together, smoking out back on their breaks, or whatever.

Then Elliot nodded. "Yeah, I can see that. Guy's weird."

I'd gotten away with it! Definitely not time to press my luck. I needed to change the subject. I held up a two-sided menu card that had been laying on the bar. "What's good?"

Elliot didn't hesitate. "Get the hushpuppies." He barely waited for my nod before he turned around to put the order in and grab my beer from below the bar.

I didn't really want to drink before my own bartending shift, but I considered it the price of admission for a seat at the bar and a conversation with the bartender. I took a sip and relaxed. I hadn't realized how tense I'd been. I flipped over the menu card to the happy hour specials and scanned for the hushpuppies. "Three hand-battered southern-style hushpuppies, served with a harissa aioli dipping sauce—$18." I groaned. Talk about the price of admission. Oh, well. It just strengthened my resolve to learn something interesting. With that kind of sunk cost, I wouldn't allow myself to chicken out.

Elliot served a few other customers and then drifted back my way while wiping down his work surface. I smiled at him, trying to concoct an opening. Everything I could think of sounded lame, so I just had to go with something.

I picked up my beer bottle and used it to wave vaguely at the entire atmosphere. "Nice place. Been meaning to check it out. I did some work for somebody recently, and I guess she's the girlfriend or fiancée or something like that of the guy who owns the place. I didn't get many details, but it made me realize I'd never been in here before."

Elliot frowned again. Probably his thinking face, not actual displeasure. "That must be Will Forester's fiancée. I can't remember her name, but she's been in a few times." He glanced along the bar, to make sure no one needed him, and leaned on his elbows in front of me. "You work for her?"

"I walk her grandmother's dog, and I've talked to her a few times. Don't really know her."

"She's quiet. Will's brought her in a few times, and she's really quiet. I thought maybe she was stuck up. Or maybe she's just shy. Flip a coin." He shrugged. "Doesn't matter much, I guess. Will's a good guy."

"Oh?" I raised my eyebrows. "I got the sense he was, like, an absentee owner. More like an investor. I thought she said he was part owner of a lot of different places."

"Nah. He's got three places, but he's pretty involved in all of them. They all have different vibes, so they complement each other, if you know what I mean. A lot of us know each other. You know, cover shifts at the other places when we need to." Elliot straightened up to close out a tab for a tall white guy in a pink collared shirt, and then walked out of sight, returning with my hushpuppies.

I was less upset about the price tag when I saw the plate. Each of the three was the size of my fist, with a deep golden brown craggy crust. I made the mistake of biting directly into the first one. The waves of steam pouring out warned me I was about to burn my tongue, but didn't give me enough time to prevent the damage. I, a model of refinement and dignity, let the bite fall out of my open mouth and back onto the plate.

Elliot laughed good-naturedly, and slid over a stack of napkins and a glass of ice water. "Should've warned you. They'll be a little hot at first."

"Thanks for the tip," is what I tried to say, but it was hard to make myself understood while holding my mouth open. I gulped the water.

"Anyway, no, Will's pretty hands-on with the day-to-day operations. I respect the guy. He came up working in restaurants. He knows his stuff." Elliot had leaned down to continue our conversation. He talked to me like a coworker, not a stranger. "Do you know MacKenzie?"

I shook my head at his question, making another assault on the hushpuppies. I really was hungry. I used my fingers to pull off a bite-sized chuck and blew on it. Nobody can say I don't learn from my mistakes.

"MacKenzie's the other owner. She's the investor of the pair. I think she handles more of the business side of things."

Distracted, I barely heard him. What I was eating was essentially just deep-fried cornbread, and it commanded most of my attention. Subtly sweet and salty and greasy, but not too greasy. I pulled off a second chunk and dipped it cautiously into the sauce. I'd already forgotten how the menu described the dipping sauce, but it was creamy and spicy, which balanced the hushpuppies and made me very grateful for my cold beer.

"I think she thought a restaurant was a pretty safe investment, at least with Will's experience. Of course, she's gotten more than she bargained for with this place."

Elliot looked at me meaningfully and, distracted by the delicious food I was shoveling into my mouth, I didn't have to pretend to be unaware what he was talking about. I'd lost track of the conversation, and really, anything not cornmeal-based.

He straightened up and looked around. The happy hour attendees all clustered together, talking about golf or real estate or the stock market or something.

"You heard about the accident? Last spring?"

My mouth opened in genuine surprise, because I'd forgotten my entire purpose in coming here. I clapped a hand over my mouth to prevent anything from spilling out, and nodded, trying to chew and swallow as quickly as possible.

"Of course I remember that," I said as soon as I could. "How horrible. I don't think I realized it was here."

Elliot nodded sadly. "Poor Jake. He was a good kid. They were being nice to him, hiring him, I mean. He wasn't really cut out for working in a place like this. He'd do OK as long as nobody talked to him. We all knew to leave him alone." His voice wavered, and he took a deep breath before continuing, staring in the direction of the front window with unfocused eyes. "We knew to leave him alone and let him get on with his duties, but of course the customers don't know anything about that. They see somebody in a uniform shirt and that's the guy to fix their problem."

He glanced at me, and I looked back with what I hoped was a look of resolute and sympathetic solidarity. Anyone who'd worked in hospitality knew what that was like.

"But he was doing OK. Everybody knew that when he'd get upset, he'd go down to the basement. He just needed a few minutes to collect himself. It's not like he was hiding down there for entire shifts, trying to get out of work. That's what some of the news reports made it sound like—like he'd clock on and then beat it down there to hide until it was time to tip out. Nothing like that."

I was suddenly very glad I'd acted on my impulse to come here. What Elliot was describing was exactly the impression I'd gotten from the articles I'd read. Knowing the truth about Jake Hernandez didn't really change anything, after all, he was just as dead, but I appreciated the chance to change my attitude toward this person I'd never get to meet. Elliot hadn't said anything that changed my opinion of Will. I mean, my initial impression that he was a pretty good guy. The accident at Afterhours sounded like just that—an accident. I suppose Will could still have murdered Mrs. Van Meer, but I couldn't see any reason to leave him at the top of the suspects list.

Chapter Twenty

The vibe in Franklin's Tower was about as different from Afterhours as you could imagine. For starters, it doesn't cater to the happy hour crowd, so it was still dead by the time I showed up, and it wouldn't pick up until after dinnertime. The wood-paneled walls were covered with . . . well, kitsch, really: concert posters, license plates, cheap memorabilia, strange artwork, fake flowers. A couple of strands of beads hung down on either side of the front door, which was propped open. The fire marshal's office had told the owners to take down the full beaded curtain they'd originally had up. I guess, in the event of an emergency, they don't want people to have to distinguish between solid obstructions and permeable, decorative ones. Fair enough.

Like I said, it was mostly dead when I showed up, so I chatted with Tim, the bartender whose shift was ending. I hadn't met him before, and I spent most of the conversation dreading the bad karma I'd earned by implying he was a creep. I'm sure I wasn't a sparkling conversationalist. I stuck my bag under the bar and washed my hands. Sasha must have heard our voices, because she stuck her head out of the back office, with a phone to her ear. She waved hello to me and goodbye to Tim, then made an exasperated gesture at whoever was on the other end of the telephone line, who wasn't letting her get a word in edgewise.

Once alone, I tried to look busy, wiping down the clean bar top and stacking some glasses. One of the few customers in the place, a middle-aged man in a patch-covered denim shirt, came up for a refill. Tim had briefed me on what people were drinking, so I served him without either of us having to say anything.

A couple came through the front door right as Sasha came out of the office, her phone call over. She waved at me again and crossed the floor to greet them and show them to one of the many open tables.

Sasha was easily the most gorgeous woman I had ever known in real life. It wasn't even close. Inside the dimly-lit bar, her skin looked black and velvety, and when she crossed into a beam of light from the setting sun shining through the front windows, her face became luminous with reflected light. I'm sure she had a dedicated skin care regime, but it looked effortless. She changed her hair frequently. That day, she wore thousands of impossibly thin braids that flowed down past her shoulders and swished when she walked. She had an indefatigable husky named Bloodhound and a pair of lovebirds named Nick and Nora. We'd been friendly in high school but really became close friends a few years ago. I was still working as a vet tech then, and Bloodhound had to have a hind leg amputated. I honestly don't know if Bloodhound really noticed for more than a few days, but it was tough on Sasha.

"Do you know the owner of Afterhours? Will something?" I asked Sasha after I fixed drinks for the new arrivals.

"Met him a few times. God, he's hot. It's a good thing my mother never met him. She'd drive herself crazy. On the one hand, she'd want his genes for her grandbabies, and on the other, she'd tell me it would never work out." Sasha came behind the bar to help stack glasses.

I laughed at that. "Yeah, it's a damn shame. I met his fiancée, too. Oh, well."

"Girl, you think some fiancée would stop my mother? She could care less about something like that. No, problem is, he's American." She laughed and slipped into the accent she always used when quoting her mother. "Sasha, you stay away from American boys. You need to find yourself a nice Nigerian man." She dropped back into her normal voice. "How'd you meet pretty boy Will?"

"The fiancée's grandmother. I'm walking her dog."

Sasha narrowed her eyes, annoying perceptive. "And this grandmother introduced the dog walker to the extended family?"

"Not exactly. It's a little more complicated than that."

We were interrupted then, when a regular came up for a refill of his rum and Coke.

"And make this one strong, sweetie," he said, pushing his empty glass across the bar at me.

"You want a double?" Sasha asked. From her frosty tone, I think she'd had trouble with this guy before.

He shook his head without looking at her, and took his drink, with its single shot of rum, back to his table without another word to either of us.

The few seconds it had taken to pour his drink gave me an opportunity to decide how to tell Sasha about getting mixed up with Mrs. Van Meer's death. With some people, my earlier nonanswer and an immediate interruption would be enough to ensure the subject dropped. Not with Sasha.

I found myself telling her not just about Mrs. Van Meer's death and her will, but also about my ridiculous urge to solve the mystery. Sasha would banter back and forth with you, probably better than anyone else I know, but she had an uncanny ability to only tease you about things you didn't mind being teased about. Some people made exploratory jabs until they found a weak spot, and then focused all their attention on your insecurities. Sasha did the opposite. She was safe to open up to.

"Have you ever heard of the Show-Me-State slayer?" she asked, after I paused for breath.

I shook my head, not sure I wanted to hear the answer. Sasha was into true crime, the kind too gruesome for me.

"It was a while ago, like thirty years, in a small town outside Kansas City. I listened to a podcast about the investigation. They found three bodies in the same part of town over the course of, like, a week, and the police had no leads. The brother of the first victim was super enthusiastic about helping find the killer. He kept dropping by the station with new suggestions and bugging the lead detective and the other victims' families. Then one night, they caught him sneaking around the area where the bodies had been dumped. He said he was just trying to catch the guy red-handed, but that was enough for the cops to focus on him. They decided he'd killed all three people and was trying to direct the course of the investigation away from himself."

"Was it him?"

"They got a conviction."

"Yeah, but was it him?"

Sasha shook her head. "He served seventeen years of a life sentence before the gun that was used turned up and was linked to similar gang-related execution that had taken place in downtown KC around the same time. Some gunman for the Crips was clearing out rival drug dealers and didn't mind driving out to the boonies to do it."

I picked up a cardboard beer coaster, with a skull on one side and roses on the other, tapping it against the bar. "You're telling me not to stick my nose into the police investigation."

Sasha shrugged. "You do you. I'm just saying there are a bunch of ways it can end badly, and probably not very many ways for it to end well."

Good advice, and we both knew it. But a true crime junkie can't ignore a true crime when it's dangled in front of her. Sasha held out as long as she could. I poured a few more drinks and served a round of beers for a larger group that came in and pushed two tables together, while Sasha kept busy in the office. When the next lull came, everyone contentedly nursing their drinks, Sasha slid onto a barstool in front of me.

"So, do you want to tell me the facts?"

I grinned. I didn't need her to explain further.

It didn't take long to bring her up to speed. With my elbows leaned on the bar, I told her about the various people I'd met, and about my feeble attempts that afternoon to solve the thing with pen and paper.

"I've got motives for just about everybody, for what it's worth. But I don't know enough about what killed her to tackle means or opportunity, so there's no way to narrow it down."

"Hmm. What motives do they have?"

Sasha was already shaking her head and frowning before I'd gotten halfway through my explanation. I stopped.

"None of those are good enough. You're not thinking about it the right way. Motive isn't just a conceivable reason somebody might be better off, or might think they'd be better off, with the victim dead. For most people, except, like, a serial killer killing for the thrill of it, that's not going to be powerful enough to make them murder. You should reframe it as . . ." Her eyes glanced around the room, looking for exactly the right phrase.

She certainly had me on the edge of my seat. I mean, she was sitting down, and I was standing, but she had me eager to know what she would say next. Who knew I was friends with a murder investigation guru?

"Look for ticking clocks," she said. "Look for someone who not just profited from her death, didn't just want her to die, but really needed her to die when she died. Look for a motive with a time element—an external pressure bearing down and leaving somebody with no other option than murder."

I tapped my fingers on the bar and thought about my suspects. I could think of two ticking clocks right off the top of my head, or maybe three. Mrs. Van Meer had been working on selling the house. As soon as that happened, Kevin and possibly Bonnie would be out of a job. Ali and Will had a baby on the way and a house under construction. If they needed money to finish their house, they couldn't satisfy their builder with vague promises of a future inheritance. And if the motive had something to do with their relationship and the hints Teri had been dropping, maybe someone had needed to act before their baby was born. I desperately wanted to pull my bag from under the bar and start making notes, but that would have to wait.

I think Sasha saw on my face that she'd been helpful. She grinned at me. "And I want updates!" Then she looked more serious. "But remember what I told you about the Show-Me-State slayer."

"I'll be careful!"

When I got home, Jai had already gone to bed. He'd fallen asleep, but the sound of the front door opening woke him, and he came out of the bedroom to meet me.

"How was it?" His question was obscured by a massive yawn right in the middle of it, but I was fluent in Sleepy Jai.

"It was an easy shift. I opened a lot of bottles of beer. Nobody ordered a drink with more than two ingredients after about nine o'clock. Why'd you get up? Go back to bed." As I talked, I herded him toward the bedroom, pulling off my coat and dropping it, along with my bag, on the couch as we passed it. His thick hair was overdue for a cut, curly and tousled from the pillow. His eyebrows, which he smoothed down throughout the day with an unconscious gesture, were bushy. I felt a surge of protective affection. "Sleepy head, back to bed," I said, in a sing-songy voice. Tomorrow I could tell him all about my visit to Afterhours and Sasha's suggestions.

Chapter Twenty-One

If I'd thought the neighbors eager for gossip the day after Mrs. Van Meer's death, it paled next to their overwhelming curiosity Thursday morning. The day before, they'd watched a fire truck and two police cars park in front of the house. That's to say nothing of the forensics team after I left, presumably in a white van marked "Crime Scene Unit," if TV police procedurals were to be believed. Jackie, the next-door neighbor I'd met the day after Mrs. Van Meer's death, was waiting for me at the end of her driveway when Reginald and I set off on our walk. It was all I could do to escape with my life. I was sorely tempted to pretend I couldn't speak English, but I didn't think she'd buy it.

When I'd arrived that morning to pick up Reginald, I'd seen the great room deserted for the very first time. No humans anywhere to be seen, although Reginald trotted toward me from some other part of the house as soon as I stepped inside. By the time we returned, the room had filled up. Will, Brett, and Teri sat at the kitchen island, together with Kevin, who looked very aware of being out-of-place.

Bonnie sat by herself on one of the couches, holding an open magazine but not looking down at it.

A uniformed police officer stepped forward when I entered the room.

"Ms. Jackson-Ramanathan? Would you please take a seat? Detective Tanghal would like to speak with you."

I flushed, horrified at being singled out. Then I registered the miserable looks on everyone else's face and realized they'd all received the same instructions. I nodded at the officer, who withdrew back into the hallway, out of sight, although I got the sense she hadn't gone far.

I released Reginald from his leash and put it away on its hook. Will wordlessly offered a cup of coffee, and then I recrossed the room to sit with Bonnie, who was still not reading her magazine.

"How long have the police been here?" I spoke quietly, like we were at a funeral held in a library. If you pushed me, I'd admit I didn't care how long the police had been there, but I needed to say something, and—shockingly—no other topics sprang to mind.

She shook her head. "They only just arrived. They're going to question us one by one, and they started with Ali." She turned the page in the magazine without glancing down. "This waiting is horrible."

I sat beside her and did my best to wait patiently, but fidgeted like my clothes had been laced with itching powder. I deserved a medal for not just running away. And of course, the whole time I had Jai's voice in my head, telling me I should have called in AJ when I had the chance. After a while, Ali came out, and they called Kevin in. I tried to rehearse a script in my head, for when my turn came, but I had no idea what they would ask me. Would the others talk about Mrs. Van Meer's will and the pet trust? Probably. They didn't have any reason not to.

Ali had joined the group at the kitchen island and was talking to them in a subdued voice. She must have been telling them what she'd been asked, because what else would she possibly be talking about at a time like this? I wished she'd have the decency to speak up a little. Bonnie and I were just as interested. By mutual, unspoken agreement, we sat as quietly as we could, hoping to hear anything useful.

"A lighter?" asked Will, looking at Ali. "I've never seen your grandmother smoke."

Ali shook her head. "I think that's the whole point. I told them Grandma didn't smoke. However, that lighter got there, it may be connected to everything else."

"And you're sure it was Kevin's? What did it look like?" Teri spoke in a hushed, shocked tone.

Ali shrugged. "That's the problem. I told them I've seen him with lighters like that one, but it was just a normal, cheap-o lighter. Nothing fancy or distinctive."

Teri started to answer, but something made her turn her head toward the couch where Bonnie and I sat. Bonnie glanced down at her magazine, but I wasn't fast enough. Teri caught me staring at the group at the island, listening. She immediately forgot about whatever Ali had been reporting and poured out her anger on me.

"What are you even doing here?" She stood and shouted across the room at me. "You've got your money. Why don't you get the hell out of my house?"

I found it surprisingly easy to remain calm. She was angry and frustrated at the entire situation, and if she chose to take it out on me, this was where I'd want it to happen, in front of as many witnesses as possible, including a lurking police officer.

I opened my mouth to answer, without the slightest idea of what to say, but Ali jumped in first.

"It's not your house; it's our house."

Teri whirled to face Ali and forgot about my existence. "You don't even want it! You're building your own house and moving out!"

Ali crossed her arms. "Doesn't matter. Grandma left everything to both of us. Equally."

Teri waved her hand, dismissively, but Ali kept going.

"Look, we can talk it over with Brett, but I'm pretty sure—"

"Brett!" Teri spat his name in utter disgust, not softening her tone at all for Brett sitting three feet away from her. "Oh, I bet you want to talk it over with Brett!"

"What's that supposed to mean?"

"You know exactly what that's supposed to mean!" Teri leaned over the island, pointing a finger in her sister's face.

Ali took a deep breath to regain her composure. "Anyway, since we've both been left the house equally—"

"But you don't want it," sputtered Teri again.

"Since we've both been left the house equally," Ali continued, as though Teri hadn't interrupted her, "the correct way to handle it is to sell the house and split the proceeds."

"Sell the house!"

"Or you could buy me out," added Ali sweetly.

I thought Teri might literally explode. Her face went bright red, and if we'd been in a cartoon, smoke would have poured out of her ears. Her fists clenched and unclenched a couple of times, as her anger threatened to spill over. "What the hell, Ali?! You've never cared about this house, and you don't need the money. Are you just doing this to hurt me?"

Ali sounded close to tears. "Yeah, right. Me trying to hurt you. That's exactly right." Her voice caught in her throat, and she struggled to continue. "You and Grandma have spent the last, what, year, shutting me out of your lives? And now you're shocked I don't want to spend one second more than I have to with you? You think joint ownership of a house is going to work out fine when you haven't spoken to me, I mean really spoken to me, in months?"

"That is just like you! Little Baby Ali playing the victim card!" Teri laughed in her face, and it sounded forced and harsh. "You can't possibly take personal responsibility for your actions, because then you'll have to confront the fact that you aren't Little Miss Goody-Two-Shoes."

"What are you talking about?" Ali's voice mixed bewilderment and righteous indignation.

"You want to do this here?"

"What are you talking about?" she repeated.

Teri glanced around the room, seeing me and the rest of her audience and dismissing us. Then she let her gaze linger for a meaningful second on Will. "You really want to do this right now?"

Ali dashed the back of hand across her eyes, though no tears had actually spilled yet. Her voice climbed an octave. "I don't have any idea what you're talking about."

I guessed what Teri was hinting at and wanted to be anywhere but here. With no graceful way to make it to an exit, I settled for making myself as still as possible, trying to melt into the decor.

Teri's voice sounded calm, but rage and despair simmering under the surface. "Grandma didn't want to get involved. She wanted to leave you alone to make your own choices, even if they were stupid and destructive. Well, she's dead, and I'm not going to stand by and watch this charade anymore. I'm sorry, and I know it's way too late to do any good, but I love Will like a brother, you know that."

Will stood and crossed the room to Ali, putting an arm around her shoulder. He didn't say anything but stood at Ali's side as she faced her sister.

Teri addressed him instead of Ali. "Will, I'm sorry, but I can't keep quiet any longer. Ali's cheating on you. She's been sleeping with Brett for months."

Will's fingers tightened on Ali's arm, and he drew in a sharp breath, but he still didn't say anything.

It was Ali who burst out, "I'm not! What are you talking about?" She looked away from Teri up to Will. "I'm not! I don't even like Brett, you know that! I love you!"

"I know, baby." Will responded to Ali without looking at her. He was staring at Teri. "Why do you think she's cheating?"

Teri took a tiny step backward, as though one of them had slapped her. She saw her statement as a huge revelation and didn't expect to be challenged on it.

"Brett said . . ." she started, but her voice trailed off.

"Brett's full of shit," Will answered her. "You know that. Why would you listen to him?"

Teri nodded slowly, almost as though Will had hypnotized her with his words. She dragged her gaze back to Ali. "So . . . you're saying Brett just made it up? Out of nothing? For no reason?"

Will opened his mouth to respond, but Ali pulled away from him and his calming influence. She took a quick step forward into Teri's face. "So, you're saying Brett claimed he was sleeping with me, and you believed him? Just like that? *Brett*? And Grandma believed him, too? And instead of, you know, asking me about it, you two just sat there and judged me, and what? Waited for my relationship with Will to fall apart?"

She stood still, breathing heavily, waiting for a response. But her sister just gaped at her, unable to form any words. Ali turned and stormed out of the room. In a second, we could hear her stomping up the stairs.

Will shook his head at Teri. "I wish you hadn't said you loved me like a brother. Not if that's how you treat your sister." Then he followed Ali from the room.

What a great parting line! I wished I could come up with stuff like that on the spot, but I'm always floundering in the moment and then coming up with devastating replies hours later. Not Will. He left Teri standing rooted to the spot, shame and confusion clear to read on her face.

It took all my self-control to not whip my head around and look at Brett right then. Oh, who am I kidding? I don't have that kind of self-control.

Some parts of Brett's face had gone pale, while others were flushed. His mouth hung open, and he swallowed a couple of times before managing to croak out, "I didn't . . ."

"Oh, shut up, Brett," Teri said, storming out of the room in the opposite direction Ali and Will had taken.

If there'd been any graceful way to consult my suspects chart, I would have, right then and there. So I'd been right that Teri thought Ali and Brett were having an affair. But not only was that not true, Ali and Will hadn't even suspected the rumor was going around. If that was the case, it couldn't be a source of motive for either of them. And the only motive I'd been able to come up with for Brett was based on him *actually* having an affair and needing to keep it quiet. Looked like my chart needed some serious reworking.

Chapter Twenty-Two

With Kevin in the study being questioned, Bonnie and I were left alone with Brett. Well, except for the uniformed police officer, who looked like Christmas had come early. She scribbled in a notebook so frantically I thought her pen might tear the paper. She would have quite the report for her superiors.

Brett stuttered out an explanation, even though the people who really mattered had all left. "It was a joke . . . I was teasing . . . I had no idea she took me seriously . . . Ali and I . . . I was just teasing . . ."

Bonnie and I exchanged a look, and I rolled my eyes. Brett was around my age, maybe a couple of years older, but I felt much closer in age to Bonnie, who had to be in her sixties. A case of age versus maturity, I guess. In any case, some of the tension in the atmosphere evaporated. Ugly feelings had been stirred up, but I couldn't help but think it better that they'd been aired, instead of left to simmer below the surface.

Bonnie whispered, "Oh, dear. Ruth would have hated all this uproar."

It didn't seem like the most promising start to a conversation, but talking to Bonnie seemed preferable to sitting in stony silence, waiting for more emotional outbursts.

"I'm sorry I didn't have the chance to get to know her better."

Bonnie's eyes glistened with the possibility of tears, but she smiled at me. "She was a wonderful lady. You should have known her in the old days. Things have been hard for her lately, and after Frank, that's Mr. Van Meer, passed, she really went downhill. Well, I don't have to tell you, do I? The Ruth I used to know, I don't see her going out and wasting her money on some so-called expert because a dog howled."

She said it gently, not like she intended to offend, so I took it that way, but I did move the conversation along. If we continued along this vein, I was likely to get my feelings hurt. "How long did you know her?"

"Oh, years and years." It sounded like she might leave it at that, but after a few moments she continued. "I had a job filing in Mr. Van Meer's office. I was terrible at it. Really terrible. Just couldn't focus. Kept setting down important papers and forgetting where I'd put them. Instead of firing me, he introduced me to his wife. This was right before the girls were sent to live here, and she wanted some help. She had a nanny lined up already, but she wanted someone to help her manage the household." Bonnie looked fondly toward the kitchen island, remembering happier days with the two little girls. "She knew how much her life was about to change and wasn't sure she was up to the task alone."

My phone beeped and I glanced down to see a text from Ruby.

You still coming?

Crap. I'd forgotten Ruby was expecting me today. We were going to get some work done while keeping each other company. I composed and deleted three replies before hitting on wording that might convey I'd been held up by forces larger than myself, without mentioning alarming words like "murder," "police," and "interrogation." With those restrictions it was bound to be vague, but I think I did OK.

So sorry! I don't know how much longer they're going to keep me here. Can I come by after?

Her reply, when it came after a few seconds, was breezy. *No worries. Whenever.* But her burning curiosity came through in the pause before the reply.

Before I knew it, it was my turn to be questioned. As I stood it hit me that I'd completely mishandled my time by chitchatting with Bonnie. I should have been sitting quietly, devising a strategy for dealing with the police. What was I going to say to them?

Obviously, I would answer all their questions about Mrs. Van Meer and the others, but what was I supposed to say about myself? Was there any chance none of the others had brought up the will? If none of them had, I could present myself as a dog walker and keep things simple. I'd be in and out in three minutes, tops.

But if any one of them had mentioned the will, I'd be better off admitting it upfront. Otherwise, I might not even be given a chance to defend myself.

If I'd had this chain of thoughts last night, I could have Googled something about, what was the term AJ had used?

"Undue influence." Could I argue that I hadn't used undue influence without a clear idea of what it was? What if I admitted something that was an element of the crime? Although, on second thought, if this went far enough, could they subpoena my browser history? A quick surge of panic rose, and I pressed a hand to my chest. There's no way all this was worth three hundred thousand dollars in dog supplies.

The uniformed officer leading me knocked once on the door of Mr. Van Meer's study and then opened the door without waiting for a reply. She stood to one side and gestured for me to enter.

Detective Tanghal and a second plainclothes officer had seated themselves at the small round table in one corner, just as Brett had done when he told me about the pet trust in Mrs. Van Meer's will. None of them must have felt like usurping Mr. Van Meer's desk either. A wooden chair with a green leather seat was pulled out invitingly for me. A phone lay facedown in front of Detective Tanghal. The other officer, a large white man with a shiny, bald head, rested his hands on top of an open notebook on the table.

Instead of being blank at the start of our interview, the page was covered in small, neat handwriting with my own name written slightly larger on the first line. I can't put into words the sensation it caused, reading my name, upside down, in this nameless officer's deliberate handwriting. Like the feeling at the very beginning of a horror movie, before anything out of the ordinary has appeared, but because you know it's a horror movie, you're obsessively anticipating the first sign of something wrong. My heartbeat thudded in my ears.

"Good to see you again, Nikki," Detective Tanghal said. "This is Officer Hooper. We're going to ask you some questions about Ruth Van Meer."

When she paused, I nodded. An automatic action, just acknowledging another human being had said words in a language I understood. Nothing in her words suggested she was asking for my permission, or even my cooperation. She took it for granted.

"Please bear in mind this is just an informal interview, for background information. We may well need you to swear to a more formal statement, at the station, later. But for now, could you tell us how you met Mrs. Van Meer?"

I swallowed, hard, inexplicably caught off guard. For some reason, I'd assumed they'd start with her death or the finding of the body and work backward. Instead, I had to think back to the week before, and I was absolutely certain that every second I wasn't answering the question I looked more and more guilty. Did they think I was concocting the world's most elaborate lie? Why else would it take me so long to answer a simple question?

Words finally came to me. "She called me to arrange a consultation about her dog, Reginald. I'm not sure how she got my information." I frowned, more trying to decide if it mattered than trying to decide the answer. "She may have mentioned visiting my website. I don't really remember."

Officer Hooper lifted one hand to read a line in his notebook. "NikkithePetWhisperer.com?"

I decided to ignore the obvious derision in his voice. "That's right," I answered, trying to sound like an eager small business owner, glad to get the word out. This wasn't just a police interrogation; it was a valuable networking opportunity. "I'm a pet behavior consultant. She was concerned about the grieving process he was going through for her late husband, his late owner."

"When was this?" Detective Tanghal's tone held none of Officer Hooper's derision. She wanted facts.

I thought back. "She called me last Monday, and we scheduled the consultation for the next day, last Tuesday."

"Monday, the seventh?"

It took my brain a second to confirm the date, and then I nodded.

Officer Hooper jumped back in. "So, she called you last Monday, and exactly one week later, she was dead?"

There didn't seem to be any good way to respond. If only I had AJ with me to lean forward and say, "My client doesn't have to answer that."

If they were doing a classic good cop/bad cop thing, I could expect Detective Tanghal to jump to my defense, but she just watched me. Seemed like they were doing that little-known variation: sarcastic cop/stone-faced cop. An urge to squirm in my seat almost overwhelmed me, but I mastered it and waited for the next real question.

It came from Officer Hooper, looking down at his notebook again. "Had you met any of the others before last Tuesday? Had any contact with any of them?"

Something about the way he consulted his notes felt intimidating. As though he was testing me on my lines for a play. He had my answers written down in front of him and was ready to catch me if I got any of them wrong.

I shook my head. "I met them all for the first time last Tuesday." Detective Tanghal watched me, and I corrected myself for complete accuracy. "Well, I didn't really meet Kevin. I saw him, but I didn't know his name or talk to him until Sunday night, at the party."

Officer Hooper picked up his pen and made the smallest possible mark next to a line of text. I think it must have been a check mark, and I felt an irrelevant swell of pride.

"What was your impression of Mrs. Van Meer?" asked Detective Tanghal.

I gaped like a fish. Once again, she'd caught me off guard, and I really have no excuse for that. In hindsight, it was an incredibly obvious thing to ask, but I'd assumed we'd be dealing with facts. I'd tried to remember who said what and when and to whom. It hadn't occurred to me they might also want my impression of the people involved.

Time for a different strategy. Instead of sitting in excruciating silence until my brain caught up, I decided to verbalize the entire terrible process. (I hope AJ never finds out about me using that particular maneuver.) "I'm sorry, you caught me off guard with that question, and I'm not sure why. I've just realized that I talked to the woman three or four times and never really formed an impression of her. I guess the first time we met, I was so focused on Reginald I didn't pay too much attention to her, except in her capacity as his owner." I thought back. "I was a little . . . disappointed in how neglectful she'd been of Reginald since her husband's death. But that says more about how judgmental I am than it does about her. I should have taken into account her own grief at his passing. And she obviously did care about Reginald, because she went to the trouble of hiring me. She was a little abrupt. I basically got steamrolled into walking Reginald daily. I mean, she was perfectly willing to pay, but I really didn't feel like 'no' would ever have been an acceptable answer." I hesitated. Time to go all in. "I'll be honest with you. When Brett told me about the pet trust after she passed, I was shocked. We hadn't spoken more than a few sentences to each other, not since that first consultation. I have no idea why she decided to do that. It really made me wonder about her relationships with the others, I mean, for her to pick some stranger she'd just met."

Officer Hooper snorted, but he wiped his nose with a handkerchief immediately afterward, so there was an outside chance genuine nasal congestion was involved. Detective Tanghal's face gave away nothing about her thoughts.

Next came the part of the interview I'd been expecting. The police officers guided me through each and every time I'd been to the Van Meer house, encouraging me to remember times as precisely as possible. Officer Hooper made notes frequently, flipping back and forth to various pages of his notebook. As we got closer and closer to the night of the NFL watch party, the night Mrs. Van Meer was killed, his note-taking rate increased.

I told them about arriving at the house and following a cluster of neighbors around back. I told them about trailing Reginald to the garage and my encounter with Kevin, omitting any mention of pot, just in case. I told them as well as I could remember where people had been and when, and about Mrs. Van Meer coming out to say goodnight to everyone. When I mentioned the text conversation with Jai, about the weather in Kansas City, Detective Tanghal asked if she could read the exchange for herself.

I hesitated. Wasn't there something about never unlocking your phone for the cops, because that's allowing them to search your whole phone, which ordinarily they'd need to get a court order for? That's the kind of advice that seems reasonable when you're reading an article about defending yourself against heavy-handed police tactics, and a lot less applicable when you're seated in front of two pleasant but openly armed officers. I couldn't remember anything incriminating on my phone, but that could have been my mind going blank in general.

It turns out I'm way too meek for criminal activity. "Sure," I said, my desire to please overriding my abstract commitment to civil liberties. "My bag's in the other room."

Officer Hooper stood and spoke to the uniformed officer who'd been waiting right outside the door. While he was gone, Detective Tanghal didn't stop looking at me. Uncomfortable, I turned my head to look at something else, anything else. My gaze fell on one of the prints I'd noticed the last time I'd visited the study, for a different uncomfortable talk around this table. The smallest painting, with the couple praying in a field, drew my eye again. The light in the sky was ambiguous, representing either dawn or dusk or a change in weather from sunny to stormy. The figures looked tall relative to everything else in the frame, even the distant church steeple, and their focus on the ground between them only exaggerated their size. Something about the painting made me feel an unidentifiable emotion. I wished I was alone in the room, free to study it for a few hours, or at least a few minutes.

But only a minute passed before Officer Hooper returned with my bag, from which I retrieved my phone. I went to the beginning of the conversation with Jai from last Sunday night and slid the phone across the table to Detective Tanghal.

She didn't pick it up, or even touch it, except for using a single finger to scroll to the end of that night's conversation. From where the phone lay between us, I could tell she stopped reading as soon as she reached a message from the next morning. She read two timestamps out for Officer Hooper, who dutifully scribbled them into his notebook.

"Thank you." She withdrew her finger from the phone. I retrieved it and put it back into my bag. "Your information about the events of the football game was very helpful. We've been able to pinpoint the time Mrs. Van Meer announced she was going to bed. These messages might give us insight to another snapshot of time. Do you remember what was going on while you were texting?"

I really, really didn't. I knew I'd told Will about Jai being stuck in Kansas City, so I must have talked to him right after I got the news. Other than that, all I could say was that people I didn't know well were swirling around me as I texted. Not particularly helpful.

"I'm sorry. Maybe if it had been a more exciting football game, I could pin it down, but the game was mostly a whole long blob of nothing special."

"What time did you get home Sunday night?"

"Maybe ten thirty? Somewhere around there?"

"Can anyone confirm that?"

I shook my head.

"Any neighbors who might have heard your car pull up? Seen your lights come on?"

I shook my head again. "I guess it's possible that someone in another building saw me, but I don't know. We're in a duplex, and the other apartment had been vacant for a while.

Our new neighbor didn't move in until Monday morning." Another reason to be annoyed with McKayla. She had terrible timing. She would have been the perfect witness to support my alibi. I wouldn't be surprised if she kept a journal of our comings and goings, with a title like "The Natural Rhythms of Life at 3943 Spring Ave."

"Do you smoke?"

The question didn't catch me off guard as much as it might have, since I'd overheard snippets of Ali's conversation with the others. From what I gathered, the police had found a lighter that seemed relevant. I shook my head.

They showed me a photo of the lighter. Just like Ali had said, the most basic, cheap lighter you could imagine. This one had a purple plastic body but had probably been one out of a multicolor pack of three or five, like you can pick up at any gas station. Ali was also right in that it was just like the one I'd seen Kevin use, except his had been bright green. The only other member of the household I'd seen smoking was Bonnie, and, try as I might, I couldn't conjure an image of the lighter she'd used. I may not have even seen it.

I was about to ask where they'd found it, when Detective Tanghal volunteered the information. "We found this on the floor beside Ruth Van Meer's bed. We have no indication Mrs. Van Meer was a smoker, and there were no candles in the room. The fireplace is gas and has a pilot light."

"Could one of the paramedics have dropped it?" I pictured the one paramedic leaning over the bed to check for vital signs. I hadn't stuck around until the body had been removed, but surely that had involved a certain amount of reaching and pulling, during which a lighter could have fallen out of a pocket.

I felt like I was grasping at straws, but Officer Hooper said, very seriously, "We're checking that possibility."

A few more questions came about the lighter, but I couldn't offer much else. Once done with me, they instructed me not to leave. I don't know exactly what that was about. Maybe they thought their later interviews might bring up something new they'd want to question me about. And then, after an arbitrary amount of time, the uniformed officer told me I was free to go. I did not wait to see if anyone else was being released at the same time. I speed-walked out the patio door without a backward glance.

I had already left Ruby waiting way longer than I could justify, but when I got outside, Teri sat on one of the patio chairs, staring into the depths of the pool. Oblivious to the chill in the air, though her nose and ears were bright pink. No doubt she was replaying the fight with Ali. I wanted to pretend I hadn't noticed her, get into my car, and drive far, far away, but something dragged me over. She reminded me of a wounded animal. I couldn't just leave her there.

I approached her exactly as warily as I would have if she actually were a wounded animal, knowing that she might lash out, not realizing I intended to offer comfort.

"I'm sorry. I guess that didn't go the way you thought it would," I said, gesturing back at the house. I had to say something, and my brain had decided inanities were the way to go. Fantastic.

But she wasn't listening to me. "Stupid Brett," she muttered to herself. "Why in the world would I have listened to Brett?"

I eased myself onto a chair beside her. "Did you listen to Brett? Or did you listen to your grandmother?"

"Thank you." She managed a genuine smile for me, if small and fleeting. "Yes, I guess I listened to Grandma. But why did she listen to Brett? She knew him just as well as we did."

I didn't have an answer for her. It was a waste of energy to speculate about the thought processes of a dead woman. "Why would Brett lie about something like that? What was the point? And he had to know you'd confront Ali at some point and figure out he'd lied."

She shook her head. "That's just Brett. I don't know why I didn't realize before. I can totally see him teasing Grandma about Ali coming on to him, and when she believed him, spinning it into a whole story based on nothing. And no, he had no reason to believe we'd ever confront Ali about it." She laughed, sounding bitter and exhausted. "He knows our family well enough. We never talk about anything. Didn't you hear? You heard everything. Grandma and I thought Ali was having an affair for months, and what did we do? We judged her and helped plan her wedding. We made spiteful comments behind her back and threw her a baby shower. We cut off all lines of communication as punishment for her silence."

She shook her head again. "No, Brett was perfectly safe, at least until Grandma died. She was predictable. She cared about propriety, about appearance. I'm a loose cannon. You saw that, too. Confronting Ali in the heat of the moment, in front of Will, and hiding behind a facade of acting in his best interest. That's really crappy behavior."

I sat with her for a few minutes, but my emotions were not sufficiently churned up for me to ignore the cold. Some heat drifted to us from the surface of the pool, but it wasn't enough. Wishing I could be finished with these people and their drama, I muttered something about having to go and snuck away.

Chapter Twenty-Three

On the way to meet Ruby, I stopped off at a bakery on her block and picked up a couple of almond croissants. Since I'd inconvenienced Ruby, there was no better remedy than some glazed, buttery, flaky goodness.

I rang the bell, and waited, listening to distant thudding. She must have been up on the third floor, where she typically worked. It was a long way down the two steep staircases to the front door.

She answered the door with a smile and laughed when she saw the box in my hands. "Don't tell me!" She grinned. "Almond croissants?"

"I'm so sorry I stood you up! I thought this might make it up to you."

She had already turned and was disappearing toward the back of the house. I closed the door behind me and followed her, when she reappeared, holding a box identical to mine.

"They smelled so good, didn't they?" she asked. "I guessed from your text you could maybe use a little pick-me-up, so I ran out for some almond croissants."

We both laughed this time, and I trailed her back into the kitchen. The current crop of foster kittens, three little black puffballs, darted under the kitchen table when they saw my unfamiliar shoes. But within a couple of seconds, the bravest of them was creeping forward to check on me. When the other two saw their sibling getting petted, they gamboled across the tile for their share of attention.

I gave them each as much attention as their tiny hearts could desire, trying to focus on their little faces and forget about the police interview. Their watery blue eyes watched my hands, trying to anticipate my movements, so that they could fling their bodies into position for pets.

"Have you picked names yet?"

Ruby had cleared some counter space by pushing aside a heavy molcajete, and was pouring us two mugs of coffee to go with the croissants. She shook her head. "I'm for Gomez, Morticia, and Wednesday, but AJ has her heart set on Noche, Notte, and Noctis."

"For what it's worth, I'm with you. Gomez, Morticia, and Wednesday are much better names."

"I know! Her argument is that they're all little girl cats, so we can't name one of them Gomez. Oh, AJ! Imagine having such a narrow-minded heteronormative outlook!" said Ruby affectionately. "Alright, tiny no-names! We'll leave you alone now, so we can get some work done! You can go back to your business!"

We stepped out of the kitchen, trying not to spill coffee, drop croissants, or step on kittens. The kittens had no such concerns and seemed to be trying to get our shoes to pet them. Then we stepped over the baby gate at the foot of the staircase, hardening our hearts to their piteous mews, and climbed up the stairs to the third floor.

AJ and Ruby live in an old Victorian-era house that's been remodeled countless times over the last century and a half. Thank goodness all their furnishings are brightly colored and cheerful, because most of the house gets very little natural light. What windows there are look directly onto the brick walls of the too-close neighboring houses, and the whole place could feel gloomy.

Their third floor makes up for all that. It may be my absolute favorite place in the whole world. I can't imagine any of it was original, but at some point, the third floor was renovated into something more like a conservatory or greenhouse, with windows on every single wall and skylights in the ceiling. The staircase deposits you right in the middle, so you can look in any direction and see the outside.

November was the least spectacular time to see AJ and Ruby's third floor, with only bare tree limbs and telephone poles visible against the sky, but they've got houseplants everywhere, that, somehow, all appeared to be flourishing. It created an impression of either spring or the tropics, at least if you squinted.

Ruby's ancient orange cat, Fred (short for Frederick Barbarossa), was curled up on one of the couches, in the perfect spot for every single inch of his body to be warmed by a sunbeam. He opened his eyes as we came up the stairs but held his position with kingly dignity. He knew that I'd come over and scratch his head. No need for him to debase himself and beg for pets, like some absurd younger cats he could name.

I gave Fred a quick pet on the top of his head and then crossed the room to set my backpack and bag down at the table that had become my designated workspace at Ruby and AJ's house. I hadn't fulfilled my obligation to Fred, so his green eyes watched my progress. When I came back toward him, he blinked at me slowly and extended his head forward just a tiny bit, in case I'd somehow forgotten to scratch his cheeks with both hands. I had not forgotten. He closed his eyes and purred as I gave him my full attention.

Ruby, who'd settled into her usual chair, laughed at me. "He's got you trained."

"He's a good boy."

"He's a very good boy," she agreed. "Today, he and Pete are knights, and they're up against a mighty dragon. They'll be OK, though."

Fred and Pete's activities relate to Ruby's webcomic, and were not a sign Ruby had a tenuous grasp on reality. Whenever Ruby said anything odd, you could be pretty sure she was talking about fictional cats, inspired by Fred and his late brother, Pete. Her webcomic stars two housecats who always find themselves having implausible adventures while their human owner is away at work. When Ruby started out, her cats were rambunctious teenagers, and she'd get excited if one of her posts got five views. Now, the webcomic had become popular enough that she'd launched a line of merchandise and quit her teaching job, and she'd lost Pete to kidney failure. Fred was still hanging on, though. The cats in the strip have never aged.

"Is everything OK? Did you have something going on this morning?" Ruby had picked up her tablet to start working before asking the question. The implication was clear. If I didn't want to talk about it, that was totally fine with her.

I'd abandoned Fred to return to my work table. But I changed course and sat down on one of the couches instead, shifting a stuffed llama with a thin, upturned mustache to make room.

"I told you Tuesday night about the old woman who named me in her will?"

Ruby nodded and took a bite of almond croissant.

"Well, now everything's a huge mess. The police are investigating. I don't know too many details, but they're saying it was either suicide or murder. They questioned everybody this morning."

Ruby's eyebrows shot up. She set both her tablet and her croissant plate to the side. "Have you called AJ yet?"

"That's what Jai said!" I answered more loudly that I'd intended. Obviously, in hindsight, they both told me to call AJ because that was the best course of action. In the moment, I gritted my teeth and ignored the suggestion.

I told Ruby a little about Mrs. Van Meer's death and what I knew about the investigation. I didn't allow myself to go into too much detail, because I needed to get some work done. This mess couldn't suck up my whole afternoon, as had happened the last two days.

Ruby nodded throughout, with a look on her face that said I was being an idiot for not consulting the criminal defense attorney I was friends with and she was married to. But she'd told me once already, and she wasn't going to tell me again, unless I asked for advice.

"But I really don't think I have much to worry about. I know the whole thing with the will and the pet trust looks bad, but that's just motive. I don't think there's anything else pointing to me, and I'm not the only one with motive."

That sounded a bit more optimistic than I felt but served its purpose in that Ruby had to immediately ask about all the other motives swirling around the Van Meer house, which directed her attention away from me. I told her about the emotions stirred up by Mrs. Van Meer's decision to sell her house, and about the big blow-up that morning about an affair that Brett and Ali may or may not be having. "It's just so pointless. If they'd had their big shouting match months and months ago, they wouldn't have had to waste so much energy being resentful. It's like, 'C'mon people. Communicate.'"

When I ran out of news, I stood, put the llama back in his place, and returned to my work table. Ruby took another bite of almond croissant and focused her attention on the tablet and stylus she used for her art, while I started unpacking my gear. I loved all the equipment I used for calligraphy, the papers and pens and nibs and inks, but when I looked at Ruby's sleek device, my stuff all felt so unwieldy. Like I'm standing awkwardly in a Victorian deep-sea diving suit, while she lounges in a state-of-the-art racing swimsuit.

I couldn't worry about that now. I was working on an order of place cards for a wedding. Two hundred and fifty guests, and each of them would have a hand-lettered card showing them where to sit. I crammed an unreasonable amount of croissant into my mouth and switched on my lightbox. The bride had settled on an ink color, a card size, a lettering style, and had sworn that she'd double-proofread the list of names. I didn't have anything to think about, no decisions to make. I just needed to sit and churn out the work. I wrote the longest of the names a few times on scrap paper, to loosen up my shoulder and my wrist.

One of the reasons I love working in the same space as Ruby was her ability to focus on her own project, as if I wasn't there. She's content to exist in the same room as another person, without interacting. Jai, and I don't mean this as a knock because I love him to death, but Jai always wanted to keep up a steady conversation if we were both working on our own things. For example, on a place card project like this, every three or four cards, I stop and look up for a few seconds, to make sure I don't get a crick in my neck or go cross-eyed. He used to always ask "What is it?" when I'd do that. He used to do that. I've addressed it, and he's better now, but sometimes I can feel his urge to talk like a physical presence in the room. Ruby doesn't have that kind of energy. I bet if you asked her to describe my work process, she'd say, "I've never noticed." It's delightful.

I had resolved to keep my mind firmly on my work and not let it drift back to Mrs. Van Meer and the prospect of a murder. This was my intention, and I was doing well, until during a brief neck stretch between the cards for "Mrs. Marianne Lu" and "Ms. Rebecca Henderson," my gaze wandered to a print hanging on the south wall of the studio.

I yelped in surprise, and Ruby looked up as I stood for a closer look. Ruby's favorite artist was Salvador Dali, but AJ claimed that surrealism makes her feel "unmoored," so all of Ruby's collection of prints was displayed in her studio. The art in the rest of the house met a minimum standard of rationality. I'd seen all the Dali prints before, in the hours I'd spent working in this room, but one had just struck me powerfully.

It showed two abandoned stone towers, ruins, really, jutting up from a vast desert plain, with impossible architecture reminiscent of something designed by an ancient incarnation of Dr. Seuss. Two tiny human figures, an adult and a child, stood in the foreground, looking up at the huge towers looming above them. It wouldn't have looked out of place as the cover art for a science fiction novel set on another world. Not as interesting, or as colorful, or as weird, as most of the other prints on the wall, but I found I couldn't look away.

"What is it?" asked Ruby, who had stood to join me.

I shook my head and passed a hand across my face. "Just a feeling of déjà vu. I don't know how to explain it."

She sat back down but didn't pick up the tablet. She could tell I wanted to talk about it, even if I wasn't sure how to start. Putting into words the sensations caused by art is always a challenge.

"I saw a painting earlier today, a print, I mean. I saw it a couple of days ago, too. At Mrs. Van Meer's house, in her husband's study. He died about a month ago, I guess. Anyway, I never met him. But the police were questioning us in his study, and I noticed one of the paintings. Most of the rest of the house, the parts I've seen anyway, have pretty pictures, lots of flowers and still lifes and landscapes. In Mr. Van Meer's study, it was all religious art."

Ruby sat up a little straighter, "Go on."

"You know what I mean, angels and crucifixions and the Madonna and saints. But there was one small print my eyes kept coming back to. It showed a man and woman, standing in a field with their heads bowed, I guess praying over a little basket at their feet."

"Potatoes," said Ruby.

"What?"

"The basket, it's a basket of potatoes. I think so anyway. I think I know what you're talking about. Keep going."

I stared at her. Ruby knew more about art history than anyone I'd ever met, but this was a little much. I'd given an incredibly vague description of a painting, and she knew which one I'd seen. She had to be bluffing.

I shook my head. "Anyway, it felt familiar, like I'd seen it before, and more than once. But probably hanging up on the wall in Catholic school or something like that. So I forgot all about it. And then, when I was staring over there"—I waved a hand at the wall—"I realized that those towers are kind of the same shape as the people in that other painting, and maybe that's why it looked familiar. Kind of dumb."

Ruby laughed triumphantly. She typed something on her tablet, nodded her satisfaction at it, and passed it over to. "Is this the painting?"

It was the same picture from Mr. Van Meer's study, with five identical thumbnails running along the left side of the screen and creating a strange echo effect.

"It is!" I looked back toward the Dali print and did a double-take. "And they are really, really similar! I wasn't imagining it. What a weird coincidence."

Ruby came to sit beside me on the couch, taking her tablet back. "It's not a coincidence at all. Salvador Dali was obsessed with this painting." She zoomed in on the face of one of the figures. "It's called The Angelus and it's by a French painter named Millet, from the eighteen hundreds. Dali reworked its elements at least a dozen times, including in that one there." She pointed back at the print hanging on her wall. "I feel weirdly proud of you for noticing."

I looked back and forth between the wall and the screen a couple times. I wasn't sure how to word this question, since I knew how much respect Ruby had for great artists. "It seems a little . . . boring. I mean, it's beautiful, but I don't see why someone, especially Dali, would get obsessed with it."

Ruby nodded, unoffended. "What do you feel when you look at Millet's painting?"

I shrugged. I felt something, deep down, but not something that I could put into words. "I'm sorry. I don't know."

"That's OK. Dali thought the painting didn't make sense."

"That's rich, coming from him," I jumped in, glad the focus was off me and my feelings.

Ruby smiled at me but continued. "He was convinced the atmosphere of the painting was too somber for its subject matter. He thought the figures were too mournful for what they were doing, saying a ritual prayer over a basket of potatoes. He was convinced Millet had originally painted a burial scene and then reworked it to be less of a downer."

I squinted at the tablet's screen. "I could see them at a funeral."

"Do you want to know the funny thing?" asked Ruby, with a mischievous glint in her eye. "When Dali said all this, there was no way to know. But then, decades later, we made a bunch of technological advances, and the Louvre x-rayed the original painting."

She paused for dramatic effect. It worked. I waited.

"Before there was a basket of potatoes, it looks like there was originally a different object on the ground between the man and the woman as they prayed. It's impossible to know for sure, but it looks like a child-sized coffin."

I breathed out. "How awful." I held up a hand to block the lower half of the tablet, hiding the basket of potatoes, and focusing just on the figures. Everything about their posture worked for a scene in which they're praying over the coffin of their lost child.

Ruby sat silent for a moment, also looking at the picture. "Millet was such a great painter that he imbued the whole picture with a sense of loss and sadness so strong it survived the repainting. He removed the coffin, but he didn't scrub out the echoes of the earlier story."

What did it say about the late Mr. Van Meer and me that we were attracted to a painting with such an atmosphere of death? Creepy. With the murder only a few days old, I decided I'd had enough death and resolved to put the grim painting out of my mind.

Chapter Twenty-Four

The next day was Friday, and I thought about not going to the suburbs. I wanted to block Teri's number and disappear from these people's lives forever. But that could make the police more likely to focus all their attention on me. I had to stick to the routine I'd fallen into. So, once again, I drove to Mrs. Van Meer's house that morning, hoping against hope to get in, walk the dog, and get back out again.

That was not the case.

I mean, I got in just fine. Ali and Will occupied their habitual spots at the kitchen island, back to looking at selection books for their new house. They nodded at me, but we didn't talk. Reginald was ready and waiting, so I escaped back outside seconds after entering.

As Reginald and I walked across the driveway, someone called my name from the direction of the garages. A harsh, carrying whisper that made me whip my head around, looking for the source. Kevin, the handyman, stood on the far side of the massive stone four-car garage, which shielded him from view of anyone who might have been watching from the house. He stared intently at me but didn't say anything else.

"What?" I called back to him, after waiting a moment.

He flinched at the sound and waved for me to come toward him.

I responded with a lower tone but didn't move. "What do you want?"

He muttered something under his breath, shifted from one foot to the other, and then answered in that same stage whisper. "I need to talk to you. Without them"—he tossed his head toward the house—"hearing us."

He had on the same battered gray hoodie and the same paint-stained blue work pants as always. He still wore a bandage on his right hand and held the hand a little away from his body. I guess he had a habit of shoving his hand into the front pocket of his hoodie, a motion that would cause him pain until his hand fully healed.

I didn't love the idea of being alone with this guy, but I was confident I could outrun him if needed. I wrapped Reginald's leash around my hand a few times to keep him close to me and followed Kevin into the garage.

When I'd seen the inside of the garage last, on Sunday night, it had an air of abandoned seediness. Most of the lights had been off, and Kevin's set-up, with his folding chairs and old TV, had looked like a squatter's camp in a warehouse. Daylight revealed a normal, even remarkably clean, garage. A giant pegboard held well-organized tools, a row of large plastic trash cans stood waiting for yard waste, and a stack of folding tables leaned against the wall. The two antique cars now had an air of sad disuse, in contrast with the slightly ghostly effect they'd created when shrouded in darkness.

"You're Nikki Jackson, right? Mindy Hale's cousin?"

Whatever I'd been expecting this man to say, that wasn't it. Hale was my mother's maiden name, so that part made sense. Since my mother was one of eleven children, I've got dozens of cousins, but I'm not close with anyone on that side of the family. "Mindy?" I repeated to buy time. Then I placed the name. "That's Carol's daughter?" My Aunt Carol was one of my mother's younger sisters, who had a daughter about ten years younger than me. I thought her name was Mindy.

"That's right!" A smile spread across Kevin's face. "I married Carol after Mindy's father left."

"Oh. Oh, right." This was ringing some bells. Carol's husband had moved away some years ago, and she'd remarried. There'd been some talk about it, but I didn't remember any details. I'd never met the new husband, but I'd heard his name at the time. I racked my brains. It could have been Kevin. The new husband was from somewhere up north.

"From Wisconsin? Or Minnesota?"

"Michigan! That's me!" He pointed two thumbs at his chest, looking overjoyed.

"Great! Nice to officially meet you, Kevin." I had no clue why he'd called me in here. Some people might be excited to make contact with a distant relation. Let me repeat. My mother is one of eleven children. And my father's family is just as big. In the right part of town, I would be more shocked to find a group with no relatives.

He walked to the still-open door and looked out. Apparently, the coast was clear, because he came back to me and spoke in a hurried whisper.

"I thought you should know you can't trust any of them." He jerked his head in the direction of the house. "They all think you did it or at least think they can blame it on you."

"It?"

His face was almost laughably serious. "They think you might have killed Mrs. Van Meer. I understand you got some money out of it, and they think you might have done it for that."

This was rich, coming from the guy whose lighter had been found beside the body. I mean, sure, he was probably right. They probably did think I'd done it, but surely, they'd bet more money on Kevin as the murderer.

I tried to sound grateful and forced a smile. "Well, thanks for the heads up. I don't know what I can do, but I appreciate you telling me."

He was all smiles again. "See! I knew you wouldn't get all hysterical. Most girls, you tell them bad news, and they fly right off the handle, crying and stuff. But Mindy always said you had a good head on your shoulders. That's why I didn't mind mentioning your name to Mrs. Van Meer, even though the whole thing about a dog grieving sounds like foolishness to me."

His blatant misogyny almost distracted me from the point of his statement. But as he went on talking, my sense of dread grew. My stomach clenched, but I fought for calm. Maybe I'd misunderstood him.

"You mentioned my name?" There was absolutely no hint of panic in my voice.

"I sure did! Your cousin Mindy saw somewhere, Facebook, I think it was, that you'd set yourself up as some kind of pet whisperer, and she told us about it, just as an interesting thing, you know. I remembered that. Then when I got back into town last Monday, I came here first, of course—it's where I keep all my tools. But first thing I saw was Bonnie's windbreaker—that white one she always wears, you know, so I headed up to the house to give it to her. But when I got there, Mrs. Van Meer was freaking out over that dog. The others were telling her to wait it out, and he'd get over it, or take him to the vet, but she didn't like any of that advice. I remembered about you, and I figured, no offense, that it probably wouldn't do any good, but it might make her feel better, so I looked up your website for her."

OK. This was bad. This was really, really very bad.

Mrs. Van Meer hadn't called me out of the blue and then named me an executor in her will because she didn't trust the rest of the family. Instead, a relative of mine, who had already insinuated himself into the household, talked Mrs. Van Meer into calling me.

I thought about the afternoon before, when I'd blithely assured Ruby that the only black mark against my name was motive. Now I was in cahoots with the handyman who had the run of the place and surely the mechanical know-how to rig up a carbon monoxide death trap.

Had Kevin already told the police about our connection? Surely not, or we'd both have been hauled down to the station for an interrogation. If he had, did the police think I'd lied to them when I said I'd never met any of these people before? Would they believe that I'd never met my aunt's husband? That I had no idea who this guy was until he'd introduced himself just now? On the other hand, why wouldn't Kevin mention it? He didn't seem to recognize the importance.

I looked into his eager face. He reminded me of nothing so much as an overgrown mutt puppy who'd just ripped open an expensive throw pillow, spread the stuffing all over the living room, and was waiting with excitement to be praised for his redecorating efforts. He had no idea he was delivering bad news.

"Thank you so much!" I tried to match his enthusiasm, then sound offhand and unconcerned for the next part. "Do any of the others know you recommended me?"

He laughed and shook his head. "I sure hope not! I mean, since they think you killed her and all." He laughed again, glad we'd surmounted that conversational hurdle and could joke about it now. "I don't want to get caught up in any of that. I'd be surprised if she didn't tell Bonnie, though."

From all I'd heard about Bonnie's central role in running the household and Mrs. Van Meer's life, I would be surprised if she didn't know how my name had come up. Bonnie was the next threat I needed to head off. Before I left Kevin, though, what were the chances of him mentioning this conversation to the police? It would look suspicious if I asked him outright not to tell anyone.

"Yeah," I said, "I'd hate if you got caught up in any of this. I can handle the others, but we'd better not tell any of them about our connection."

He nodded and used his finger and thumb to zip his lips shut, a playground gesture that made me smile in spite of this new source of stress.

"Did you tell Mrs. Van Meer I'm your stepdaughter's cousin? Or just show her my website, without saying how you heard about it?" If he hadn't told Mrs. Van Meer, Mrs. Van Meer couldn't have told Bonnie. I didn't think the police could stumble on our family connection on their own. It was my mother's side of the family, so everyone involved had a different last name. And "Jackson" wasn't unique enough to narrow things down. Every branch was large and tangled, just like you'd expect from a Catholic family on the south side.

Kevin rubbed his stubbly chin. "Not too sure. Lemme see." He stared at the wall behind me, concentrating hard, which I appreciated. "I said, 'I don't set much store by this kinda thing, but I'll show you a thing.' I pulled it up on my phone, and passed it over to her, and she looked at it longer than I thought she would, if I'm honest. She said your name out loud, to herself, like, to remember it, and then she gave me my phone back and said 'thank you.' No questions. So, no. I must not have told her about Mindy and how I came to find you."

I breathed a little easier then. "Why didn't you tell me who you were when we hung out that night? When I came in here during the party?"

He shrugged and looked a little sheepish. "I was a little messed up. Honestly? I think I forgot that you didn't already know. Sorry about that."

I grinned. "No worries. I get it. Looking back, you were talking like we already knew each other."

As soon as I said goodbye to Kevin and led Reginald out of the garage, my grin slipped. Now I had the whole walk to brood on what Kevin had told me. I tried to imagine the scenarios the police could conceivably put together if they found out Kevin had recommended me.

Kevin was disgruntled about Mrs. Van Meer's decision to sell the house, which would put him out of a job. He got me hired in, so I could work my way into the will and then one of us killed her, splitting the profits. It wasn't exactly plausible, but I didn't like imagining the police entertaining it for even a second.

It all hinged on whether Mrs. Van Meer had told Bonnie how she heard about me, and whether Bonnie had passed the information along to the police. If Bonnie knew, but hadn't told the police, it must be because she considered the information inconsequential. I couldn't think of any way to find out whether she knew without alerting her to the importance of the fact, if she did know.

Could I make up some kind of new customer survey and ask her to fill it out on Mrs. Van Meer's behalf? Explain that I know it's awkward, but I'm a newish business, a small business, and I really need to gather as much information and feedback as possible. I could bury a question about referrals in there.

But if she answered, "Yes, you were referred by a landscaper/handyman named Kevin," would that really affect my actions? It would satisfy my curiosity, but there wasn't anything I could do about it. If she answered anything else, I could assume Bonnie didn't know where the referral had come from, and I could relax a little on that front. Of course, if Bonnie did know that Kevin had gotten me the gig, I'd jog her memory and send her running to the police. Then, the only question would be, which of us would they arrest first?

Chapter Twenty-Five

As Reginald and I meandered our way through the neighborhood streets, my brain kept chanting "means, motive, and opportunity" at me. Although I had motive because of that damned pet trust, there had been no reason for the cops to think I had means or opportunity. I wasn't particularly familiar with the house, didn't have free access to it, and had no special knowledge that indicated I could have rigged up a source of deadly gas. But now everything had changed. With Kevin as my accomplice, it would have been the easiest thing in the world. He would know the garages inside and out, as well as any other possible sources of carbon monoxide in the house. He was around the night of the party, but no one was keeping tabs on him. His lighter had been found at the crime scene. He was around the next morning and could have cleaned up after himself whenever he wanted.

I thought back to the morning we'd found Mrs. Van Meer's body. Bonnie had been up a ladder, pruning the ficus tree, and Kevin had been . . . what? I closed my eyes and pictured the scene. I couldn't see his face.

My eyes snapped open, and I looked around, reassuring myself that I wasn't being followed.

He'd been on his hands and knees at the *fireplace*, tools in hand. He'd given the police some innocuous story about a minor repair, but couldn't he just as easily have been clearing his tracks, reversing the telltale signs of sabotage he'd put in place the night before?

I wish I knew more about things! The fireplace in Mrs. Van Meer's bedroom backed up to the much larger fireplace in the great room. Did that mean they were somehow connected, like with a shared chimney? Was gas exchanged between them, or were they separate from each other before they vented out of the roof? My brain very helpfully produced the word "flue," but without any understanding of what exactly that meant or if it was relevant. I shouldn't really complain too much about my brain coughing up tangentially related vocabulary words, because the alternative was subjecting me to a recitation of the chimney sweep song from *Mary Poppins*.

But the police knew Kevin had been working on the fireplace, and they hadn't arrested him immediately, so maybe fireplaces don't work the way I imagined. They might have tested the chimney or possibly the flue, depending on what a "flue" was, and determined it wasn't a possible source of carbon monoxide in Mrs. Van Meer's bedroom.

I slid the loop of Reginald's leash up from my hand to my elbow and texted Jai.

How do fireplaces work?

While waiting for an answer, I tried to remember what he'd said his day would be like. If he was stuck in meetings all day, it might be hours before he could get back to me.

But he replied almost immediately. *Depends.* I waited another second. *Is it connected to the Floo network?*

I laughed. No wonder I knew the word "flue" without knowing anything else about fireplaces.

I clarified, confident his joking answer meant he wasn't in the middle of anything important. *Two fireplaces, back to back. Can you do something to one to make CO leak out the other?*

Don't know.

Now, with some people, I might have taken that answer at face value. I could have thought, "Oh, well. Jai doesn't know. I'd better find out another way." But I knew he was even at that very moment Googling ferociously.

The answer, when it came, was inconclusive. I read two of the links he sent me before I gave up and asked for the CliffsNotes version. Apparently, if the chimneys were improperly designed, they could leak deadly gases, including carbon monoxide from one to the other. No blueprint existed for rigging a well-designed fireplace into a murder weapon, but that didn't mean it wasn't possible with some knowledge and ingenuity.

I was still wondering about the inner workings of chimneys when I approached the house. Despite the back of the house being almost entirely windows, I somehow missed that the great room was now full of people. When I opened the back door, Detective Tanghal and Officer Hooper were exiting toward the front of the house.

"Detective Tanghal!" Will called out, stopping them. "There's just one more thing. Could I speak to you for a minute?"

The officers exchanged a quick glance, and then headed in the direction of the study, with Will trailing after them. I was surprised to see a flash of weariness cross the detective's face. She was exhausted, and all of a sudden, I felt much less adversarial toward her. Without realizing it, I'd built her up in my mind as this indefatigable bulldog in pursuit of the truth, making her an intimidating character to have to confront. Instead, she was a woman doing her job, and right this minute, she was tired. She may have been up late the night before poring over evidence, or up early preparing to take witness statements. Or, for all I knew, up late watching a marathon of bad movies or up early because her basement flooded. If I thought of her as an actual person, the possibilities were endless.

Ali sat with her arms folded on the kitchen island, watching her fiancé following the police. As Will left the room, she dropped her head onto her arms. As the one closest to her, I laid a tentative hand on her back and sat on the chair next to her.

"Are you alright?" I whispered.

She didn't speak but moved her head in answer. Unfortunately, because of her posture, I couldn't tell whether she was trying to nod her head or shake it. I stayed where I was, feeling the eyes of the others on us.

After what seemed like ten minutes, but may have only been twenty or thirty seconds, Ali lifted her head and gave me a weak smile.

"Thank you, Nikki. You're really nice."

That was gratifying to hear. As far as I knew, everyone in this room hated me and had, at least at one point, suspected me of murder. But, no, I was really nice.

"Will's been dealing with a lot recently, and it doesn't have anything to do with Grandma, but he figured if he went any longer without telling the police, it would count as lying. They're going to make a bigger deal out of it than they should."

She'd been talking quietly, directing her words to me, but now Brett broke in from across the room.

"He's telling them about the busboy at Afterhours?" He sounded concerned. "That doesn't have anything to do with this."

"That's what I've been telling him," said Ali. "He's been so worried that the police will think they're connected."

Maybe these people were all naive, or maybe I was paranoid. Since this whole police investigation started, I'd been assuming the police knew everything about us in the public record. There were news stories on the internet that I'd been able to find within seconds of learning Will's full name. Wasn't it a certainty there'd been a police report of the accident? And yet Brett and Ali, and apparently Will, were acting like this was private information that Will was choosing to divulge. Unless there was some aspect of the accident that hadn't made it into the newspaper reports or that hadn't turned up in the official investigation. Were they referring to the bare fact that a busboy had died at one of Will's restaurants, or was there something I'd missed?

As far as the others were aware, I didn't know anything about any busboy at Afterhours. I decided it wouldn't sound unnatural to pry, just a little.

"A busboy?" I directed the question to Ali but made sure to speak loudly enough that Brett and Teri could hear, just in case Ali didn't feel up to answering and one of them wanted to jump in with some facts.

"It was terrible." Ali's voice was faint. "Something went wrong with one of the carbon dioxide tanks. They need them for the soda machines, I think. Or maybe the beer taps. I don't really know how it works."

Brett jumped in here, sounding very much like someone cutting off a client about to say something they might regret in front of a jury. "It was a tragic confluence of events. A faulty gauge, a deteriorating gasket, and a young man who, while he was supposed to be working, sneaked into a disused portion of the basement. He was in the wrong place at the wrong time. Unfortunately, his poor work ethic proved fatal."

I hadn't liked Brett much from the start. He seemed like one of those guys who know how to be charming but only bother to make the effort when they want something. But there must have been a way to emphasize that his friend, Will, was not legally or morally culpable for his employee's death without quite so much victim-blaming. Elliot, the bartender I'd met at Afterhours, had taken such pains to emphasize Jake Hernandez had been a good employee, overwhelmed for a moment, rather than the irresponsible work-shirker Brett described.

To his credit, I think he realized almost immediately he'd chosen the wrong tone for his audience. He rushed on. "Of course, what matters now is making sure nothing like this ever happens again. Will and the other owner of Afterhours have replaced the entire carbon dioxide system: tanks, gas lines, gauges, everything. They've overhauled the ventilation systems servicing the basement of the restaurant. They've even set aside scholarship money for the younger brother of the victim, as a gesture of good will to the grieving parents."

I nodded, still not loving his pompous tone, but recognizing he was making an effort. "Why mention all this to the police?"

"Exactly!" Brett flung a hand out. "Why is he dredging all this up now?" he demanded of Ali. "The police investigation has been over for months."

I noted with interest Brett's need for accuracy outweighed his loathing to admit a possibility of wrong-doing. If I'd only heard his earlier statements, I might have assumed the innocence of Afterhours was so obvious there was never any need for an in-depth investigation. But he hadn't said the whole thing had been over for months. The wrongful death suit referred to in the text message I had glimpsed must be ongoing.

Ali looked sick. "Will's in charge of the overhaul at the restaurant. He's been studying up on building codes and safety systems and, really, everything to do with handling gas safely within an enclosed area." She wasn't looking at any of us, but instead stared at her engagement ring, twisting it around and around on her finger.

This may not be the most appropriate moment to mention the size of the diamond on her engagement ring, so I won't. Except to say that it was huge.

"If Grandma's death wasn't an accident, and it wasn't suicide," Ali's voice shuddered on the last word, and then she gathered herself. "They're going to look at who knows how to do something like this. They might even think the restaurant was just an excuse, and he was researching all that stuff for . . .

for this. Or that the accident at the restaurant gave him the idea. Oh, I don't know! Maybe he's got himself all worked up about nothing."

Teri and Brett both tripped over themselves reassuring her that knowledge of gas safety wouldn't attract the attention of the police. The very idea was absurd! They were pretty convincing. I kept very quiet, glad I hadn't let any of them catch wind of my suspicions of Will, which had indeed been founded solely on the gas-based accident at a restaurant he co-owned. It had felt like a rock-solid basis for suspicion, a connection that demanded attention, but maybe it was just a coincidence after all.

Of course, I'd pretty much already moved on from Will. I'd shifted most of my suspicions onto Kevin, so he had been foremost in my thoughts lately. But that was back when I thought him a random landscaper.

Now everything had changed. He was my cousin's stepfather and had, unbeknownst to me, gotten me the job at the house. If he had murdered Mrs. Van Meer, I didn't think my innocence would be enough to keep me from being implicated right along with him.

I'd started out looking for the killer for the police, to end this quickly. Kevin had been a fantastic candidate. All of a sudden, I needed to shift focus, divert attention from both Kevin and me.

If I ignored the two of us, which I planned to, I was left with Teri, Ali, Will, Brett, and Bonnie. What information did I have that would point to any one of them? Looking for facts to fit my conclusion. That wasn't the way to do it, I knew. Wasn't that what AJ was always railing against the police for? They'd decide on a culprit and look for evidence to prove them guilty. Not very scientific. I'd always agreed wholeheartedly with AJ on this topic, but now I had to admit some sympathy with the method.

Well, of course you're not going to find evidence if you don't actively look for it, I told myself. That was logical, right?

Time for me to start looking harder.

Chapter Twenty-Six

Preoccupied with my thoughts as I drove away, I came close to killing Jackie, the gossipy neighbor. Today's tight-fitting velour track suit was purple. I'm a hundred percent sure of that, because a streak of purple dashed out of the way as I rounded the curve beyond the Van Meers' house. I slammed on my brakes and rolled down my driver's side window to apologize to Jackie, who stood in the middle of the road, with one hand on her chest as she tried to catch her breath, and the other hand already waving away my apology.

"I'm so sorry! I don't know why I didn't see you crossing! I was thinking, and I didn't see you, and I'm so sorry," I babbled at her.

"No, no, no," she said, getting her breath back. "I thought you'd seen me and were slowing down to talk, otherwise I never would have come out in front of you. Don't you worry about it at all. We're both fine."

I took a few deep breaths and gulped. "I'm sorry."

"Don't you worry about it at all," she said again. "I missed you both times when you walked by with the little doggie this morning, because I was on the phone with my son and daughter-in-law, and we've kind of fallen into our own little routine, haven't we, and I wanted to make sure to say 'hello' to you, if I could manage it."

She put both hands on the edge of my open window and leaned her weight on them. I could see her looking around the interior of my car, relishing the glimpse into another part of my life. I don't know exactly what conclusion she would draw from the piles of crap in the backseat. She knew I was a dog-walker, so presumably she wasn't surprised to find threadbare bath towels serving as makeshift seat covers, spare leashes looped through the seatbelt holders, and enough miscellaneous dog paraphernalia to stock a small shelter. Fabric scraps spilled out of the tops of two plastic bags. I'd picked them up from someone clearing out their sewing room, and I hadn't had a chance to sort through them yet. A stack of not-yet-folded cardboard shipping boxes had fallen over when I'd braked and now lay strewn over everything.

She took a good long look. When she'd committed everything to memory, she dragged her eyes away the detritus of my life and looked at me. "And how's everything up at the house? We haven't seen Bonnie since it happened, you know."

I wasn't surprised Bonnie hadn't snuck next door for a friendly chat. As far as I'm concerned, if you want to gossip with someone after a death in their family, you don't wait for them to come to you. You show up on their doorstep with a casserole. That's just basic etiquette.

"Yes, I believe she's pretty upset."

Jackie shook her head sadly. "If you look at it another way, it's a blessing, don't you think? Wouldn't we all rather go peacefully in our sleep, and avoid a lingering illness and long decline?"

Either Jackie was in the dark about some key elements about the police investigation, or she was trying some advanced information-gathering techniques. She made it sound like Mrs. Van Meer had died of natural causes. If she didn't already know that a murder had taken place next door, I certainly wasn't going to be the one to tell her. I wasn't sure whether she would be terrified or horrified or exhilarated, and I didn't want to deal with any of those reactions.

I don't have any way of knowing what went on at the Van Meers' house after I drove away. Whatever happened, the police must have stirred something up, because I got a text from Teri after I'd been home for only a minute or two.

Can you meet?

It seemed like she'd messaged me by mistake. Surely the less she saw of me, the better.

I just left there. What's up? I replied.

Not here. Starbucks at Clayton and Lindbergh?

I didn't feel like driving right back out there, especially not to meet someone so openly hostile to me, but my curiosity was piqued. If I ignored her, I'd drive myself crazy with wondering for the rest of the day, if not for the rest of my life.

So, instead of wasting time pressing her for details, I tried negotiating the location, suggesting a Starbucks halfway between us. We went back and forth, and I imagined the rising frustration behind her bland messages. But, hey. She's the one who wanted to meet. We settled on a location a tiny bit closer to me than the one she'd originally suggested. I never said I was a good haggler.

Besides, I'd been distracted. As I stood at the kitchen window, texting with a woman who hated me about which soulless corporate coffee shop we'd meet at for mysterious reasons, my eye had been caught by movement at the back of the house. McKayla, our new downstairs neighbor, walked, not in circles, but back and forth, crossing from one falling-down fence to the other, and then back again.

McKayla's manner was so baffling I ended up replying "fine" to an arbitrary one of Teri's texts, just to put an end to the conversation. I wanted to focus all my attention on whatever the hell was happening outside. I leaned past the kitchen wall to check on Jai. If he wasn't engrossed in something, I'd pull him over for a second opinion. But he was staring at his screen and typing intermittently, probably doing something I shouldn't interrupt.

McKayla crossed and recrossed the yard—her head bent, eyes focused on her feet, and taking such unnaturally long steps she had to whirl her arms every now and then to keep her balance. I would not have been surprised in the slightest if you told me she was talking to herself. Something about her attitude of total concentration was endearing to me. I felt a surge of protectiveness, like watching a very small child, deep in a serious game of make-believe.

Time to tell her about the rule against pets. It would be like ripping off a Band-Aid. The sooner I said something, the better. Standing here now, watching her from our second-story window, I couldn't explain why I hadn't managed to say anything yet.

Without letting myself think or plan anymore, I flipped the bolt on the back door and stepped onto the deck. I immediately wished I had let myself think or plan just enough to grab my jacket. McKayla clearly had more tolerance to cold than I did. I waved to her, and walked down the wooden stairs, making sure to step only on the left side of the fifth one down, the one with the rotted tread Dwayne hadn't gotten around to fixing yet.

"Nikki! I'm so glad to see you!" She turned toward me, and I saw with shock a tiny, furry face poking out of one of the pockets on her droopy cardigan. It ducked back down, so I didn't get a good look at it. A ferret maybe? McKayla patted the outside of the pocket and smiled blissfully at me. "Come on inside, won't you? It's too cold out here."

The ferret, if that's what it was, had disarmed me to such an extent that all I could do was follow meekly after McKayla to her own back door. The giant white cat sat in the back window, watching us approach, his eyes fixed on McKayla's cardigan pocket. Something predatory filled his gaze, like maybe he knew that, whatever that thing was, it was probably delicious.

The layout of the downstairs apartment mimicked ours, with the back door opening into the kitchen. The cat didn't budge from his post in the window as we entered, but his eyes tracked McKayla and her pocket as she entered and crossed the room.

I'd found my perfect opportunity. After all, I couldn't keep pretending that I hadn't noticed the cat.

"Oh, what a beautiful cat! What's his name? I thought Dwayne doesn't allow pets?" I forced my pitch up at the end of the last sentence, trying to sound curious instead of censorious.

"Yes, he is a beautiful cat, isn't he? He started living with me a few months ago. I don't know his name, yet, but I call him Mr. Cat, when I need to call him something."

I laughed, an automatic reaction to not knowing what to say. In my old job at the vet's, I'd met plenty of cats who hadn't been named yet. The most common scenario was a family with multiple children, who'd just adopted a new pet, and each of the kids had their own suggestion, but no one was willing to compromise yet. Usually, the parents rolled their eyes as they explained the situation to me. McKayla had sounded utterly sincere. I didn't doubt that she was waiting for Mr. Cat to warm up to her enough for him to share his True Name with her, or something like that.

Laughing had been the wrong reaction, but McKayla didn't seem to care. She sat down on one of the red plastic kitchen chairs and waved at me to join her. The kitchen looked well used already, the counter crowded with mason jars and bags from the bulk aisle of the grocery store. These apartments had a four-inch-wide strip of counter between the stove and the refrigerator, the result of a design mistake, or the changing sizes of appliances over the years. In our place, that strip was where junk mail sat until Jai moved it away from the open flame of the gas burners. Here, that space held a tall green bottle of oil, a bowl full of salt, and three wooden spoons of different sizes. Some dishes rested in the sink, and some pots sat out on the stove, but the kitchen didn't feel messy, just like it was being used as a kitchen.

"I'm so glad I ran into you," she said. "I was just taking some measurements out in the backyard. I think there'd be enough room for five or six chickens to live comfortably. I've always wanted to have chickens, but I've never lived somewhere with a nice, fenced yard like this one." She waved a hand toward the back left corner, where our shared dumpster faced the alley. "That would be the perfect spot for a cozy chicken coop."

I was momentarily speechless. The "backyard" she referred to was not deserving of the term. It was a narrow ten-by-twelve strip of dirt between the back of the building and the alley. It featured a single hickory tree that looked perpetually sick, probably because it didn't get enough light. The buildings squeezed too close together for it to get more than a couple of hours of sun daily. In spring and summer, it filled out just enough to shade the ground and prevent any grass from growing. In the fall, somehow more dry, brown leaves fell off it than had ever been attached to it. In that way, it was kind of magical, I guess. I don't know if scientists could find a way to harness the Miracle of the Miserable Hickory to solve our energy crisis.

She'd blown past my reference to our landlord's rules against pets and was doubling down by suggesting a flock of poultry. Although, to be fair, Dwayne couldn't claim chickens in the backyard were a danger to his original hardwood floors. At least, not with most tenants. I could totally see McKayla bustling the feathery ladies inside to roost in her bedroom on a cold night.

"Dwayne doesn't allow his tenants to have any animals," I said, giving up on conversational segues. "It's in the lease."

"Oh, leases! That's all standard landlord boilerplate." She flipped a hand airily. "He probably downloaded the whole thing from some website and never bothered to read all the way through it. I saw somewhere that eighty-seven percent of landlords have never read their own leases. Anyway, nobody would ban pets. We need animals in our lives. They're like us, but not so complicated, you know, so they help us remember that we can be like that, too, you know?"

I squinted one eye. I did, kind of, know what she meant. About the value of animal companionship, not about her cavalier attitude to legal contracts. But I also knew our no-nonsense landlord, and I could imagine how he'd react if he saw Mr. Cat, or whatever she still held curled in her pocket, or whatever was making that squawking noise from the front room.

"Look, it's not like I have a problem with it, or anything. I'd love to be able to have pets here. I'm just saying, you might want to be a little more . . . subtle."

McKayla stared at me wide-eyed. I don't think she'd ever encountered the concept of subtlety before. I really, really didn't want to get more involved, but she somehow awakened my protective instincts.

"Like, maybe cover your front windows, so that people can't see Mr. Cat from the sidewalk." I waved an arm toward the area I'd first caught a glimpse of the cat. "And maybe don't get a flock of chickens for the backyard. You know, little precautions like that."

"Oh, wow. Thank you, Nikki." Coming from literally anyone else that would have sounded sarcastic. But sarcasm must have been covered in the same class as subtlety on that day McKayla skipped.

"But Dwayne's not stupid. And he'll have to come into your unit now and then for maintenance and inspections and that kind of thing. You're really just stalling. You need to find a pet-friendly place to move, if you're serious about keeping Mr. Cat and the others." Easier said than done, I knew from long experience, but no reason to point that out right now.

She shrugged, letting my advice fall off her shoulders and slump onto the floor. "Would you like some tea?" she asked.

"Actually, I have to go. I have an appointment. Thanks, though." I'd done my best and couldn't do anything else.

She followed me to the back door Mr. Cat still guarded. "Another time, then. We need to have a girls' night soon."

I forced a smile. "Sounds great. See you!"

My instinct was to slip around to the front without disturbing Jai, but my imagination was too morbid to allow that. If Teri slipped cyanide into my Frappuccino, shouldn't someone know where I'd gone? So I climbed the wooden stairs and reentered our apartment.

When I laid a hand on Jai's shoulder, he pulled himself out of whatever he'd been working on, blinking as he looked away from his computer screen.

"Don't work too hard," I told him. "Listen, I'm going to meet Teri for coffee. I have no idea why she wants to meet, but I can't imagine it'll be too long. I'm sure I won't be gone more than an hour or so."

Jai looked worried but just nodded. "Love you."

"Love you, too," I answered, and went off on my own to meet someone who thought I was a murderer.

Chapter Twenty-Seven

Teri's coffee mug was almost empty by the time I showed up. She'd stationed herself at a table by the window and was scrolling through her phone. She went to put it away when she saw me, but I waved from a few feet away and then pointed at the counter.

"I'm going to get something. Want a refill?" I kept my tone pleasant and cheerful, enjoying the impatient frustration on her face. She didn't answer, so I placed my own order, put my change in the tip jar, and then stood at the counter to get my drink. No other customers waited right then, so the barista and I chatted about the weather until my drink was slid across to me.

Teri was fuming by the time I took a seat. I'll give her this, though, she stayed in control of herself. I thought back to something Brett had said and felt relieved to be in a public place. She wouldn't explode in front of witnesses. Instead, she funneled all her impatience into a no-nonsense attitude, getting straight down to business with no small talk or pleasantries.

"The police think my grandmother killed herself."

"Oh, really?" I tried to keep the relief out of my voice. Given that the alternative was murder, this was fantastic news, but I could tell from Teri's face she didn't agree.

"Yes!" She stood, jolting her chair backward and attracting stares from a nearby table. She strode once around our table and sat back down, like an angry parody of a dog circling before lying down to sleep. "They think she took her sleeping pills and then went into the garage and started Grandpa's old Studebaker and sat in there and breathed in the exhaust and died."

"But that doesn't make any sense!" Maybe I should have latched onto this theory, but my brain couldn't even pretend to accept the story. "We found her in bed. She'd gone to bed that night, not to the garage."

"The police found evidence in the garage," Teri replied.

"What kind of evidence?"

She leaned back in her chair and narrowed her eyes. All her suspicions of me had come flooding back, and I couldn't blame her. Was it natural for me to have asked about the evidence? It felt natural as the words left my lips, a logical extension of the conversation, but maybe that was the kind of question only a murderer would ask, trying to determine how close the police were on their tail.

I remembered all too clearly what Sasha had said about how the man convicted of the Show-Me-State killings had gotten himself mixed up in the whole thing, by being too eager for details of the investigation.

Teri, thankfully, seemed not to be familiar with the story of the Show-Me-State slayer, because after a moment's contemplation, she answered me. "They found a wad of duct tape."

"That could be anything!"

"No, they found a wadded-up ball of duct tape under my grandfather's old Studebaker. It was apparently far enough back that the rear passenger tire would conceal it from view no matter where in the garage you're standing."

I found myself nodding. It didn't seem like a smoking gun. I could think of dozens of uses for duct tape in a garage. But I could picture the scene perfectly. The small wad of tape, kicked just out of sight, lying forgotten under the dusty black car.

"Then they found the residue of duct tape adhesive on the tailpipe. Then they searched the whole property and found matching duct tape residue on one end of some tubing we keep to use for the pool system. It had been coiled up and put away with the other pool equipment."

One half of my brain was listening to Teri, trying to digest her words. The other half focused on the duct tape under the car. Something about her description had resonated with me. I could picture it—like I had seen it.

I snapped my fingers, interrupting Teri in the middle of a sentence. I *had* seen it. Reginald had sniffed at a sticky gray ball Sunday night during the party, when we'd been in the garage talking to Kevin. That must have been it. I felt a little sick, realizing I'd seen . . . it seemed grandiose to call it the murder weapon, but at least the detritus of a death, and I hadn't known.

Thanks to my snap of triumphant realization, Teri was looking at me expectantly. I came out with the first thing that popped into my head, a repeat of my earlier objection. "But we found her in bed. She was in bed, not in the garage."

Teri rolled her eyes and spoke to me like an elementary school teacher at the very end of her patience. "They think she had help. Do you understand? They think someone helped her plan it and then helped cover it up, to make it look like an accident or death by natural causes. After she was dead, they moved her into the bedroom. She would have hated for us to find her that way. In the garage. Suicide." Teri shuddered.

"Oh." I couldn't think of anything more intelligent to say, and, if I'm being honest, I only managed that after opening and closing my mouth a few times. It certainly could have happened that way. The possibility hadn't occurred to me, but that didn't mean much. "Do they think you were the one who helped her?"

Teri pulled a napkin from a dispenser on the table and wiped up a microscopic droplet of coffee from the table. She wadded up the napkin and held it inside a tight fist for just a second or two, and then relaxed her hand, letting the ball of paper fall soundless on the table. We both watched as it relaxed and expanded, free of the pressure of her hand.

Just when I'd decided she wasn't going to answer me, she finally spoke, dragging the words out like I'd forced her to admit some long-buried secret. "The stuff in the garage . . . the tape residue . . . that's not all they found."

Great. Time to wait again. I got that she was dealing with some stuff, so I didn't push her, but a person can only sit still and quiet for so long. Do detectives carry fidget spinners for times like this? I couldn't picture Detective Tanghal resorting to such measures during a long interrogation. I could tough it out.

Finally, Teri sighed again. "The police found an envelope in Grandma's bedside table. In a drawer, shoved all the way in the back." She looked at me. "Did they already ask you about it?"

I shook my head, baffled.

"It was full of magazine clippings, newspaper clippings, a couple of print-outs from websites, all about euthanasia and assisted suicide and right-to-die and all that kind of thing. They didn't show it to me, but they showed me pictures."

I was still lost. "So, your grandmother was interested in euthanasia?" But even as I said it, my mind was working. "Isn't that kind of thing all about people who are terminal anyway? Like, they decide there's no point in lingering around in horrific pain, and they'd rather just go quickly?" My brain tried to follow this thought to its logical conclusion, but my mouth was already there. "Why do they think she was interested for herself? Didn't your grandfather just die of some lingering fatal cancer? Maybe she saw what he was going through, and looked it up, or maybe he even asked her to look it up for him."

I wasn't expecting Teri to smile about such a bleak topic, but she did, just barely. "That's what I said, too. I said no way she was looking to end her own life. She wasn't sick. But Grandpa hated being in the hospital, and I'm sure he would have taken any way out." She smiled again. "Devout Catholic, at least up until it mattered."

That was the brand of Catholicism I'd grown up with, too. "But then . . . that makes sense."

She shook her head. "Some of the articles are too new. Last couple of weeks. From *after* Grandpa's death."

"Is there a chance she was sick, and you didn't know it? Maybe she'd just found out, gotten some terrible diagnosis, and hadn't told people yet." Suddenly something Bonnie had said that very first day clicked into place for me. I sat forward. "I bet that's it. I bet her doctors told her she didn't have long, and she didn't know how to tell you and Ali, but she told Bonnie. When we were making arrangements for me to walk

Reginald, Bonnie said something that made it sound like your grandmother had one foot in the grave. I thought she just meant . . . you know . . . she *was* pretty old . . ." I trailed off.

Teri had leaned forward excitedly when I had, expecting some profound revelation. As I talked, she slumped back in her chair. "No, that's just Bonnie. She's always made comments like that. Or at least as long as I've known her. You know the type, right? Disaster is always looming and every silver lining has a cloud."

Fair enough. I did know the type. When I was a kid, we had a neighbor who wandered over during my ninth birthday party to make sure we knew the story of that time somebody burned their house down with unattended birthday candles.

"Don't get me wrong. I love Bonnie. My whole childhood, she was the one who was waiting for us when we got home from school. She was the one we could talk to if we needed someone, if we got lonely or scared. She's had a really rough time with her mother." Teri's gaze had wandered to the window, and she no longer sounded like she was speaking directly to me. "Her mind started to slip when she was in her late seventies. I get the impression Bonnie and her brothers ignored, or think they may have ignored, some very early signs of what was happening. Then when the dementia was obvious, it progressed incredibly quickly. Within a matter of months, she couldn't recognize her own children. She's been lingering like that for years and years, in a nursing home."

Teri dragged her gaze back to me. "I think that experience colored how she saw my grandmother. Every misunderstanding or tiny bit of confusion was the looming specter of Alzheimer's. I think she thought it was inevitable. I don't know how Bonnie's thinking affected my grandmother. If I were her age and truly believed that Alzheimer's was inevitable, I might contemplate suicide when I felt it creeping up. Before Grandpa's death, my grandmother was extremely levelheaded. But loss has been known to change people. I don't know." She tilted her head to one side as a new thought struck her. "I mean, she did change her will on the basis of what? Three days of knowing you? Maybe four conversations? Maybe that does point to some kind of cognitive slip."

I ignored that comment. "So, the police think Bonnie convinced your grandmother to commit suicide? And what, dragged her body from the garage to the bedroom afterward? That doesn't seem likely to me." It wasn't impossible to picture the scene, but if a wealthy woman decided she'd like to die, surely there were more dignified ways to go. Don't they have some kind of death pod in Switzerland? Or maybe it's Sweden. Whichever. Surely Mrs. Van Meer could have shelled out for a one-way ticket. The idea that she would choose that dusty garage, and then to be lugged unceremoniously through the frost-covered grass in full view of any member of her family who chanced to look out the window . . . I shook my head to clear the visual and tuned back into Teri.

"The clippings were from magazines Bonnie reads, and the envelope was from a pack of stationary that she keeps in her desk."

"But even if Bonnie found the articles and gave them to her, isn't it a massive leap to go from researching something like assisted suicide to dragging a dead body across the yard in the dead of night?" I didn't want to say it out loud, but if things happened the way Teri was saying, I doubted it was a plan Mrs. Van Meer and Bonnie had truly come up with together. Teri was making Bonnie sound a little unhinged, like maybe she had convinced an otherwise healthy old woman to off herself. Manipulative, subtle hints building and building over the weeks, months, or years, and suddenly the unthinkable seems inevitable. I shuddered a little.

Teri shrugged. "The police didn't tell me everything they were thinking. Just enough to ask questions about it. But I could tell where they were headed. They kept circling back to Grandma's relationship with Bonnie."

We sat in silence for another few moments. I assumed Teri's thoughts were fixated on death and suicide. My thoughts stuck on the scene in the garage. Something about the duct tape continued niggling away at my mind. I felt like the noise of the coffee shop kept me from thinking clearly. Just as I would order my thoughts, the barista would call out a name, or the espresso machine would let out a burst of steam, and my brain would scramble.

"I'll be right back," I said, standing up. I didn't wait for any kind of reply but headed to the bathroom.

The bathroom smelled of industrial cleaner, which was probably the best-case scenario, really. I locked the door behind me and stood staring at my face in the mirror. I looked pale, with dark circles under my eyes. Hopefully, an effect caused by the overly bright florescent light bouncing off the beige walls. I didn't really look like that.

I shut my eyes tight and pictured the duct tape. A small, gray ball lying under the big, black car. Reginald had sniffed it. It had stuck to his nose, and he had shaken his head to dislodge it. All of that was fine. Why was it bothering me so much?

Relax. I took a deep breath. The only way to cope with thoughts tickling the back of your mind was to avoid thinking about them directly.

Everything Teri had said to me made sense. Duct tape residue on the tailpipe. Someone must have pulled the tape off the tailpipe, wadded it up, and then dropped it out of sight. The one clumsy moment in an otherwise well-orchestrated effort to cover up a suicide. Bonnie, or whoever, would have had plenty of time after the guests left—

My eyes snapped open. That was it. I dug in my purse for Detective Tanghal's business card. I needed to call her, tell her she was wasting her time, looking in the wrong direction.

Someone knocked on the door, startling me back to my surroundings.

"I'll be out in a minute," I called, starting to wash my hands.

Should I tell Teri? She was under a lot of stress, and maybe I could relieve some of it. But I might be wrong. I may have misunderstood her, or she may have misunderstood the police. I'd go back out there, finish my conversation with Teri, and then call Detective Tanghal as soon as I could. She'd have to rethink everything.

Chapter Twenty-Eight

I returned to the table, and bolstered by my realization, decided to address the elephant in the room. Teri had been talking to me so candidly, latching on to me as a disinterested outsider.

"Does the fact that you're telling me all this—" I started to ask, then faltered when she looked at me. I told myself she wasn't challenging me or scrutinizing me or judging me, just looking at me. That wasn't scary. I started over. "At one point, you thought I might have murdered your grandmother." She looked away, and I kept going. "You thought I'd done it to get my hands on Reginald's pet trust."

"I didn't. Not really." Her reply sounded automatic, and we both knew it was a lie. She sighed and tried again. "I was overwhelmed with grief and anger. I don't know what I was thinking. You were an outsider benefiting from her death, and it was easiest to push all those negative feelings onto you."

"And . . ." She'd gone back to playing with the napkin. "You wouldn't understand. But, to me, my grandmother's generosity toward her dog was like a slap in the face." She sighed again and opened her mouth to continue but then seemed to consider something and looked up. She stared directly into my eyes. "Ali doesn't know about this."

I nodded. She hadn't explicitly asked me to keep a secret for her, but that's how I understood it.

"I think I told you that our mother sent us to live with Grandma when I was six and Ali was five. From then on, Grandma took care of everything for us. We got cards from Mom, and talked to her on the phone sometimes, but I can count on one hand the number of times she's come to St. Louis in our lifetimes."

"Thank god for your grandma."

Teri laughed. I'd heard her laugh like that before, and I would have described it as bitter, except this time, she sounded more tired than anything else. "Yeah, and that's what Ali would say, too. 'Thank god for Grandma.' Except she wasn't old enough to see, or maybe she just didn't want to see how transactional the whole thing was. Grandma kept track of every little expense for us, I don't know, on a spreadsheet or something, so she could be sure to collect from Mom. I realized what was going on in third grade, when we were going on a field trip to the science center, and there was some fee, just a couple of dollars, for I don't know what exactly, maybe like the IMAX movie. The school didn't give enough notice for Mom to transfer the money to Grandma, so I didn't get to go."

I winced.

"Yeah, exactly." Teri laughed again, this time sounding a little more lighthearted. "The sad thing was, I thought it made perfect sense at the time. Oh, I don't mean about that particular field trip. That was a heartbreaking injustice for a little nine-year-old. I just mean that their system made sense. We were Mom's, so it made sense that she would pay for us. It was like Grandma was babysitting us. Of course, she wouldn't pay out of pocket for our stuff."

"But she was your grandmother!" I never thought I'd be put in the position of saying good things about my family, but one byproduct of messy, complicated families was you get people raising children who aren't their own. And in my experience, people just got on with it, because somebody needed to.

I would have said more, but Teri held up a hand. "I know, I know. I'm just saying the logic made sense back then. As I got older, I started to realize how messed up it was. The saddest part is, they both just pulled their money from different sections of the same family trusts. It's not like either of them were hurting for cash or even spending their own hard-earned money. It was all money earned five or six generations back, and since then, everybody's just been squatting on the hoard."

She drew a deep breath. "Anyway, that brings me to the point of all this, why I got you here today. I wanted to say I'm sorry. I was thinking about how much energy my mother and grandmother wasted arm wrestling over the family pile, and I realized I was about to start the exact same thing with you. It's money. Whatever."

Now, I had heard similar sentiments before, downplaying the importance of money. But never when the sum in question was more than about ten bucks. "You'll get me next time," when not bothering to ask for split checks at a restaurant, or something like that. Not waving away multiple hundreds of thousands of dollars. I didn't dare speak in case I was misunderstanding her.

"The idea of some long, drawn-out court battle? It could be years, I don't even know. The idea makes me sick to my stomach. I want to get her in the ground and move on with my life."

I nodded. That, at least, was a stance I could identify with. I wasn't sure what to say, though. Should I thank her? Wouldn't that make me sound money-hungry? My deep-seated need to justify myself won out instead. "You know I really didn't know anything about the pet trust. Brett only told me about it the day after she died."

Her gaze had drifted out the window again, but now she snapped her attention back to me.

"She told you about it," she said. "My grandmother told you she'd named you the trustee. She'd only known you for a few days, but she could tell how responsible you were and how devoted you were to animals and that Reginald would be guaranteed to get quality care if you oversaw the trust. The implication was that obviously she couldn't trust me and Ali to do the same."

I opened my mouth and then shut it again. Why had I even brought this up? We'd been getting along so well, and she'd said she didn't suspect me anymore. Now I had to call a dead woman a liar? Why should Teri believe me? I had nothing to offer except a flat denial. "She didn't. She never said anything to me."

Teri scoffed and shifted in her chair.

"Did she say when she told me? We were never even alone together." I ticked off on my fingers. "That first day, Ali and

Will were there the whole time. Ask them. When I got back from walking Reginald, your grandmother was up with the stager. I only talked to Bonnie. Wednesday, you were there. I never even saw your grandmother." This recitation should have been a feat of memory, but I'd been over all this with the police just the day before. "Thursday, you screamed at me in the street, and Ali and Will invited me to the party. Never saw your grandmother. Friday, I talked to her for a long time about Reginald, and Bonnie was there the whole time. Ask her. Brett apologized for you and invited me to the party again. Ask him. Saturday, it was Ali and Will again, no sign of your grandmother. Sunday morning, she was there, doing water aerobics. Ask her personal trainer what we talked about. At the party, I never saw your grandmother until she came out to say goodnight to everybody."

Teri had looked like she'd wanted to interrupt a couple of times while I spoke, but I hadn't given her an opening. Now she looked ashamed. I don't think she enjoyed the reminder of her attitude toward me.

"Well, maybe Bonnie was right after all. Maybe Grandma thought she'd talked to you, but she got confused and never actually had the conversation." She paused for a moment, and when she spoke again, her tone was less defensive. "The point is, I really do think you'll do what's best for Reginald and that's obviously something Grandma valued, at least after Grandpa died. So, . . . you have my blessing." She waved a hand vaguely in the air over the table and smiled self-deprecatingly at the pomposity of it all.

As much as I appreciated Teri's new outlook, I was positively wriggling with suppressed tension by the time she actually got up and left. The instant the door swung shut behind her, I dove into my bag, digging through crumpled receipts, notebooks, and grocery lists for Detective Tanghal's business card. She'd handed them out to all of us and said that we should call if we thought of anything that might help. I had thought of something that might help. But I hesitated. My instinct was to lie low. Surely, they could solve this themselves. Don't call attention to yourself. Don't invite scrutiny.

That was absurd. The longer this investigation dragged on, the more scrutiny we'd all be under. If I could find the killer and hand them over the cops wrapped up in a neat little package, this would all be over.

I dialed Detective Tanghal's number. She picked up on the second ring, answering with her name.

"Hi. It's Nikki. Um, Nikki Jackson-Ramanathan. I walk the dog for Mrs. Van Meer?"

"The dog whisperer. What can I do for you?" Her voice sounded preoccupied.

"Oh! Yes, sorry. I was just talking to Teri, and she told me about the theory that Mrs. Van Meer died in the garage." I paused here, waiting for Detective Tanghal to say something, but she didn't. I pulled the phone away from my ear to check the call hadn't dropped, then continued. "Well, it's just that, I was in the garage Sunday night, you know that. I think I saw . . ." My voice trailed off. It felt wrong to blurt it out over the phone. What if she didn't believe me?

"Where are you?" She heard my hesitation and took charge.

"Uh . . ." I looked around, as if I had no idea where I was, but then my brain clicked back into gear, and I gave her the address. "Teri just left."

"I could use a cup of coffee." A slight pause, and I could picture her checking her watch. "I can be there in about fifteen minutes. Can you wait for me?"

I nodded as I said, "yes," and then went up to the counter for another drink. I got a cinnamon steamer. Unlike Detective Tanghal, I had already had way too much coffee for one day.

Even though she'd said she wanted some coffee, I kind of assumed she'd march right in and get down to business. But, although she nodded at me as she entered, she only joined me at the table after ordering. I've apparently seen way too many cop dramas in my lifetime, because I also expected her to turn the empty chair around and straddle it backward, but of course she sat in it like a normal person.

She didn't say anything, and I'd rehearsed my opening line, so I went first. "Teri said you think Mrs. Van Meer died in the garage, and then somebody took her back to bed, to cover up either a suicide or a murder."

"It's one theory, certainly." Detective Tanghal wasn't giving anything away.

"Teri said one reason you think that's what happened is you found a little ball of duct tape under the black Studebaker, by the rear passenger tire. She said you found duct tape residue on a long section of hose used for the pool system, so you think Mrs. Van Meer or someone taped the hose to the exhaust pipe and filled the car with carbon monoxide that way."

Detective Tanghal's eyes narrowed. "Teri certainly shared a lot of information with you. Information that she was told confidentially."

"She was really upset. I don't think she even realized everything she was saying." I had absolutely no idea why I was defending her. A nonzero percentage of her brain had thought I was a murderer. "But I was in the garage the night of the NFL party, early in the evening. Mrs. Van Meer was definitely still alive then, and that wad of duct tape was already there."

"Describe it," commanded Detective Tanghal, leaning forward. I expected her to pull out a notebook, or for that matter, to pull out Officer Hooper to take the notes. But she just sat, leaning forward in her chair, arms resting on the table in front of her, eyes boring into mine.

I opened my mouth and closed it again without saying anything. It was a wad of duct tape, what did she want from me? But I did my best to picture the scene. I could see Reginald with his nose against the silvery ball. That gave me scale. "It was about the size of a golf ball or ping pong ball, or maybe a little smaller. Not bigger than that, for sure. Originally lying right up against the tire, but Reginald sniffed at it, and it stuck to his nose, and when he shook his head to get it off, I think it landed a few inches farther under the car, and a few inches away from the wheel. I was sitting in a lawn chair across from the car. I don't think I could have seen it if I'd been standing up. There was nothing else under the car, not that I could see anyway." Was that true? "At least, Reginald didn't explore under there anymore, not after he was done with the duct tape."

"You were across the room. How did you know it was duct tape?"

"I don't know what else it could have been. It wasn't smooth, it was obviously sticky, and it was the right color. It never occurred to me it could be anything else." I squinted, thinking hard. "I guess it helped that it was in a garage. Duct tape belongs in a garage. If I'd seen the same thing somewhere else in the house, maybe I wouldn't have recognized it."

"Did you see the same thing somewhere else in the house?"

I shook my head. I don't know why I'd said that.

"You were with Mr. Driscoll when you saw it?"

"Kevin? Yes."

"Did he see it, too? Did you call it to his attention? Was he watching the dog?"

I shook my head again, slowly this time. "I don't think I ever saw him look over there. When we came in, he was playing a video game, and then he got up to get a treat for Reginald, and then he sat right back down, facing toward the TV and away from the cars."

"Can you be more precise with the time?"

I did my best to remember when exactly I'd wandered toward the garage. It couldn't possibly matter, because Mrs. Van Meer had definitely been alive and well long afterward.

We went back and forth over it a couple times. I assume she was trying to get me to contradict myself or remember that Kevin had picked up my ball of duct tape and thrown it away, and so they must have found a new ball of duct tape, or something like that.

Finally Detective Tanghal leaned back in her chair, out of questions, but her narrowed eyes still bored into me. I shifted my weight on the chair, and worried, even as I did it, that my nervousness indicated guilt to her.

I forced out a laugh. "I swear I don't know anything else. I've told you everything."

She nodded but kept staring. I shifted again.

"I'm trying to decide if Teri put you up to this," she said.

My eyes widened. "Why in the world would I lie for Teri? She doesn't even like me." I was shooting for "reasonable" with a hint of "logical," but I think my tone was a little too whiny.

Detective Tanghal leaned forward, and her tone, in contrast, was perfectly reasonable. "Maybe she threatened you." She spread her hands. "Maybe she has something on you, something she can hold over your head. Maybe you should go ahead and tell me why Ruth Van Meer wrote you into her will."

Now it was my turn to stare at her. We had suddenly waded into deep waters. I had momentarily allowed myself to forget about the will. A virtual stranger made a beneficiary after a couple of days? Yeah, I should be easy to manipulate. I wasn't going to be able to convince Detective Tanghal she was wrong. Heck, it seemed like Teri still half believed I'd pressured her grandmother into naming me, but had just decided it wasn't worth fighting over. I knew I hadn't had any 'undue influence' or whatever AJ had called it, but that wasn't the kind of solid, provable fact I could convince the police of. Instead, I held firm to two other facts: I had seen that ball of duct tape on Sunday night while Mrs. Van Meer was alive, and Teri wasn't pulling my strings behind the scenes.

"Look, I have no idea why Teri decided to confide in me about all this. I think she just needed someone to talk to. Some people think I'm a good listener. When I realized that what I saw might be important, I didn't have to call you, but I thought it might be helpful. I'm sorry if I'm wasting your time."

Thankfully Detective Tanghal didn't choose to press the issue further. I still have no idea whether she left our little meeting believing I'd seen a ball of duct tape on the garage floor Sunday night while Mrs. Van Meer was still alive. If the woman didn't play poker, she was wasting her talents.

Chapter Twenty-Nine

Saturday morning, I planned to sleep in. I didn't have so much dog walking on my schedule that I needed to start at the crack of dawn or anything. It was a rare fall weekend when Jai wasn't out of town at a mock trial tournament. Not that they didn't have a tournament that weekend, just it was in town. So although his weekend would be fully eaten up by his coaching duties, he could at least sleep in his own bed.

But it was barely eight o'clock when two loud, sharp cracks came from outside. As I lay in bed, struggling to get my eyes open, I tried to imagine what could be going on out there. On a brilliant sunny day, it would be a waste to shoot off fireworks. They'd probably been gunshots, which you'd think would be worrying, but was a normal part of the soundtrack of this neighborhood. Then I heard a loud engine noise, like a souped-up vacuum cleaner or a generator, followed by two more sharp cracks. Can generators backfire?

I stumbled out of bed, annoyed Jai hadn't been woken up by the racket. Life was unfair sometimes. I looked out the front windows. Nothing there. I went into the kitchen and looked into the backyard. Dwayne, our landlord, was crouched on the wooden steps leading down from our balcony, wielding a nail gun that looked like a prop weapon from some over-the-top action movie. When I appeared in the window, he looked up and gave me a cheery wave.

I grabbed a sweatshirt of Jai's draped over the back of the couch and pulled it over my head as I stepped out. Like I said, the sunlight was brilliant, but it was cold enough that I could see my breath. No matter the weather, I've never seen Dwayne wear anything other than shorts.

"Good morning!" he called. He started to say more, but, just as he opened his mouth, the compressor hooked up to his nail gun started up its deafening noise again. He held up a hand apologetically and hobbled down the stairs to switch it off. The noise had been so loud that, in the silence that followed, the air seemed to vibrate.

"Good morning," he said again. "How're you?"

Some tiny part of me wanted to complain he'd woken me up, but I couldn't really bring myself to say it. "Doing good. It's chilly," I added, hugging the sweatshirt more tightly around myself. "What are you doing?"

He looked down at the nail gun, like he'd forgotten it. "Oh, just fixing this step. Did you know you had a rotten tread on one of these stairs?"

I stepped forward to be able to see where he'd been working. The fifth step down, which yesterday had been rotted to such an extent you could look straight through it and see the ground, had been replaced with a new tread, its bright yellow wood in stark contrast to the gray, weathered wood on every other part of the deck.

"Looks great! Thanks so much."

He shrugged, looking, for some reason, a little bashful. Maybe he just realized that he'd been making a lot of noise early in the morning? Or maybe he'd just realized that the step must have been in that condition for a while? "I was over fixing a few things for McKayla. You've met McKayla, right? She said you two had met. I got her stuff taken care of, and she mentioned seeing you take these stairs very carefully, and asked me to have a look." He pointed toward the stairs again with his nail gun. "I had some wood in my truck. So I fixed it."

"Looks great," I said again. "Thanks so much." Dwayne was super friendly, but I never knew how to end conversations with him. I waved at him and walked back inside.

Jai came out of the bedroom.

"Oh, you're up!" I said in surprise.

He looked ruefully at me. "Yeah, kinda hard to sleep with you guys talking out there."

Of course. Jai's selective hearing was some kind of weird superpower. He hadn't heard the nail gun or the compressor, but I had a conversation at a normal volume outside the apartment, and that he heard.

I recounted my conversation with Dwayne as we made breakfast. "And now I know he's seen her animals, or at least the cat, unless she got rid of them since yesterday. I'm glad I didn't say anything. I told her he'd find out all on his own. Do you think he gave her thirty-days' notice?"

Jai scratched his head and shrugged. "It kind of sounds like he has a crush on her."

I made an involuntary noise somewhere between amusement and disgust. "He's thirty years older than her. At least!"

He shrugged again. "She's an adult. He didn't come fix a bunch of stuff for us the first week we moved in. Have you seen him do that for any of the other tenants who've been in that unit?"

It wasn't impossible. I scrunched up my face, thinking hard. If he was right, I should use the situation to my advantage. "If he's going to let her have pets, because he likes her, doesn't he have to do the same for us? Equal treatment under the law, or something? If he treats us differently, isn't that sex discrimination, or something?"

Jai swallowed a bite of Pop-Tart. "None of those words mean what you think they mean." He stood up and kissed me. "You're beautiful, even when you're pouting. We have to follow the lease we signed and ignore what anyone else is doing." He ducked back into the bedroom to get dressed and was out the front door within just a few minutes, not to return for hours and hours and hours.

I could have stayed there all day, sitting at the kitchen table. The sunshine fell through the streaky window over the sink, illuminating the three cheerfully painted pots of desiccated succulents on its sill. I sipped my coffee and daydreamed about never having to go anywhere ever again. Then Dwayne's compressor kicked on again. The noise was ever so slightly less painfully loud than when I'd been standing outside, but loud enough to serve as a kick in the pants.

If I sat here all day, I'd have to hear that until he finished whatever he was working on now. I sighed and stood up. I was going to have to walk Reginald at some point. Might as well get it over with.

The police were back. When I turned onto the Van Meers' street, Detective Tanghal's silver car sat in the driveway, and two squad cars were parked on the street. I almost drove past the house. No one would see me go by. I really didn't feel up to dealing with all this again today. But if they wanted me, they'd get me one way or the other. It would be easier to get it over with, rather than go back home and wait for them to knock on the door. I parked behind one of the police cars and trudged up the driveway.

Once again, everyone was gathered in the great room. This was starting to feel like *Groundhog Day*. But as soon as I opened the door and slipped in, I could tell something was different this time. The last time they'd all been gathered here, waiting to be interviewed by the police, the vibe had been sullen watchfulness. Now the air had a sense of excitement.

"What's going on?" I asked Teri, as I sat down next to her. I kept my voice low, more out of habit than anything else.

"They're reinterviewing everyone," she explained. "Sounds like they'd been focused on the idea that . . . someone had helped Grandma commit suicide, but now they've gotten information that's pointing them in another direction." She turned away from the others and faced me. She mouthed "What did you tell them?" and I pretended not to understand. I didn't see how I could possibly answer her, not right then and there.

My tip about the duct tape must have been helpful for the police, after all. I didn't know if Detective Tanghal had told Teri the information had come from me, or she was just guessing, but I didn't mind one way or the other. Anything to convince Teri we were on the same team was fine by me. I mean, unless she was the murderer and the whole apology had been an elaborate ruse on her part to throw me off the scent. But I'd never managed to come up with a plausible motive for her. I was also struggling to imagine Ali or Will in the role of killer. They seemed too even-keeled to resort to something as drastic as murder.

"They've searched the house again," Teri continued. "And now they have a new theory for how it was done."

"Oh, really?" I sat forward, fascinated. "How?"

Teri shook her head. "They're not saying. At least, they didn't tell me. They're just going over everybody's whereabouts again."

I looked around to see who was with the police just then. It must have been Ali, because the others were all there. Brett and Will sat around the kitchen island, not making eye contact with each other. Bonnie sat on one of the couches, a magazine lying open and neglected on her lap. Kevin stood uncomfortably by the French doors leading out onto the patio. Reginald was lying in his dog bed, watching me. He'd popped up when I came into the room but had sat down when I did.

I couldn't just sit there and wait my turn, not with Reginald's baleful eyes boring into me from across the room. I stood and approached the uniformed officer stationed in one corner of the room to keep an eye on us. I'd seen her around the house but didn't know her name.

"Excuse me?" Everyone in the room leaned my way to listen, just because there was absolutely nothing else happening. "Hi, my name's Nikki, and I'm sure they'll want to interview me, and that's totally fine. But if it's going to be a while before my turn, do you think I could go ahead and walk Reginald? I'll come right back."

The officer looked at me as though this was a carefully orchestrated plan designed to distract her and spring the others. I gave her my best earnest and trustworthy face, which isn't particularly good. She glanced at her watch, and then around the room, then fixed her eyes on a spot behind me, near the floor. I watched her face soften, and glanced back in confusion. Reginald had come up behind me to give this poor defenseless officer literal puppy dog eyes. She had no choice at that point.

Maintain law and order or disappoint a sweet hound dog with watery brown eyes? We were out the door before she'd finished her curt nod.

Chapter Thirty

As we passed Jackie's house, I stalled, moving even more slowly than the pace set by arthritic old Reginald. I'd done a complete one-eighty in my opinion of Jackie, the gossipy neighbor. The first time I'd been sucked into conversation with her, I'd done my best to get away. Now, I was eager for her insights into the dynamics at the Van Meer house. Something she'd said the first time we met had been echoing in my head since my heart-to-heart with Teri the day before.

"Well, Reggie? Do you think Ms. Jackie is at home today? She didn't strike me as a lady with a bulging social calendar, so I wouldn't be surprised at all if—oh, yup, I think that's her coming around the side of the house now. Was she lying in wait for us? Don't worry, old man. We'll be on our way soon." I reached down and patted Reginald on the head and pretended to notice Jackie for the first time as I straightened back up.

"Good morning!" I called. "How are you doing today?"

Jackie trundled toward me as quickly as she could, so she had no spare breath to answer until she reached me.

"Just fine, just fine. And how is everyone up at the house?" She pointed with her chin in the direction of the Van Meer house, while arranging her features in an expression of sympathetic concern.

"Oh, they're holding it together, just about," I said, matching her expression. "You know, I think you were right. About what you said, I mean."

Who could resist a conversational opener like that! Certainly not Jackie.

"What do you mean, dear?"

I leaned forward and lowered my voice. "Poor Bonnie! She's taking it harder than anyone."

"Oh, I just knew she would!" Jackie exclaimed. She laid a hand to her heart and shook her head. "Has she told you about her mother, Bonnie's mother, I mean?"

I widened my eyes and shook my head. I suspected Jackie would be more than happy to tell the story from the beginning, and might give me more detail than Teri had.

"Well, it was just awful! Her mother, Bonnie's mother, I mean, wasn't even that old when she started to decline. I mean, she was old enough, obviously, but she wasn't that old. She just went downhill so fast once it started, you almost couldn't believe. Of course, the same thing happened to Henry's uncle, Alzheimer's, you know, and his kids had to put him in a home. Bonnie's mother couldn't live on her own, either, and it happened so quick. I know she thought the same thing was going to happen to poor old Ruthie. I mean, the same thing as her mother, Bonnie's mother, I mean. Bonnie didn't know Henry's uncle, or maybe I told her about him, but I can't remember now." She stopped, having delivered a string of words confusing enough to confuse herself.

"My great-grandmother was just about the same," I said. "She lingered, you know. All her siblings, they went quick as anything when their time came, and that was awful, of course, but I somehow think it was much better that way. Quick, I mean."

I was lying through my teeth here. Most of that generation died before I could remember, and from what I understand, they did their best to get a clean sweep of every possible iteration of liver failure and lung disease. I made a mental promise to donate some money to a worthy cause to counteract any bad karma I was attracting.

"Oh my, yes, sweetie. That's just what I think, too. And Bonnie's said the same thing about her mother many, many times. 'I wish she didn't have to go through that,' she'd say. Or 'I wish it could have all been over right as her mind started to go, because that was truly the end of her life, as far as any reasonable definition of life.' Things like that. Oh, Bonnie has had such a rough time, dealing with all that."

Jackie, predictably, went on this vein for a while longer. I didn't listen to all of it. She'd confirmed what Teri had said. There was a chance Bonnie had decided Mrs. Van Meer was heading inexorably toward a hopeless battle with dementia. If that were the case, would Bonnie have helped Mrs. Van Meer avoid all the pain and confusion with a swift exit? Was there any chance Mrs. Van Meer had asked her to do it?

Sure, my report meant that the little ball of duct tape in the garage had no connection to the crime. The idea of Mrs. Van Meer gassing herself in her late husband's Studebaker and Bonnie or someone else lugging her corpse across the yard to tuck her into bed, always farfetched, no longer had any basis in evidence. But that didn't necessarily clear Bonnie.

Bonnie had an unhealthy obsession with death, seeing it as an easy out before the realities of old age settled in. Teri had said as much, and Jackie had confirmed it. Even if I didn't understand exactly *how* Mrs. Van Meer had died, Bonnie just felt right as a suspect. Either Mrs. Van Meer had wanted to end her life and had sought out a long-time companion for help or Bonnie had been poisoning her mind for years, convincing her that death would be a simple solution to life's inconveniences. She must have stepped up her efforts in the month since Mr. Van Meer's death, or maybe Mrs. Van Meer became more receptive to the idea.

Teri seemed to think that, if Bonnie had been involved, her motives were pure. That Bonnie truly believed that Mrs. Van Meer was teetering on the cusp of an inexorable decline and that Bonnie had only done what she hoped someone would do for her were Bonnie to find herself in a similar situation.

I didn't know about all that. More important, I didn't know if the police would buy that. If I was going to present Bonnie as a viable suspect, to draw attention away from Kevin and from me, it had to be plausible to the police. Did Bonnie stand to gain from Mrs. Van Meer's death? I'd speculated that maybe her position would be unnecessary if Mrs. Van Meer sold the house and moved into a condo. I guess I could have tried to ask Jackie whether Bonnie had been worried about that. Or was there a provision in either of the Van Meers' wills for Bonnie? That sounded more promising. I could figure out a way to ask Brett about that. Casually, somehow, so he didn't feel like he was divulging confidential information.

I didn't get a chance to talk to Brett at all when I got back to the house. Will was just coming out of the study, and it was my turn. Detective Tanghal's first question to me wasn't about wads of duct tape or about Bonnie or, as far as I could tell, about the murder at all. "Could you tell us about Reginald's movements during the party?"

My hackles rose. I flashed back to the derision in Officer Hooper's voice as he confirmed my web address. Sure, "pet whisperer" was a cutesy marketing gimmick, but I was an animal behaviorist, a valuable and skilled position. Just look at Reginald! Before I'd been brought onto the case, he'd been grieving, howling in the middle of the night. And now? Now he was a relatively healthy and happy old man. I hadn't heard him howl even once. So if the cops wanted to mock my focus on animals, well, that just proved how narrow-minded they were.

Apparently, seasoned homicide detectives can read facial expressions. Detective Tanghal smiled at me. "I really do need to know where the dog was that evening, and it seems like none of the others paid any attention to him. I know you followed him to the garage early on, and thank god you did, as it turns out."

The muscles in my neck relaxed. "I wasn't making it up? The duct tape was already there?"

She leaned forward. "This doesn't leave the room, understand?"

I nodded.

"With your hint that the garage may have been a blind, we started hunting for corroborating evidence. An analysis of the fine particles stuck to the duct tape indicated it had lain in that position for longer than seventy-two hours. I won't go into detail, but the layers of accumulated particulate matter suggest it may have been there for more than a week." She consulted her notebook. "It's nothing conclusive enough to be brought up in court, but it made it more likely than not that you were telling the truth. It was a good observation."

I raised my chin like a smug dog accepting a pat on the head. It may sound mild, but to me, that felt like the strongest praise from Detective Tanghal. I'd earned a gold star. Maybe that's why she kept going.

"The coroner's initial analysis revealed that the cause of death was likely carbon monoxide poisoning. Although there are other possible explanations, our focus had to be on the garage as the source of the gas. We've now received the full report on the deceased, and without getting too technical, the blood sample was lacking the methemoglobin we'd expect to see alongside the carboxyhemoglobin, if car exhaust really was the source of the poisoning."

At least she'd said "without getting too technical," which suggested she was already dumbing things down for me. The terms, utterly foreign to me, tripped off her tongue with easy familiarity. I wished she'd write her explanation down for me, so I could read through it later, with as much Googling as I needed. I was going to sound like an idiot recounting this conversation to Jai tonight. "She said Mrs. Van Meer's blood didn't have a thing it would have if she'd died in the car." That didn't sound that bad, but with one well-placed follow-up question I'd crumble like a house built on sand.

"So." Detective Tanghal pressed both palms onto the table. "I've given you some information, probably more than I should, to say thanks for your earlier help. Now I need more help. Please tell me about the dog's movements at the party Sunday night."

I did my best. Starting with Reginald's trip to the garage, and leading all the way through the evening, until Mrs. Van

Meer announced she was going to bed and she and Reginald had disappeared inside the house together. Gaps existed in the timeline, moments when I'd lost sight of Reginald during conversations with other partygoers. But on the whole, I did better than I had when asked to remember the movements of the human guests during the party.

"Thank you," said Detective Tanghal when I finished. "You're sure she said she was going to put him in the study?"

I nodded and then thought back. I nodded again, more firmly. "Yes. She called him. 'Here, Reginald. Time for bed.' And then as he walked through the door, Mrs. Van Meer looked over toward someone, Teri, I think. She said, 'Don't worry about Reginald. I'll put him in the study.' Anyway, she did put him in the study, because I'm the one who let him out the next morning. He was eager to get outside to relieve himself, since no one had let him out at his regular time. He's such a good boy."

"But we found a dog bed in Mrs. Van Meer's bedroom. And there's a dog door in there, leading out into the backyard. There's nothing like that in the study. Do you know why the dog was shut up in the study?"

I nodded. "The whole reason Mrs. Van Meer consulted me was that Reginald was grieving Mr. Van Meer's death, which I understand was about a month ago. They had a problem with him howling in the middle of the night but moving him to Mr. Van Meer's study seemed to comfort him. Familiar scents, and that kind of thing, you know."

"It was your idea?" asked Detective Tanghal.

"Actually, no. This was before I was called in. Mrs. Van Meer took him to the study in the middle of night, I think just because it was what made her feel better when she was missing her husband. It's funny, but people assume animals are different from us, but they're really, really not, especially domesticated animals, like dogs and cats. They experience and sense our emotions and feel similar things themselves. When Mrs. Van Meer told me that sleeping in the study had seemed to calm Reginald down, I told her it was a good idea, and there was no reason to stop letting him sleep in there."

"Hmm." Detective Tanghal tapped her chin with a pen, staring at me with the same intensity as in the coffee shop yesterday. She was intimidating. I couldn't imagine sitting across from her if I were guilty. "Did Reginald sleep in the study every night from that point on? Or just some nights?"

"I have no idea." I thought back. "He was always up and about when I came over. Until that Monday morning." She knew what I meant. Of course she knew what I meant. She couldn't not know what I meant, but my mouth wouldn't stop talking. "When we found her. Found her body. Dead. You know."

Detective Tanghal must have been used to people blabbering about obvious things. "You were never here at night, when the dog was put to bed?"

"No, just in the mornings. Oh, except for the football watch party, of course. But that was it."

"Hmm," she said again. Then she rose but gestured for me to stay where I was. She crossed the room and stuck her head out the door. "Officer Hooper? Could you join us please? And bring the evidence bag with you."

I hadn't registered Officer Hooper's absence until then. Detective Tanghal had jotted down a few lines, especially as we went back over the timeline of Sunday night, but she was missing her dedicated note-taker. I didn't like the way she said, "Bring the evidence bag." It sounded ominous.

Officer Hooper entered the room holding something small, wrapped in plastic. They'd show it to me, in their own sweet time, but I still squinted and craned my neck and cursed my lack of X-ray vision that could have seen through Officer Hooper's meaty fingers.

He laid it on the table in front of me, unfurling the bag, so that only one thickness of clear plastic covered the object. It was about eight inches long, dark teal, cylindrical, like a pencil, or—"Oh! My pen!" The instant I recognized it, the words escaped, without a thought given to what it might mean that the police had it in an evidence bag.

Unhelpfully, my only thought in the next moment was, "if this thing gets to trial, my defense attorney will be pissed!" I pictured my beleaguered attorney, bizarrely not AJ, but an overweight white man in a dress shirt with pit stains, like from *To Kill a Mockingbird* or *Twelve Angry Men*, or something else in black and white.

"You identified it?!" he'd say. "Why did you identify it?" Then, sinking his head into his hands, "The jury's going to have a field day with this one."

Like I said, not really a helpful train of thought.

"Where did you lose it?" asked Detective Tanghal, snapping me back out of whatever antiquated movie I'd wandered into.

"I didn't! I mean," I corrected myself, "I don't know. I didn't know it was lost." I shook my head and tried to remember the last time I'd used it. I'd had it on Thursday, and I hadn't seen it today. What about yesterday? And more importantly, could I prove it? "As far as I knew—until just now—it was still in my bag."

"I'll go fetch your bag, then, just so you can double-check," said Officer Hooper. His tone sounded matter-of-fact, but I dreaded having to look through my bag for a pen that wasn't there. Because of course it wouldn't be in my bag. How could it? It was lying on the table, in an evidence bag, between me and two police officers.

I wondered what the others would think, when they saw Officer Hooper come into the great room and pick up my bag from where I always dropped it, just inside the back door.

A shiver went through me. Except, one of them must have already identified the pen.

Most of them had seen me writing with a similar pen, when making notes about my initial consultation with Reginald. And they each knew the others had seen my pen, too. If the police had found my pen somewhere incriminating, someone must have stolen it out of my bag and planted it.

I was being framed.

A complex series of emotions must have raced across my face as these thoughts raced through my head, because Detective Tanghal held up a hand. "Just . . . where did you last see it?" The "calm down" was implicit.

"I don't know," I said again, taking a few deep breaths. "I know for sure I used it Thursday afternoon, but I'm trying to remember seeing it after that."

Then the absurdity of the situation hit me. My heart stopped pounding. "Listen," I said, as Officer Hooper reentered the room and passed me my bag, "I'm not stupid. You're investigating a murder that happened Sunday night or the early morning on Monday. You show me something in an evidence bag, so there's gotta be a link between the two, right?" I leaned back in my chair, sure that I had them. "I bought that pen on Wednesday afternoon, two days after Mrs. Van Meer's death. I didn't get a receipt or anything, but

I can show you the transaction, and Alex, from the art supply store, might remember."

Neither of them said anything, which I fully understand was an interrogation technique, but it's one that works. I couldn't let the silence drag on. I had to make sure they got it.

"So somebody must have stolen it from my bag in the last day or two and planted it wherever you found it. To frame me. It's not like I could have dropped it while I was murdering Mrs. Van Meer, or anything. Because I didn't—murder her, I mean. Or have the pen then."

Detective Tanghal nodded. "That's one possibility. Why don't we tell you where we found it, and see if you can come up with any other explanations?"

I didn't like her tone now. I nodded and forced myself not to gulp.

"Officer Hooper?" Detective Tangal kept her eyes on me as he consulted his notebook.

"Saturday, November nineteenth, oh-eight-hundred approximately." He glanced up at me. "That's this morning at around eight o'clock. The item was discovered outside 45 Timber Haven Lane. It was in a small utility area, to the east side of the patio."

"You mean, where the trash cans are?" My mind raced, but I tried to keep my voice calm. I could picture the narrow space, brick walls on three sides shielding it from view. What else was in there, besides the trash cans? The air conditioner, a hose spigot, some mechanical boxes that must be related to the pool, some coils of black tubing. That must be it. Teri had mentioned that the cops had found duct tape residue on a hose from the pool system.

And they'd found my pen there.

Neither Detective Tanghal or Officer Hooper said anything. They kept staring at me, probably willing me to confess to murder.

I shook my head at them. "I can't help. I don't have any idea how my pen ended up there. I know the place you're talking about. I throw away the doggy bags there every day. You know, after our walks? Reginald's poop?" Oh, my brain was offering up some wonderful dialog here. I willed myself to take a deep breath, to regain control. "But I keep my pens in my bag, and whenever I walk Reginald, I leave my bag just inside the back door. It was there now. I don't think I've ever even had my bag with me when I've been over by the trash cans."

"You mentioned you thought someone was trying to frame you." Detective Tanghal had been quiet so long her words jolted me. "Who?"

"I don't know." I mean, Teri knew that the police were specifically interested in the pool hoses. Was she trying to point the cops at me to protect Bonnie?

"You must have a guess, if your first thought was that someone was deliberately trying to implicate you."

"I mean, it'd be whoever's guilty, right?" It had been three or four days since I'd confidently decided I could crack the case before the police, and this was the best I could offer. *Astounding, Nikki.* "I don't know. But I do know I only bought that pen on Wednesday. It can't be connected to Mrs. Van Meer's death."

"Oh, I have no doubt that, if we check up on it, you will have purchased a pen matching this description on Wednesday," said Detective Tanghal, holding the pen, still in its bag, up to the light and squinting at it. "But, the question is, did you buy this pen, or did you buy a replacement since you lost this one?"

I gaped at her. She had me. I couldn't poke a hole in her logic. The only way I could prove my innocence would have been to prove I hadn't owned a pen like that one prior to my trip to Crosshatch on Wednesday. I couldn't prove a negative.

Was it too late to call AJ? It probably was, although she'd do her best for me. How embarrassing to have ignored all the advice to get a lawyer and then have to call my friend and let her know I was the prime suspect in a murder investigation. Not only had I already talked to the cops twice, I'd given them a tip. She would call me a complete moron, and I wouldn't be able to argue with her.

Detective Tanghal opened her mouth, and I would have bet all kinds of money she was going to read me my Miranda rights. Instead, she said, "It's irrelevant. The pen must have been put there sometime between Thursday afternoon and this morning at 8 AM. My officers did a thorough search of the house and the grounds, which concluded Thursday afternoon. We've crosschecked all the photographs that were taken. The pen was not there."

I blinked. Was this how Alice had felt when she fell down the rabbit hole? I'd been expecting a life in prison, and now she told me the evidence her officers had collected and stuck in a bag and labeled was irrelevant? Why had they bothered?

"So, it's entirely possible that someone, possibly someone involved in Ruth Van Meer's murder, planted it there with the intention of implicating you. Or," she said, dropping her voice to a sterner register, "it's possible you dropped your pen when you were snooping around. Have you been playing Nancy Drew at my crime scene?"

Her tone suggested amateur detective work was a much greater crime than mere homicide. I shifted in my chair. I had been playing detective, in a way, but only on a theoretical level. I hadn't been poking around the house, although, now that she mentioned it, I really should have.

Later, when I get some free time, I'll examine what self-destructive tendency makes me want to do something only when an authority figure tells me not to. In the meantime, there was still a murderer on the loose, and that bastard had tried to frame me. Me! I was going to catch them, if it was the last thing . . . well, let's not go too far.

Chapter Thirty-One

The cops finally let me out of that stuffy office. I made my way back down the hall, trying to calm down my breathing. I took two long, deep breaths just before I entered the great room, expecting everyone in there to stare at me as I entered.

Instead, everyone had gathered around the kitchen island. A woman who looked vaguely familiar, but whom I couldn't place, had a laptop open on the counter. She sat in front of it, with Teri and Ali on either side of her. Brett and Will stood just behind them, leaning forward to see the screen. I exchanged a glance with Bonnie, who stood on the opposite side of the room, holding a pile of mail and listening with rapt attention.

The woman leaned forward to point at something on the screen. "I know this is awful news. I don't understand it myself, but I've double-checked every way I know how."

I recognized the woman's high fluttery voice. Mrs. Van Meer's real estate agent, who I'd met Monday morning, right after we found the body. I couldn't remember her name. I drifted deeper into the room, staying behind the group at the island. On some level, I told myself I was being unobtrusive to avoid interrupting them. In reality, I wanted to hear as much as I could.

"But Grandma was planning to sell the house!" protested Teri.

The realtor shook her head. "I know! That's why I was so surprised. This would have turned up when I went to list the house—turned up in the title search. We hadn't gotten that far yet." She shook her head again. "I just don't understand. Maybe she forgot?"

I crossed the room to stand next to Bonnie and shot her a quizzical look. I didn't know whether I had enough goodwill banked to merit an explanation. Thankfully, I think Bonnie's urge to gossip in that moment was strong enough she would have brought anyone up to speed.

She turned slightly, so that her back faced the kitchen island. She shuffled the mail in her hands and barely moved her lips. "After the girls' fight, they called in Ruth's realtor, Debbie, for a consultation about selling the house. It turns out"—she glanced back at the island to make sure we were unobserved—"that Ruth and Frank didn't actually own the house. They must have realized their time on this earth was coming to an end. It sounds like they took out a reverse mortgage a few years ago, and from what I gather, it will cost the girls a fortune if they want to do anything other than walk away from it."

My eyebrows shot up. I'd heard of rich people living beyond their means, of flashy lifestyles built on a precarious pile of credit, but I hadn't thought the Van Meers were that kind of rich people.

"Are you sure you're looking at the most recent information?" asked Brett. "This loan should have been settled ages ago."

Teri pushed back in her chair to look Brett in the face. I think it was the calmness of his tone as much as his words that caught her attention. "You knew about this?"

He shook his head. "Knew that they'd gone through with it? No. But I knew they were considering it. Must have been, oh, I don't know, three years ago?" He ran his fingers through his hair, and I was struck by how tired he looked. "Your grandfather came to me and asked me what I could tell him about reverse mortgages. I told him what I knew, which wasn't too much, and that was the last I heard about it."

"But they weren't in financial trouble," said Ali. "Were they?"

Brett shook his head again and pointed to the laptop. "No. And that's why this is so surprising to me. If I understood your grandfather correctly, they weren't dealing with any trouble like that. He wanted to get a whole lot of cash, quickly, for some investment opportunity. I don't know the details. I told him he'd lose so much in the closing costs, it would never be worth it, but it looks like he went ahead with it anyway. But he was adamant he'd be able to pay back the loan amount almost immediately." He shrugged. "It sounded screwy to me, and I thought I'd convinced him not to go through with it."

"But how could Grandma have been planning to sell the house, then?" asked Ali, turning back to Debbie. "Or," she added, with realization dawning on her face, "is this something Grandpa did behind her back?"

Debbie shook her head. "I don't think so. Both of them would have had to sign off on the reverse mortgage. It's possible she forgot about it, or that she didn't fully understand the implications. The way a loan like this works, the homeowners would have received a lump sum representing a large percentage of the value of the house. They have to maintain the house and pay taxes and insurance, but other than that, they don't have to make any payments toward the loan. Once the homeowners pass away, or if they decide to move away, the entire loan amount, plus interest and fees becomes due." She cocked her head to one side. "I suppose it's possible Ruth knew about the reverse mortgage, but Frank told her he'd paid it off."

Debbie shook her head again, as if to clear it, and closed the laptop. "I'm sorry, girls. I know this is terrible news and coming at a terrible time. We have a little bit of time to decide how to proceed. Think about what you'd like to do, and call me if you come up with any other questions. I'll check back in in a few days and see where we are. Make sure to talk to Ruth's attorney as soon as you can about the escrow process for the estate."

Teri, Ali, and Will all turned to Brett, who raised a hand sheepishly. "That'd be me. I'll go over all the details with them. Don't worry."

Debbie nodded and slipped her computer into a bag. Ali walked her to the front door while the rest of us stayed silent, listening to the fading clack of her heels on the marble floor.

No one spoke until Ali came back into the room, a hand on her stomach. "Well, that sucks," she said, looking at Teri. "What do you want to do?"

Brett drew in a deep breath. "Your options are—"

"Don't." Ali stopped him before he could get started. "You're still on thin ice with me. Teri and I can handle this." She looked around, seeing me and Bonnie for the first time.

She stepped back into the hall and addressed the uniformed police officer lurking there. "Could you please find out if Detective Tanghal is finished with questioning for today? If people are free to leave, I'd like to know that. Thank you."

It took a few minutes before the all clear was handed down through the chain of command, and Bonnie and I didn't dare talk to each other while we waited. As we left, I got the impression Brett wanted to hang around, despite the icy reception Ali had given his last attempt to speak. But as I walked down the driveway, I saw him trudging out the door, following Bonnie to the garage and their cars.

There was too much money floating around in this case. I'd always assumed there was a financial motive for the murder, based mostly on the fact that the victim was rich. And now I'd found out the Van Meers had sold their house for a wheelbarrow load of cash just a few years ago. Where had that money gone? Is that how Teri had gotten her business off the ground, or how Ali was paying for a house? But neither of those seemed urgent enough to justify a reverse mortgage. If the Van Meers needed money that quickly, it sounded more like they were the victims of blackmail or a Ponzi scheme or something. Whatever was going on, I didn't want to get dragged any further into it.

My dashboard clock showed it was still early in the day. I felt like I'd been inside the Van Meer house for hours and hours, but it was only around lunchtime. If I went home, I would turn into a useless lump on the couch, and I would do nothing except stew about the murder investigation and someone's attempt to frame me.

Ruby was never home on Saturday afternoons, but she let me use her studio whenever I wanted. I texted her that I was going over, picked up some soup dumplings from a take-out Chinese place, and let myself into Ruby and AJ's house using their door code. It was a struggle to keep Fred away from my food, but once I finished eating, he left me alone, and I was able to be productive. I finished the order of place cards I'd been putting off for days and whittled down a mountain of business-related emails I'd ignored.

When I left their house, the sun was down, which isn't saying too much, given the time of year. I'd forgotten Jai wouldn't be home, so I called out happily to him, then remembered he'd be tied up with mock trial stuff until late. While I'd been in Ruby's bright, spacious, plant-filled, art-filled room, it'd been easy to focus on work. As soon as I settled on my own couch, I lost control of my brain, and it went straight back to Mrs. Van Meer's murder. I wasn't going to solve it, and it seemed like someone was determined to pin the whole thing on me.

I don't know how long I sat there, trying unsuccessfully to force myself to think about something else, anything else. Finally, I gave up. I grabbed my phone and texted Sasha. *You in the middle of anything? I wanna pick your brain.*

I stood up and stared out the front window into the dark street. An orange cat sat beside a parked car, illuminated by a streetlight. He had white paws and a white patch on his chest and looked reasonably well-fed for a stray cat. I'd seen this cat around plenty of times before, sometimes close enough to see his cropped left ear, a sign that he'd been neutered and released, an irredeemably feral cat, much more at home on the streets than in someone's home.

Instead of hunting or grooming or stalking or doing any of the important business cats needed to take care of, he stared at our building. My rational brain told me he was having a good, old-fashioned staring contest with Mr. Cat in the downstairs window, a giant, furry neon sign proclaiming "McKayla Has Unauthorized Pets." But that was my rational brain. Standing here alone after dark, contemplating a murder, I'll admit that my rational brain wasn't in complete control of my consciousness.

The eyes of the feral cat outside seemed to bore into mine. Maybe he had supernatural information about Mrs. Van Meer's death to impart to me, or maybe he was the familiar of a witch who had decided I was her archnemesis. Or maybe he was a human who had temporarily taken the form of a cat for reasons passing my understanding. Or maybe ascribing fanciful motivations to stray cats wasn't the best use of my brain power when I had a murder to solve.

Chapter Thirty-Two

My phone rang, and I jumped about a foot into the air, dropping the phone onto the hardwood floor, where it bounced a couple times and landed screen-side up. Sasha.

I answered as I checked the screen, which seemed to have avoided picking up any new cracks. "Hey, hope I'm not bothering you," I said.

"Naw, don't worry about it," Sasha replied. "I'm at the Tower, but it's hella slow for a Saturday. Figures. The one night when everybody on the schedule showed up. What's going on?" I couldn't hear any background noise, so she was in the tiny back office, where she did scheduling and ordering and the other shift managers stashed their weed to avoid having to share it with the lowly barkeepers.

"I wanted to ask . . ." I trailed off. I'd called Sasha for her expertise in crime-solving. Relative to me, that is, since I had absolutely no idea what I was doing. Actual law-enforcement officers would not consider her a colleague, but surely an obsession with true crime was better than nothing. But I hadn't bothered to formulate a question in my mind. Was I going to have to spit out every scrap of information swirling around my head, and let her solve the thing? "You know, I'm sorry. I'm not even sure what exactly I wanted to ask."

Her tone changed. I pictured her hunched over the phone, impatiently flipping her braids back over her shoulder when they tried to snake their way between her ear and the speaker. "Is this what we were talking about the other day? Your dog-walking client?"

I nodded into the phone. "I know so much about all these people. I feel like I know the answer, but I just can't put it all together."

Sasha was quiet for a moment. "You at home?"

"Yeah." I nodded again.

"Listen, can I be super rude and invite myself over? I was going to cut out of here soon anyway. I'll grab a bottle of wine and come over, and you can tell me absolutely everything, and even if that doesn't let you figure it out, maybe it'll be a relief to have it out of your head."

I nodded for the third time in this phone conversation. Telecommunications were not my strong suit. "Oh, that'd be awesome. Text me when you're here." It would be a relief to get everything out of my head. I already felt myself starting to relax.

But first, I should probably get the folded laundry off the couch. The pile had been there for the last four days, dwindling by an outfit or two at a time. Time to put it away in the appropriate dresser drawers. Or at least shift the stack onto the bed, out of sight of the living room. I won't reveal here which option was chosen that night.

I tidied up a bit, knowing that I wasn't fooling anyone. As I worked, I kept thinking about Mrs. Van Meer's death. By the time I descended the stairs to open the door, I'd formulated the question that I think summed up my frustration with the mystery.

"Why would an overwhelming majority of the evidence point to one person, and yet a pretty good amount of other evidence point to another person?"

"Hello to you, too! Got a corkscrew?" Sasha brandished a bottle of red wine.

We sat on the laundry-free couch and drank the wine while I filled Sasha in on all the details, including the fun new tidbit about the police finding my pen.

"And you're positive you didn't just lose it? You didn't stick it behind your ear and it fell out?"

In answer, I heaved my bag off the floor and dug around for another pen in the same style, finding a purple one and handing it over.

"Girl, that's not a pen. That's a marker. OK, so, you didn't stick it behind your ear." She tapped the pen on her chin. "And I see what you mean. It's pretty distinctive. If somebody knew you used pens like this, and knew other people knew, that might be exactly the thing to use to tie you to the scene. Plausible that you could have dropped it, but unique enough not to point to anybody else. Tell me again, where'd they find it?"

I described the space in as much detail as I could. Then, at her insistence, I opened my notebook to a clean page and drew a quick map, showing the brick walls on either side, the air conditioning unit on one side, the bulky pool equipment at the back, and the trash cans at the front. In the moment, it was legible, but if I were to look back at it now, I'd see a jumble of irregular boxes.

"Maybe the idea was supposed to be that the pen itself was incriminating, and I'd tried to throw it away, but missed the trash can? I don't know."

Sasha didn't say anything, but she looked thoughtfully off into the distance. After a moment, she pulled out her phone and typed something. She read for a second, frowned, shook her head, and then began typing again. This series repeated itself three or four times until her eyebrows rose and she smiled.

"What is it?" I asked.

"Hang on." She was still reading whatever she'd found, so I took a long sip of wine, just to fill the time.

"OK, I think I've got it," she said after at least six or seven hours, or maybe thirty or forty seconds. "If someone planted your pen there, that spot must be connected with the murder somehow, or otherwise why would it matter that you'd supposedly been there and dropped your pen?"

I followed her logic, if not her sentence structure, so I nodded.

"Read this." She started to hold her phone out to me, then grabbed it back as some kind of pop-up ad took over the whole screen. Once she cleared that, she handed the phone over.

She'd found a local news site, and for a second, I thought she'd dug up yet another story about the busboy who'd asphyxiated at Will's bar. Then I saw the article was seven years old and tagged "St. Petersburg, Florida." It told the story of a compounding accident at a chain hotel, when a total of twelve people died in the same room, over the course of several weeks. Through a combination of miscommunication, incompetence, and laziness, no concerted investigation was made until way too many people had already died. When the police finally got their act together, they discovered that the fatal room, room 107, backed up to one side of the indoor swimming pool. The inner workings of the pool heater had clogged somehow, and it was venting carbon monoxide into the nearest hotel room.

"That's it. That's exactly it." I stared at Sasha in admiration. "I said there were systems for the pool there. I was just thinking, like, the filter and pump and whatever else. But you're exactly right. I'd bet my whole entire life the pool heater is there, too." I pictured the steam rising up into the cold November air and remembered thinking how wasteful it was to keep the pool at a comfortable temperature this late into the year. "How did you figure it out?"

Sasha shrugged. She looked a little sheepish, like a magician who's forced to reveal the mundane trick behind her illusion. "You told me what was in that little space, so I Googled each of them plus 'carbon monoxide.' It wasn't anything too impressive."

"You're a genius. You basically solved the whole thing. Once the police know what exactly was done, they'll be able to figure out who did it, easy. It's obviously too late to call the detective tonight, but I can tell her tomorrow, and then they'll be all set."

Sasha stared at me, her head cocked to one side. "Nikki? They already know how it was done. Whether my guess about the pool heater is right, one hundred percent they know."

My eyes widened. "What do you mean?"

"You told me how they ruled out the cars as the source of the carbon monoxide—something about the chemical composition of the gas? There's no way in hell they're getting a detailed forensic analysis of the gas in a dead woman's tissues, and the report just says 'not a car.' I don't know anything about the specifics, but I bet they narrowed it down to one or two possible sources just based on science. And then once they had more focus, I'm sure they found the source pretty quickly." Sasha held up one hand. "Now, I'll admit, I've watched way more *CSI* than is healthy, but I bet this whole time they've just been killing time waiting for the scientific reports to come in."

I knew she was right. It felt almost like cheating on the cops' part. They had been able to sit back and wait for a team of forensic scientists to tell them the answer. I was stuck with only my brain, plus the brains of whichever of my brilliant friends I could sucker into helping me. Sasha downplayed her skills as good Googling, but her deductive reasoning inspired me. Wait, was it deductive or inductive? That feels like something I should know, if I plan to solve a murder. I made a mental note to look it up later.

Either way, Sasha had seen that whoever stole my pen to frame me wanted to connect me with the pool heater, which meant the pool heater was important. She's a genius.

I frowned down at the map I'd drawn of the area around the pool heater. The pool heater had been the source of the carbon monoxide. Everything fit. But that didn't quite explain everything. If it had been done in the garage, using car exhaust, there would be no unanswered questions. Run a hose to the tailpipe, make sure the garage door's closed—easy. But a pool heater? Installed outdoors? What, had someone convinced Mrs. Van Meer to lie down on the ground with her head right next to the vent and wait? The police had found duct tape residue on the coil of hose. Somehow, the murderer must have routed the gas into Mrs. Van Meer's bedroom.

Sasha said the police had already figured it out. I should be able to look at the direction of their investigation and work backward. Detective Tanghal had asked me about Reginald's movements during the watch party. She must have had a reason, even if it seemed ridiculous. I chewed on my lip and stared at the drawing.

Sasha watched me, but she wasn't going to interrupt. I picked up the pen and started sketching on the map. My idea started to form. If I continued this wall down here, the flagstone path led away from the pool and the main patio, here the brick of the house's exterior gave way to the floor-to-ceiling windows that marked the start of Mrs. Van Meer's bedroom. Then they continued uninterrupted to the corner of the house. Well, almost uninterrupted. I stopped the line I was drawing, jumping back half an inch to draw another line, this one representing the flap of a dog door.

I shivered. Horrible to imagine. Being deeply asleep in a dark bedroom, and the mouth of a black hose snaking its way through a small, square flap down by the floor. An odorless gas seeping into the room, and nothing happening. Nothing, that is, until enough time has passed to ensure a fatal dose, and then the deadly hose retracting just as silently as it came.

Goosebumps prickled my skin when I told Sasha my theory. But her exposure to true crime had toughened her up, and she just congratulated me on my solution. If we'd been standing up, I think she would have slapped me on the back, but as it was, she slapped her knees and then toasted me with her wine glass.

Method was solved. In my notebook, we flipped back to my original chart of all the suspects and went through them in as much detail as we could. Sasha wanted to see if knowing the source of the carbon monoxide changed any of my assumptions about anyone's guilt or innocence. We went back over Bonnie's alibi, which had started to annoy me. If only she'd had the decency to come to the party Sunday night, I would have been able to conclude with a clear conscience she was a murderer.

Finally, we both sat back, and Sasha rubbed her eyes. "You know, a notebook's no good. You need a giant whiteboard, with big photos of all these people."

I grinned at her. "I'll get right on that." Then I looked ruefully at my notebook. "You may be on to something." My once-beautiful chart had notes scribbled all over, arrows connecting comments with people's names. Even the motive column, which had once looked so promising, was now covered with barely legible scrawls, and many of my original notes had been scratched out, following the revelation that Ali and Brett weren't actually having a secret affair. And the worst thing about the destruction of my beautiful chart was that none of it had done any good. We were no closer to pinning the murder on anyone.

"It doesn't make any sense!" Sasha said, sighing and leaning back on the couch. "There's a pattern, but not a sensible one. The handyman's lighter, the housekeeper's magazine clippings, and the dogwalker's pen. It feels like they must all have been planted by the same person, because they all kind of fit together, or at least, follow the same pattern. But why in the world would someone try to frame three different people?"

"Maybe just trying to mess with the police? Or bury the truth in total chaos." I shook my head. "Or, wait. What about this? Especially since my pen turned up where it did, I've been assuming all the clues were fake. Like, they were all planted to frame different people. What if the murderer left behind a real clue by accident, and then planted similar clues pointing toward other people—to kind of drown out the significance of the real clue?" I talked faster than my brain worked, figuring this out as I went. "Say Kevin realized the next morning he had lost his lighter in Mrs. Van Meer's bedroom, and he thought it would be too risky to get it back. So instead, he plants stuff pointing at Bonnie and at me, knowing then the police can't take any of it too seriously."

"But the envelope of clippings from Bonnie was found in the old lady's bedside table, right? If he could get into the bedroom to plant it there, couldn't he have grabbed his lighter? And the logic works the other way, too," Sasha added, seeing me about to interrupt. "So you can't just say that then the envelope must be the real clue."

"Yeah, OK." I slumped. It had made sense for a minute. "I mean, maybe Kevin realized he lost his lighter, but thought one of us had seen it when we were all in there Monday morning. He might have thought removing it might attract more attention than leaving it." I didn't believe it. We were still missing something. I closed the notebook in frustration. Staring at it wasn't doing either of us any good.

Sasha looked around the apartment for the first time since she'd gotten there. "No Jai tonight?"

I shook my head. "Mock trial tournament. He thinks he'll get back just after midnight." I took a last gulp of wine and checked my phone for updates. Nothing, which meant they were still on schedule. I laughed. "They always head off for these things with specific plans, and it never turns out that way. This weekend, who knows? Last weekend, they got caught in that big ice storm in Kansas City and stayed an extra night. Weekend before last, they got on the highway going east instead of west on the way home and didn't realize it for three hours. Got home late . . ."

I'd started the story as a funny anecdote and trailed off at the end. Some new thought niggled at the back of my mind. Something about the weekend before last. Which one had that been? I thought back. Somewhere in Iowa? A lot of these mock trial tournaments were at schools I'd never heard of. Jai had ridden with three of the kids. He'd told me their names, but I had no hope of remembering now. But I was remembering something. Or rather, I wasn't remembering something.

I groaned in frustration. "Tell me this. Do you ever listen to podcasts about unsolved mysteries? Or only ones that've been solved?"

I'd caught Sasha right as she also drained her wine glass. She shook her head to buy herself the time to swallow. "Oh, no. The best ones are unsolved mysteries."

"Isn't that super, I don't know, unsatisfying?"

"I guess. Maybe. But it means that you listen to it and think that maybe there's a chance that you could be the one to solve it. 'The truth is out there' and that whole thing. You know?"

That made sense, at least on some level. But this case would be solved. It had to be. I couldn't live the rest of my life as a murder suspect, even if I was no longer the focus of the investigation.

Sasha read my mind. "It's been a week, Nik. Not even. They've been investigating for what? Four days? They'll solve it." She shrugged. "Hell, for all we know, they may have solved it already and are just waiting for a warrant to come through or a DNA result to come back." She shrugged again. "It'll all shake out soon enough."

She pointed a finger at me. "And when it does, you better tell me all about it. Every single detail. I'm hooked now." She stood up. "Thanks for letting me invite myself over. But Bloodhound'll go crazy if I don't get home soon."

I stood up with her. Her husky was notoriously high-strung, even for a husky. "Thank you for your brilliant detective work, and for the wine." I gestured with the half-emptied bottle as I moved it from the coffee table to the kitchen counter and then showed Sasha to the door. I still didn't know who the murderer was, but at least Sasha had talked me down from the panic that had been gripping me for the last few days.

Chapter Thirty-Three

I had vague ideas about waiting up for Jai, even though he'd told me not to bother. I still had these vague ideas as I changed into my pajamas. Not to go to sleep, but to be more comfortable. I still had these vague ideas as I got into bed. Not to go to sleep, but to be more comfortable. But at some point, midway through my third episode of a trash TV show, I drifted off.

Next thing I remember, it was Sunday morning. One slat of the venetian blinds had gotten stuck at a weird angle and perfectly positioned the sun to shine through the opening and onto my pillow. I opened my eyes and then squeezed them shut against the glare. Jai sprawled next to me, still asleep. Evidently, he'd made it home safely.

If the sun insisted on shining into my eyes, I might as well get up. I stood up slowly and creakily, and stretched, forcing myself more awake. I bent back a few more of the slats of the blinds, like I needed to get a panoramic view of the street in order to confirm the weather. The orange feral cat sat in the same place I'd noticed him the night before, in a space sheltered from wind and traffic by two parked cars. He'd been joined by another cat, one I hadn't seen around before, a black and white beauty, taller and more elegant than the bowlegged orange tomcat. The new cat was built like a lithe Siamese, although the markings were all wrong for that. They sat, side by side, looking down at a spot on the pavement between them.

From my spot across the street and two floors up, I couldn't tell what was there. It could have been a leaf or a dropped candy wrapper, but something about their posture and attentiveness told me that their eyes were fixed on prey. The two cats waited, either being deferential to each other to have the first bite, or more likely, waiting for whatever they had maimed to finish dying so they could eat in peace.

It reminded me of the painting in Mr. Van Meer's study, with the couple bowing their heads over a basket of food, or if you listen to Ruby tell it, over a casket. I took a quick picture, making a mental note to show Ruby. These alley cats had found a way to reconcile two distinct explanations for a French painting from hundreds of years ago. They bowed their heads over a corpse *and* over their next meal. In this moment, both were true.

I wished I hadn't thought of the Van Meer family just then. I'd been up for less than a minute and already those people had intruded on my consciousness. Was I ever going to be able to put this whole thing behind me? Was I a terrible person for even thinking such a thing, given that someone had died?

I rubbed my eyes with one hand and looked back out the window, forcing myself to contemplate the day ahead. Sunday morning. Besides Reginald, I had my other weekend walks, and I was criminally behind on a calligraphy order for a wedding coming up in a month. I tried to visualize the design of the seating chart, but my brain kept spinning back to the crude map of the Van Meer house I'd drawn for Sasha the night before.

I knew the notebook was lying on the table in front of the couch, open to the page with my chart of suspects. It called to me.

I slipped out of the room, grabbing a sweatshirt off the floor as I rounded the foot of the bed. The apartment was always cold in the mornings, except at the very height of summer, when we had the opposite problem. I skirted around Jai's backpack, laying where he must have left it behind the couch, and started a cup of coffee.

When the coffee was ready, I crossed to the couch and curled my legs under a blanket. I stared at the notebook, at my original attempt to pin down everyone's means, motive, and opportunity, now partially obscured by some new guesses we'd made last night. There was so much information. There was too much information.

I turned to a fresh page and held the pen poised over it, ready for insight. Willing myself to have a revelation.

I drank my coffee instead.

Lacking ideas, I doodled on the blank page, starting with a few abstract lines and curves that turned into the orange feral cat and his breakfast companion, bowing their heads over a freshly killed mouse. At least, that's what I meant for it to be. A disinterested observer might see two lumpy mountains on either side of a valley, or, with some squinting, a malformed version of Notre Dame cathedral. Basically, my artwork wasn't good. But the doodle served its purpose. It kept my hand busy and broke up the intimidating whiteness of the paper with cheerful purple brightness.

By the time Jai stumbled out of the bedroom, I'd refined the drawing to something almost recognizable. Turns out, almost any jumble of lines will look like a cat if you add pointy ears and a tail.

Jai being up was a good thing. My attempts to reason things out alone had failed miserably. Hadn't I needed Sasha last night for the breakthrough about the method? A sounding board was much more valuable than a blank piece of paper.

I turned toward Jai, already opening my mouth to bring him up to speed. He looked from me to the notebook in front of me.

"That's why you got up so early? Is there hot water?"

Absolutely infuriating. Good thing I was in love with him.

He stood at the counter, fiddling with the tea strainer. I stood at his side, making a big production out of refilling my coffee mug, but really focusing all my mental energy on willing his tea to steep faster than tea steeps.

When he joined me on the couch, I explained everything that had happened yesterday. He had trouble focusing on Sasha's brilliance. Whenever I tried to get us back on that track, he dragged the conversation back to the whole "somebody tried to frame Nikki" thing.

"Can you let that go?" I asked. "We figured out how someone committed murder! Well, Sasha did, mostly." Modesty has always been one of my best features.

He took a sip from his mug, refusing to meet my eyes. I hated that look. It meant he thought I'd missed something. And he was always right, which made it all the more annoying.

"Let me get this straight. The police are now sure that the old woman's death was murder, not suicide. The murderer has taken active steps to frame you for the crime. A crime for you which you have a plausible motive. You are actively concealing information that would suggest you had means and opportunity."

"What are you talking about?" I couldn't help interrupting.

Jai stared at me for a second before he said, "Kevin. Who is married to one of your aunts."

"Oh, that." I waved a hand, as if it was no big deal. Really, I'd let it slip my mind.

"Now," Jai continued, "you believe that you and your friend have guessed the method of murder, and you're expecting me to praise you for that? Can't you stay far away from these people? Please?" He was looking at me with earnest concern, and I felt my excitement ebb away.

I rubbed my eyes. "What if the police never solve the murder on their own? I can't just sit quietly and hope." I couldn't stomach the idea of a murderer walking free if I could have done something to prevent it.

Jai lifted his mug for another sip of tea only to find it empty. He put it back down and took my hand. "To be clear, I don't think you can just walk away at this point. I think you're right. I think you've been sucked in too deeply to just drop it. Even if the cops let you keep your distance, I think this would eat you up inside. But you're long past the point when you should've gotten legal advice. You need to be talking to AJ, not me. She's a real lawyer, with actual experience."

Somewhere in the middle of that speech, Jai had lifted his head to meet my eyes, but by the end, he'd dropped his gaze to the dregs of his tea. My heart ached for him. This wasn't the first time since giving up on passing the bar exam that Jai had contrasted himself with AJ, by calling her a "real lawyer." Every other time it had happened, I had jumped in immediately, aware he was bitterly disappointed by his career setbacks, and wanting to build him up. This time, I held my tongue, though it hurt to see the sadness in his eyes.

He wasn't disparaging himself, or at least, not *just* disparaging himself. He was pointing out an important distinction. AJ was a licensed attorney, and Jai was a guy with a law degree. For the first time in our relationship, I needed to care about the difference.

If I texted AJ right now, she'd drop whatever to come advise me. I'd put it off earlier, telling myself that things hadn't gotten serious enough yet to call in AJ. I couldn't tell myself that anymore. Calling her in was the rational thing to do. Jai knew it was the rational thing to do, and I knew it was the rational thing to do.

AJ would be the go-between for me and the police. With her help, I could find a safe path through the minefield of helping the police with their investigation while actively being a suspect myself.

But some irrational part of my brain overruled everything else. It sounds absurd, but it felt like consulting AJ would be cheating on Jai. He was my husband, and I loved him, and that was good enough for me. I leaned into him, and he put an arm around my shoulders.

Now, I'm not claiming if tested further, with, like say, prison, I might not change my mind. I have trouble imagining myself sitting in court, waiting for my sentence to be handed down, steadfastly refusing to accept licensed legal representation. But right at this moment, I decided I could muddle through on my own, based on a sense of loyalty to Jai.

The most straightforward way to clear my name would be to solve the whole thing, so that's what I'd have to do.

Chapter Thirty-Four

A knock on the front door saved me from having to come up with an answer for Jai. I glanced at the clock on the microwave as I crossed to open it. Who in the world knocks on somebody's door at seven-thirty in the morning, and on a Sunday?

If you guessed McKayla, you get a gold star.

"Hi, Nikki!" She leaned around me to wave at Jai, too. "Hi, Jai! I thought I heard you guys up."

I really didn't know how to deal with that level of energy. And she'd violated one of the core rules of peaceful living in a multi-unit building. You must always maintain the polite fiction that you can't hear your neighbors living their daily lives. I responded to this cheerful breach of etiquette the only way I knew how. I stood to one side and waved her in.

"Thanks! Listen, I can't stay long, but I wanted to invite you down in a couple hours. I'm having a couple people over for a kind of get-together, house-warming brunchy-type thing. You don't have to bring anything," she added, seeing Jai and me exchange a look. "I love cooking breakfast food, and when Dwayne came over the other day, I told him I'd cook for him sometime—he's such a sweetheart, isn't he?—and my mom hasn't really seen the place since I moved in, and I have a couple friends who live down the block, and I'd love if you two would come, too. Just head down sometime late morning. Nothing super firm."

I suspected McKayla's plans were never super firm. But I felt bad for thinking it. Her invitation was a nice gesture, and I hadn't done a good job welcoming her to the building. Between my preoccupation with Mrs. Van Meer's murder and my almost allergic reaction to McKayla's overall vibe, I doubted whether I'd even cleared the bar of civility. The least I could do was go down and eat some of her food. Besides, she'd said Dwayne was coming. I didn't want to miss the fireworks when he saw the animals in his building.

I glanced at the clock on the microwave. "I'd love to, thanks. If it really is kind of open-ended, anyway, I've got to go walk a couple of clients' dogs, and the walks themselves won't take long, but . . ." I trailed off. In no situation would it be acceptable to say I might be unable to make brunch because I might get arrested for murder. "It's sometimes hard to get out of there. People can be talkative, you know?"

McKayla nodded so enthusiastically I thought her head might fall off. "Oh, yes. There'll be plenty of food. Come down whenever you can." She looked questioningly at Jai.

He smiled. "Thanks for the invite. I'm headed out, too, but if I'm back when Nikki gets home, we'll come down together."

"Yay!" She clapped her hands and did a little twirl of happiness. She'd made it halfway out our front door when she stopped. "Oh, hey, Nikki, there was one more thing. Do you remember what you said about Dwayne and pets?

"You mean how he absolutely doesn't allow pets at any of his properties, and it's written into his leases, and he will absolutely evict you if he finds out you have pets? Yes, I remember."

"Oh, good! Well, I still think you're being a little silly. He's such a sweetheart, he can't possibly be so against animals. But, I was thinking, just in case, what if Mr. Cat and the others hung out up here while we were having brunch? It's not that I'm worried Dwayne might be mad—he's such a sweetheart, after all. It's just I don't want to be the reason any animal has to be around that kind of negative energy."

I opened my mouth and then closed it again. The answer was no. Obviously. But she'd asked with such an interesting mixture of audacity and naivety, I was having trouble formulating an answer.

"Sorry. I'm allergic," Jai lied. He had stood up from the couch to join us, ushering McKayla out with a gesture, and closing the door firmly behind her.

After McKayla was back downstairs, we both got ready to leave. I had an early morning walk scheduled, and Jai had day two of his tournament.

"Hey, Nikki?" Jai caught my hand as I headed for the door a few minutes later. I had a witty reply on the tip of tongue, a continuation of our last conversation, but it died unsaid when I saw the concern on his face.

"What's the matter?"

He still hadn't let go of my hand. "Be careful."

I pulled my hand away and put it on my hip. "I'm not even going over there yet. I've got Georgio."

"And after that?"

I really wasn't liking how serious he was being.

"Fine. Yes, I'm going to walk Reginald after Georgio. And, yes, I'll be careful." I finally forced the snotty tone out of my voice. "Promise."

Jai kissed me, longer than a normal goodbye kiss, but not quite as long as I would have liked. Still, the thought of it kept me warm as I set out for my first dog-walking appointment of the day.

Georgio was an elderly sheepdog who wasn't one of my regular clients. I'd worked with his owners in my pet behaviorist capacity to rehousetrain him after he lost his eyesight the year before. They both worked from home, so they usually had no need for a dogwalker, but were off on a quick weekend getaway to Chicago.

We made our way very, very slowly to a sunny clearing in the park, with me struggling to get used to the handle on Georgio's harness that allowed me to support his back legs. When we found a good spot, I spread out his favorite plaid blanket and we both settled down to soak up whatever warmth we could from the November sun.

While I shifted to get comfortable on the hard ground and hugged my knees to my chest to ward off the cold breeze, Georgio was utterly content. He turned his face to the sun, closed his eyes, and let his tongue dangle.

I suddenly thought of McKayla. Completely unperturbed by anything that might be going on, just existing. Just happy. Seemed like a nice way to live.

The party she was planning would be a disaster, of course. It was a miracle that Dwayne hadn't seen any of her illicit animals when he'd been over the other day. There was no chance he'd fail to notice Mr. Cat and the others when he was invited inside. She'd be evicted, and then the unit would sit empty for god knows how long again, and then we'd have some new neighbor again.

Right at the end though, it had seemed like maybe she was realizing the problem. The McKayla I'd met that first day would never have asked to hide her pets up in our apartment. She wouldn't have been capable of seeing the need for such a thing. With her animals around, the party would be a disaster. With them gone, out of the way, it would go off without a hitch.

I sat bolt upright. One of Georgio's ears twitched my direction, but he was too comfortable to move.

Why was I so fixated on McKayla's party all of a sudden? It wouldn't work with the animals there. If the animals were somewhere else, it would be fine. So obvious it hardly needed to be said. So why were there strobe lights going off in my brain?

Slowly, creakingly, I worked through the thought process. Was that what had happened? While Jai was driving three hours the wrong way and then sitting out a sleet storm in a hotel room in Kansas City? It would explain everything, wouldn't it? The conflicting clues weren't conflicting at all. They were parts of different stories. Once you saw that, they slotted together neatly. As neatly as the two feral cats bowing over their prey that morning.

It took all my willpower not to just toss Georgio into a fireman's carry and sprint back to his house. But I am a responsible person. The two-block walk from his house to the park had taken us about fifteen minutes. The return journey took, I don't know, six or seven years? I was prickling all over with nervous excitement, but Georgio couldn't walk any faster than Georgio could walk, so we trundled along at his pace.

The enforced delay was probably a good thing, as much as it chafed in the moment. If I ran to the cops with this theory still a jumbled mess in my brain, would they even listen to me? I put the time to good use, trying to think through all the possible angles. As I helped Georgio settle into his self-warming dog bed, I thought of Reginald, alone in the study, and my heart twisted. I wanted to get the murderer. And not just to save my own skin. I wanted to get the bastard.

That resolve didn't slacken as I drove to the Van Meer house. When I pulled the car into what had become my habitual place next to the front curb, it took an effort of will to loosen my white-knuckle grip on the wheel and pull the parking brake.

After hiking up the driveway, I made a wide arc around the back of the house, rather than cutting straight toward the door. I wanted a chance onsite to double-check the theory Sasha and I had come up with. All well and good to sit in my apartment after the sun went down and imagine a murderer lurking around. The test was if I could still imagine it when I looked at the house in broad daylight.

Thin yellow police tape had been stretched across the gap between the two brick walls on the east side of the patio. Unless they were taking the theft of my pen absurdly seriously, the police must have determined the pool heater as the source of the deadly carbon monoxide. Past the far wall, the French doors formed the one wall of Mrs. Van Meer's bedroom. Just like when I'd first seen them, the sun glinted off the glass. From my angle, I couldn't see Reginald's doggy door, but I knew roughly where it was.

I was satisfied. Our scenario worked. More than that, it seemed likely. I mean, not really likely, when you got right down to it. But given the facts of the case, I couldn't imagine a better explanation.

When I entered the great room, Reginald came to me, looking about as cheerful as I'd ever seen him. No one else was around. It was quite a letdown. I'd come in fully prepared to pull Detective Tanghal away from the crowd to tell her my solution to the murder. Instead, I was apparently walking a dog. If not for the tension coursing through every muscle in my body, it was much more attractive prospect.

Reginald watched with happy complacence as I dropped my bag in its now-familiar spot just inside the back door, pulled his leash off the hook, and clipped it on. Walking time!

The sun was shining, the birds were singing, and Reginald was unusually chipper.

I was less chipper. I just wanted to get this whole thing over with. Once I could talk to Detective Tanghal and tell her the whole story, then I could relax. I walked faster than normal, having burnt up most of my patience walking Georgio earlier. But I didn't want to risk getting back to the house too soon and face the prospect of having to wait there. So we explored the neighborhood, breathing in the fresh air, while I tried to relax and put the murder out of my mind for a few precious moments.

That's when I heard the squeal of locking brakes, the ca-thunk of a car hitting an obstacle, the scream.

Chapter Thirty-Five

Reginald and I were on a perfectly peaceful stretch of road, heavily tree-lined and curving away sharply both ahead of us and behind us. When we heard the noise, we both stopped in our tracks. I couldn't pinpoint the direction from which the sounds had come, but Reginald was staring off to the left, so that was a pretty good guess.

My instinct was to head toward the sound of the accident, either to offer aid or maybe just to satisfy my natural curiosity. But the way these suburban streets wound and curved it was impossible to tell where to go. It must have been pretty close, as the crow flies, but I wasn't a crow. If I kept moving forward until the next opportunity to turn left, I might find myself headed in the right direction, or I might end up on a street curving entirely the other way.

After that first burst of sound, the peace that normally reigned in these neighborhood streets had settled back into place. The birds resumed singing. I couldn't see any obvious signs of a serious disaster. There was no ominous smoke plume, no glow from a fire. But as we finished our walk along our normal route, I kept my ears pricked for the sound of approaching sirens, which never came. As much as Reginald enjoyed the walk, by the time we were back in sight of the house, he'd slowed, eager for his cozy dog bed. Thankfully, the police were there. Usually a driveway parker, this time Detective Tanghal had pulled her silver car to the curb just in front of mine, out on the street. I breathed a sigh of relief. I don't know how I would have handled the tension if I'd had to sit and wait for her after finishing my walk.

Before entering the great room, now full of people, I took one last look at the utility area, just to make sure nothing had changed with the layout of the house while I'd been walking Reginald. There, behind the six-foot brick wall, was the pool heater and there, not more than a dozen feet away, was Reginald's dog door leading into Ruth Van Meer's bedroom. I shuddered again, unwillingly picturing the scene as it must have been that night.

I unclipped Reginald and shook my head as he bounded off, headed for his dog bed. As much as I wanted to dispel the image from my mind, I needed all the details clear if I was going to convince the police. I pulled open the back door, still trying to compose the best opening to use with Detective Tanghal.

"There she is!" Teri shouted from the center of a cluster of people, pointing at me dramatically.

I barely had time to register that she was in her black running gear, complete with neon pink sneakers when someone grabbed me from behind, vise-like fingers gripping my upper arms, pinning them against my body. I twisted wildly and caught a glimpse of Officer Hooper before he swept my legs out from under me. The fall wasn't too bad, but then he landed on me with his full weight, enough to knock the wind out of me.

Teri was talking, and some of the others were too, but I couldn't hear them. Every fiber of my being was focused on drawing a breath against the burning pain in my chest. It was impossible. Something had changed about the quality of the air in the room. It was no longer a gas. It was solid and no amount of effort on my part could force it to fit into my nose or my mouth, much less down and into my lungs.

Until, of course, everything slid back into its normal and correct state of matter. My chest muscles stopped spasming, my lungs expanded, and sweet, sweet air flooded in.

And then the noise in the room flooded into my ears.

Teri was gabbling incomprehensibly, with a note of hysteria I'd never heard in her voice before. Ali was sobbing. Will and Brett were shouting. Even Bonnie and Kevin, standing a little way from the others, were trying to make themselves heard. Cutting through all of it, Officer Hooper was muttering something into my ear, rhythmic, like an incantation. In one wild moment I recognized, through his hot breath, that he was reciting my Miranda rights.

My eyes met Reginald's, the only one in the room at the right height to meet my gaze from my position splayed on the floor. I'd missed my chance. I'd solved the murder, but I'd waited too long to tell the police. Why, when I'd failed to find Detective Tanghal at the Van Meer house that morning, had I taken Reginald for his walk instead of pulling out my phone and calling her? For that matter, why had I even bothered coming over here at all this morning? Couldn't I have called her just as easily from the safety of my apartment?

No, I'd waited. And now they'd made up their minds that I was the murderer, and I hadn't had a chance to tell Detective Tanghal about the real murderer. And I hadn't called AJ. I was being arrested on the strength of my three-hundred-thousand-dollar motive and a pen found near a pool heater.

Even as I felt myself sink into despair, some part of my mind rebelled. No, they'd dismissed the pen. The police had dismissed the pen, hadn't they? Detective Tanghal thought it was evidence of my snooping around her crime scene, but not evidence of murder.

Something else must have happened.

While I'd been out enjoying the sunshine with Reginald, the murderer had been hard at work. Some other piece of evidence had been planted, something more compelling than the flimsy pen. I should have expected this. Hadn't Sasha and I just talked last night about this murderer's habit? "The handyman's lighter, the housekeeper's magazine clippings, and the dogwalker's pen." None strong enough to shove the investigation in a definitive direction. Well, now something had. What could the escalation have been?

At a sign from Detective Tanghal, Officer Hooper hauled me to my feet. None too gently, I might add.

"Can you please tell me where you've been for the last thirty minutes, Ms. Jackson-Ramanathan?" Detective Tanghal shot a look at Teri, who'd been about to interrupt. It was the kind of look you'd use if you needed to stop a charging elephant and you'd misplaced your elephant gun.

I stared at her. I couldn't see how, but this was a trick question, a trap. I hadn't even had a chance to hang Reginald's leash back on the hook. It lay half-coiled on the floor where I'd dropped it while being manhandled. "I was walking the dog." I tried to hold eye contact, to radiate sincerity, but my gaze dropped to the leash.

"And where are your keys?" This time I didn't even bother with words. Baffled, I looked at my bag, still slumped just inside the back door where I'd left it.

Detective Tanghal crossed the room in two long strides. Her steps were the only sound in the otherwise silent room. It sounded like everyone was holding their breath.

I braced myself for an interminably long wait as Detective Tanghal knelt to poke open the flap of my bag with a gloved finger. If she was going to rummage around for my keys, we might be here awhile. But through some minor miracle, they were right on top. She carefully placed them in a plastic bag, which she then held out to Officer Hooper.

"Now?" His voice, coming from behind me, sounded a little hurt and offended. I couldn't muster any sympathy. I was too confused and sore.

"Yes, thank you," replied Detective Tanghal.

"But . . . the prisoner . . ."

Detective Tanghal closed her eyes, so briefly it might have just been a long blink. "I will take responsibility for the prisoner. Please, Officer Hooper. Check the vehicle."

Finally, the crushing grip on my arms was gone. I hugged myself, trying to get blood flow back into all the spots that were tingling and throbbing.

"Why don't you have a seat, Ms. Jackson-Ramanathan," Detective Tanghal continued after Officer Hooper disappeared toward the front of the house, "and I'll let you know what's happened."

"She knows what happened!" Teri had jumped to her feet as I collapsed on the couch. I got my first good look at her and was shocked to see bloody scrapes on both her hands and her knees. "She tried to kill me!"

"Ms. Van Meer. Please try to control yourself. If I have to, I'll separate each and every one of you and take detailed statements from everyone. But I believe we can clarify a few things more quickly this way."

It hadn't been a question, but Detective Tanghal waited, giving Teri a chance to reply. Instead of answering, Teri slowly resumed her seat at the kitchen island. Brett on one side and Ali on the other quickly leaned in with comforting pats.

"Around twenty minutes ago, a white Toyota Corolla which has been identified as yours accelerated behind Teri as she ran along Hedgerow Estates Lane. She heard the car and moved to the extreme edge of the road. Its progress did not stop. The car mounted the curb, forcing Teri to fling herself out of its path. The car drove off. She did not get a look at the driver."

I'd been staring at Detective Tanghal while she was talking, but now I looked back to Teri. "Oh, my god! Are you OK?" It was all I could manage. I could see the scrapes, but it could have been so much worse. I heard again the squeal, the thump, the scream.

"She'll survive," answered Detective Tanghal. "However, we're left with the little matter of identifying the driver. It seems beyond doubt that your car was involved. Teri recognized it, and the front passenger-side tire has clearly sustained damage consistent with her story."

I groaned. Maybe I should have been worried about other things just then, but I really, really couldn't afford to do any work on my car that month.

Officer Hooper returned just then, looking a little glum and still holding the plastic bag with my keys. He nodded at Detective Tanghal and took up a post by the door.

"What time did you arrive this morning, and who was around?" Detective Tanghal resumed her questioning.

Teri jumped up again. "You're seriously just going to stand there and ask her polite questions? She tried to kill me!"

I answered Detective Tanghal's questions as well as I could, then turned my attention to Teri. "I'm guessing somebody's still trying to frame me for your grandmother's murder. All they had to work with was my supposed motive, the pet trust. You stood in this room and shouted in front of everybody that I'd never get my slimy little hands on it. You made yourself look like an obstacle. If I'd murdered your grandmother to get the money, of course I'd kill you, too, and clear the way."

Teri was gulping air. I could have demanded to speak to Detective Tanghal in the other room and told her exactly who the murderer was, but I couldn't stand the hatred I saw in Teri's eyes. I couldn't stand knowing there was someone in the world with that level of animosity toward me. If I didn't try to convince her I was innocent, would she believe the solution when it came from Detective Tanghal? We'd had such a good rapport just one day ago. I couldn't believe it had all shattered so quickly. When she'd opened up to me about her childhood, her relationship with Bonnie, her relationship with . . . Then I had it. The way out.

"Who did you tell about our meeting yesterday?" Teri shook her head dazedly and didn't answer. I prompted her. "We got coffee yesterday and talked about the pet trust. Who did you tell? Did you tell Ali or Will? Brett? Bonnie? Kevin? Who did you tell?"

Teri shook her head slowly. "I didn't tell anyone." She glanced around at the faces in the room. "No one."

When you're training a dog, you give them a treat when they do the first, the tiniest little fraction of the trick you ultimately want to build up to. I wanted to give Teri a treat. She didn't see it yet, but she'd cleared me.

"So, as far as the others know, your last word on the subject was that you and Ali were prepared for a long, drawn-out legal battle. You were going to fight tooth and nail to keep me from getting my hands on a single penny of your grandmother's money. None of them knew that you'd changed your mind. None of them knew that you'd invited me for coffee yesterday to tell me you'd decided to respect your grandmother's wishes and let the will go uncontested. You knew it, and I knew it. But none of the others knew it. Whoever went joyriding in my car this morning didn't know it."

Teri's face had changed. I couldn't pinpoint the moment it had happened. She was still furious, and she was still staring at me, but as I'd been talking, something subtle had changed, and her fury was no longer directed at me. The others were looking back and forth between us. I couldn't tell if they'd seen the change happen. Ali had leaned in closer and put an arm around Teri's shoulder.

"Well?" Detective Tanghal asked Teri after a moment of silence. "Ms. Van Meer? Can you corroborate Ms. Jackson-Ramanathan's characterization of that meeting?"

Teri's spine stiffened, and I thought she was about to call me a liar. Instead, she pulled away from Ali's embrace and Brett's hand, pushed herself to stand, limped across to the couch and dropped heavily beside me. "As far as any of them knew," she said carefully, looking at each person in the room in turn, "I was prepared to do whatever it took to keep Nikki from getting access to Reginald's pet trust. They all heard me say that. Every single one. Nikki was the only one who knew that I'd washed my hands of the whole business." She turned to Detective Tanghal. "Any one of them could have grabbed Nikki's keys this morning. We all knew her car, we all knew where she left her bag while she was out walking the dog. It could have been any one of them."

Detective Tanghal nodded to Teri and turned to Officer Hooper, opening her mouth to give him instructions.

That's when I piped up. "Not any one of them. Only the one who murdered Mrs. Van Meer would have had a reason."

Detective Tanghal didn't bother turning back to me. "Yes, Ms. Jackson-Ramanathan, thank you. We *had* managed to get that far on our own, but I appreciate the help." Her tone didn't sound particularly appreciative.

I soldiered one. "Did you also figure out how the murderer got gas into the bedroom?" No point in blurting out everything if the basic assumption Sasha and I had come up with was wrong.

"The bedroom?" Ali jumped in. "I thought she died in the garage. Isn't that what you said, that she died in the garage, and then someone put her in the bedroom?"

Detective Tanghal frowned, perhaps evaluating whether I had valuable information to offset the loss of her secrets. "That was an early theory, yes," she told Ali. "We haven't been able to find any physical evidence consistent with the body having been moved."

Teri snorted. "You've changed your tune."

Detective Tanghal ignored her, watching me now to see where I was going with this. For the first time, I appreciated how delicate a balancing act a murder investigation must be. Trying to control the flow of information must be like trying to stuff handfuls of smoke into your pockets. She could order me to stop talking, hustle me from the room, instead she watched, waiting to see what I would say next. Giving me enough rope to hang myself.

I touched my neck and regretted it. That had to be a sign of guilt, probably one they covered on the first day in the police academy.

"Through the vents?" asked Will.

I looked at him, momentarily baffled. In my mind, the conversation had shifted to the garage versus bedroom question, but he pulled us all back to my original question. How had the murderer gotten the poisonous gas into the room?

"Huh," I said. "I thought about that, but I don't think so. There were people milling around the great room for a long time after Mrs. Van Meer went to bed. And even if there'd been a few minutes with no one in here, everyone on the patio would have seen someone in here tampering with the vents into her bedroom." I waved toward the east wall of the great room, dominated by the stone fireplace. It would have been possible to direct air through this wall and into the bedroom on the other side of it, but it felt too exposed, too public.

"Now, I haven't explored the whole house, the way the rest of you have." I held up my hands. "It's possible the main HVAC system is directly under Mrs. Van Meer's bedroom, and so it would have been simple to vent gas into her room, and to seal off the other ducts to avoid contaminating the whole house." I let my voice trail off, inviting input.

Most of them looked blank, but Kevin shook his head and jerked a thumb toward the opposite end of the house. I took that to mean the furnace lay somewhere under the west wing of the house, maybe under Mr. Van Meer's study, or under the kitchen.

"The chimney?" asked Will. I'd given him a defined problem, and he focused on it like a bloodhound.

I shook my head. "How accessible is the roof? Is there a walk-out balcony, or a gabled window it'd be easy to climb out?"

Again, Kevin shook his head while the others sat silently.

I took a deep breath. "Then the answer's obvious. Teri, you told me that the police found duct tape residue on the end of a length of hose for the pool. At the time, they thought it had been used to direct gas from the car exhaust. Now they know the car wasn't used."

Detective Tanghal's face was impassive. The others were staring at me with rapt attention. It was impossible to tell if I'd said anything that was news to any of them.

I mentally shut out the others and focused solely on Detective Tanghal. "Like I told you, Reginald used to always sleep in Mrs. Van Meer's bedroom. He's got a dog bed at the foot of the larger bed, and that's been his spot until very recently. One night, not too long ago, a strange smell woke him up in the middle of the night, and a hose stuck through his doggy door. Pumping deadly gas into Mrs. Van Meer's bedroom."

A general uproar interrupted me. Everyone spoke at once, each one raising their voice to be heard over the tumult. Will won out. He wasn't the loudest of the group, but his deeper voice contrasted the most with the others.

"Dogs can't smell carbon monoxide. It's completely odorless."

"That's true." Officer Hooper's pronouncement was loud and decisive. It sounded a lot like the voice of God.

My ears started burning, probably bright red. Dogs couldn't smell carbon monoxide? That would have been fantastic to have known. My brain rushed ahead. *Wait.* That didn't destroy my theory.

"Of course, dogs can't smell carbon monoxide," I said. "The noise of the hose being put in place and the sound of gas woke him up. And the gas that was pumping in wouldn't have been pure carbon monoxide, would it?" I turned to Detective Tanghal. "It wouldn't, would it? If the murderer tampered with, say, the pool heater, blocked the ventilation to make it burn less efficiently? There would still be some uncombusted natural gas in the mix. Dogs can definitely smell that."

Detective Tanghal glanced at me sharply when I said the words "pool heater." If I'd still been in any doubt about Sasha's theory that clinched it. Her poker face wasn't so good after all.

"That's true," said Officer Hooper again in the same tone he'd used a moment ago but now supporting me. "Dogs can smell natural gas."

"Reginald wasn't even in the room that night." Teri had that look again, the one where she thought I was being particularly stupid. She'd clearly aligned herself with the wrong person. "He was in the study. You know that, you're the one who found him there the next morning."

I nodded and some snottiness crept into my voice. "Yes, obviously. When your grandmother died, Reginald had been sleeping in the study, even though normally he slept in her bedroom. But that's not the night I'm talking about. I'm talking about the murderer's first try!"

Chapter Thirty-Six

"First try?" Teri's eyes narrowed and she stared at me. Either my tone had pissed her off so much that she was at a loss for words, or she'd just gotten it. I don't know if the others had any idea, but none of them said anything.

"Yes, first try. I've never heard this dog howl. Not once. Not ever. Your grandmother called me the Monday before she died, because Reginald had woken her up in the middle of the night, howling for no obvious reason. She decided he was grieving for your grandfather." Now Ali did look like she wanted to speak. Although it was the perfect spot for a dramatic pause, I rushed on.

"One week earlier, on the night of Sunday, November sixth, somebody tried to kill Mrs. Van Meer. With the NFL watch party as a distraction, one end of a hose was attached to the vent on the side of the pool heater, and the other end was poked through the dog door into Mrs. Van Meer's bedroom. Mrs. Van Meer only survived because Reginald realized the danger and woke her up with his howling." I turned to Ali. "What did your grandmother do after Reginald woke her up?"

Ali didn't answer right away. She fidgeted with her ring and looked first to Will, then to Teri. She couldn't see where I was leading, and clearly worried I was taking her over a cliff.

Finally, she spoke. "I remember that night. She took Reginald into the study, and lay down on the couch with him, and watched some old movie until she fell back asleep. She had a crick in her neck the next day from sleeping on the couch." Ali looked down at her hands. She spread her fingers wide, then relaxed as Will reached over and took one of her hands in his. "She's done that a lot since Grandpa died. I think nights are the worst for her, and the study smells like him."

"It saved her life that night," I said with the vague hope it might comfort her. It sounded reassuring, as long as you didn't think about it too much. "She slept in the study that night, and the gas that had built up in her bedroom dissipated harmlessly over the course of the next day. There may have been enough to give someone a headache, but not a lethal dose."

Reginald got to his feet, and everyone in the room watched, hypnotized by the swinging motion of his ears as he took a few plodding steps toward me. He leaned against my legs, and then flopped, sliding down to lie with his head on my sneakers.

I pulled strength from his warm solidity. "I imagine some murderers would have given up after that attempt. It must have been a shock to see Mrs. Van Meer alive and well the next morning. Of course, when they heard about Reginald's howling in the middle of the night, they knew what had really happened. The plan could work, but it needed some editing before they tried again."

Ali spoke, haltingly. "So, you're saying that Reginald . . . that he might have seen who did it?"

Teri threw her hands in the air. "Oh, my god! What a brilliant idea! We'll all stand in a circle and ask Reginald to point out the killer."

Ali's face flushed bright red, and she opened her mouth for an angry retort even as her eyes glazed with tears.

"Not exactly," I said quickly. If this dissolved into a bickering match between the two sisters we'd never get anywhere. "Besides, that kind of test is never going to be admissible evidence, is it?" I asked Detective Tanghal.

Officer Hooper jumped in. "Well, actually, there have been cases in which the court has considered evidence from dogs, especially—"

"Thank you, Officer," interrupted Detective Tanghal. "No, you're right, Ms. Jackson-Ramanathan. A seeming accusation from a household pet wouldn't be admissible under any circumstances."

I nodded at her and turned back to the others. "Instead, I want to ask you two questions. In the week before the successful murder attempt, do you remember who suggested your grandmother up her dose of sleeping pills when the next party rolled around? Or who encouraged her to shut Reginald in the study every night?"

They looked at each other, eyes not meeting. No doubt they remembered general conversations on those two topics, but not who had initiated them. The innocent ones suspected each other, and the murderer did a very good acting job to fit in.

"Let's look at it this way," I said, taking a deep breath.

"No, I think that's enough," said Detective Tanghal. She held up a hand. "If you have any evidence, I'll have you report it to me, in private."

I'd been expecting that. No police officer would want one suspect spouting off theories in front of all the other suspects. Frankly, I was surprised she'd let me go on this long. But it had been enough. I'd gotten out the big, pivotal revelation. And none of the others had jumped in to destroy my theory. There was always the chance that Will or someone would say, "Actually, Reginald used to howl day and night, and in fact, he kept it up all last week. Weird that he hasn't done it when you're around."

That hadn't happened. Now Detective Tanghal and I would go talk privately in the study, and I'd lay out all my logic and she'd have to see the truth of it, or at least the potential, and investigate further.

"Actually, I think we'd like to hear what Nikki has to say," said Teri, "especially since she seems to have uncovered an attempted murder that the police never even suspected." She looked across the room at Ali, who nodded firmly. The color and the tears had vanished from Ali's face, which was now just as stern as Teri's. Any hint of disagreement between the sisters had evaporated into thin air. They were a united front, staring at Detective Tanghal and ignoring everyone else in the room.

Detective Tanghal and Officer Hooper exchanged a glance. Without saying anything, they both sat down, Detective Tanghal on an unoccupied couch close to the one Teri and I were on and Officer Hooper on an uncomfortable-looking chair in the undefined space between the two halves of the room.

Once they settled into their seats, all eyes turned back to me. I couldn't decide whether to thank Teri, or curse her.

"Let's look at it this way," I repeated. "The evidence pointed to the idea that Mrs. Van Meer was gassed in the garage and dragged back into the bedroom. The police found duct tape in the garage that looked like it had been used to attach a hose to the tailpipe. And the most obvious suspect was Kevin."

Everyone turned to look at Kevin, even though I'd tried to take the sting out by naming him right after mentioning a discredited theory.

"Kevin has access to the garage, to everywhere, really, and the police found a lighter of his in Mrs. Van Meer's bedroom, where it had no business being."

I waited until they all turned back to me before continuing. "But there's other evidence, too. Evidence pointing toward Bonnie. A little less obvious, but it's enough that the police didn't arrest Kevin on day one. Except Bonnie wasn't here the night Mrs. Van Meer died. So she couldn't have done it." They'd all resisted looking at Bonnie, so they didn't see her dab at her eyes.

"Kevin, how did you cut your hand?"

His face paled at my question, and I cringed. To the others, I'm sure his reaction looked like an admission of guilt, but it was the normal response to finding himself in an unwanted spotlight. I just hoped he trusted me enough to answer the question, and to do it without blurting out our shared family connection.

Detective Tanghal answered, waving a hand dismissively. "I know where you're going with this, Nikki, but no. This homicide would not have required physical strength or manual dexterity. If it had turned out the body—Mrs. Van Meer—had been moved from the garage and arranged in the bed, then maybe you'd have a point. But the injury to Mr. Driscoll's hand would not have rendered him incapable of running the hose to Mrs. Van Meer's room."

Everyone in the room looked at Kevin again, who held his hand to his chest, almost curling around it as though to protect it from our scrutiny. When I'd first seen him, my very first day coming to this house, his whole hand had been wrapped in gauze. Now the cut had mostly healed, judging by the single strip of tape that crossed his palm.

"How'd you cut it?" I asked again, ignoring Detective Tanghal.

"Cheap can opener," he whispered, clearly fearing a trap.

I heard it, but I doubted the rest of them had, so I asked again, giving him a reassuring smile.

"It was a cheap can opener," he repeated, a more loudly. If anything, more bewildered than scared now. "The cabin me and my buddies stay at when we go hunting has this piece of crap can opener, and I knew it was going to get one of us sooner or later. I was opening a can of baked beans, and it didn't get a clean cut, and the lid jumped up and cut me right across the palm." He held his hand toward me, palm up, as though he wanted me to examine the injury, although of course nothing showed except the dingy tape. "Hurt like a . . . hurt like anything."

"Where's the cabin?"

He perked up, forgetting the broader topic of conversation. "Oh, it's down in the Ozarks. 'Bout three hours southwest of here. One of my buddies inherited a little plot down there from his grandfather, and there's this falling-down old cabin we stay in. It's good enough, except for the can opener, of course."

Detective Tanghal caught on. She nodded to Officer Hooper, who raised his notebook in readiness. "We'll need the names of the other members of your party. When exactly did you arrive at this cabin, and when did you return to St. Louis?"

Kevin blinked, baffled. "Well, I rode down with one of my buddies on a Tuesday morning. He picked me up at my place and we were on the highway by ten o'clock. And we stayed out the week, and that weekend, and drove back Monday morning. He dropped me off home at about noon, and I got in my truck and came straight over here." He pointed at Teri. "You remember, because Mrs. VM was all worked up, going on and on about the dog grieving for Mr. VM."

Teri nodded, although it looked like she didn't want to. She was starting to understand what had happened as well.

"Can you give me dates, Mr. Driscoll?" asked Officer Hooper, waiting for something he could add to his notebook.

Kevin looked lost for just a second, and then pulled out his phone. He opened a calendar and scrolled back, moving his lips as he counted. "We left on the first and got back on the seventh."

"And you're confident your friends will corroborate those dates?"

"Sure, they will! They were there."

"Just one more question, if you don't mind," I said. "You told me that after you got back to town, you found Bonnie's windbreaker in the garage. Is that right?"

Bonnie's head snapped up at that. She started to say something but stopped when I held up a hand.

"Kevin? Bonnie's windbreaker?"

He nodded. "It's fine. She's free to hang out in the garage as much as she wants. Not like it's my garage or anything. I just thought it was weird, because I've never seen her in there before."

"So, if the first attempt had been successful, and Mrs. Van Meer had died sometime during the night of the sixth, and the death wasn't immediately dismissed as an old woman dying of natural causes in her sleep, what would have happened when the police investigated? The police would have found an envelope of Bonnie's full of clippings about euthanasia, Bonnie's windbreaker in the garage, and a fresh ball of duct tape near the tailpipe of the Studebaker. Doesn't it look like the original plan was to frame Bonnie, either by staging it as a murder, or some kind of assisted suicide?" I paused here, knowing I'd just dumped a lot of information on the others. I'd had a few hours to sort it all out in my head. The least I could do was give them a few seconds.

Detective Tanghal made no move to cut me off. She wasn't nodding at me, or giving me any kind of encouragement, but she wasn't trying to stop me anymore. Officer Hooper was writing furiously in his notebook, which I took as a compliment, probably the nicest compliment I've ever gotten.

"Then, when the murderer was set to try again the next weekend," I continued, "Bonnie was unexpectedly called away. They needed a new narrative to present to the police, and they needed it fast. This is where you come in," I said, gesturing to Kevin. "You were an easy target. There was no need to link you to the garage. But they still wanted something to point to you specifically. That explains the lighter. They weren't drastically changing the story; just some of the details. They didn't bother to swap out the duct tape, because it would work just as well with the new version."

I nodded to Detective Tangal. "Maybe you worked all this out already, but this case has always seemed so confusing to me. And it's because there was an older story underlying the narrative the murderer ended up presenting." I toyed with the idea of repeating Ruby's lecture about the various versions of the painting that hung in Mr. Van Meer's study.

They'd all be familiar with it, after all, and it had been the spark that had shown me the way to untangle all the conflicting strands of this mystery. One murder attempt, peeking out from underneath another. In the end, I avoided any mention of the picture in the interest of simplicity. I already felt like I'd been talking for hours.

After they indulged my lapsing into thought for a few moments, Ali couldn't take it any longer. "So," she asked, slowly, "who did it, then?"

Chapter Thirty-Seven

"Oh! Sorry!" I shook my head to clear it. I'd spent so much time trying to wind my way through the maze created by the murderer, I'd gotten distracted from the main question. "Once you eliminate Bonnie and Kevin, it's pretty obvious." I shrugged. "It was Brett."

The room erupted again. Brett jumped to his feet, shouting, while Ali pulled on his arm, trying to make him sit back down. Will moved to block the door to the yard, ready for whatever happened next. Teri crossed to stand in front of Detective Tanghal, speaking furiously, too quietly for me to hear, with lots of angry pointing. Officer Hooper stood, positioning himself between Brett and the other door. I exchanged glances with Kevin and Bonnie, who both seemed too dazed to react to any of the chaos around them. Bonnie managed a ghost of a smile for me, but I'm not sure if Kevin even registered I was looking at him.

Then Brett tugged his arm free from Ali's grasp and took two steps toward the door, not seeing Officer Hooper moving to intercept him. "I don't have to sit here and listen to this nonsense. She probably did it herself, to get her grubby little hands on a pile of money!"

"Brett!" Teri said, so sharply everyone in the room stopped what they were doing and turned to her. "I'd think you'd want to hear what you're being accused of." Teri's eyes narrowed as she looked back and forth between me and Brett. I thought she believed me. I hoped she believed me.

Maybe it was wishful thinking. I don't know.

"I can prove it," I said. "I think I can prove it. But first, remember those two questions I asked? I don't know the answers, but I think you do." I looked first at Teri, then Ali, and then Will. "Who suggested that Mrs. Van Meer take a larger dose of sleeping pills before the football watch party? I mean, the second time, when she *was* killed? And who made sure Reginald would sleep in the study that night? Did it come up in conversation? Did anyone check he was there, instead of in the bedroom?"

I honestly didn't know the answers to those questions. It was likely Brett had taken those steps, and it would have been easy to camouflage them as benign interest in Mrs. Van Meer's welfare. I looked at the others and saw hints of dawning realization in their eyes. Maybe they were remembering innocuous comments, seeing them in a new and insidious light. Nobody had anything concrete, at least not right then. That was OK. I'd just have to provide the proof I'd promised.

"Like I said, Brett had to improvise when Bonnie wasn't around for his second murder attempt. He thought he did a pretty good job. But he couldn't be sure it was enough. Would the police buy it? Would they arrest Kevin on the strength of his lighter being where it didn't belong? My guess is, the more he thought about it, the flimsier the planted evidence seemed. I don't know how long he plotted and planned before the first murder attempt, laying the groundwork for Bonnie's supposed motive. But this one was ad-libbed, and he started second-guessing himself almost immediately."

I went on, "I can't know for sure what it was that made him think Kevin might not be a viable suspect. If I had to guess . . . does anyone remember what Kevin said that day, that morning I mean, when we were all together, and Teri went off to check on Mrs. Van Meer?"

I'd started out talking mostly to Teri, but as I went on, I directed more and more of my attention to Brett. He stared at me, not with the hatred and anger I would have expected, but almost with a hypnotized look in his eyes.

He hadn't expected anyone to understand his thought process. Oh, find him guilty of the murder, sure, he must have known that was a possibility, but to give voice to his uncertainty and hesitations? I don't think he was ready for it, and it left him vulnerable.

No one answered my question. I dragged my gaze away from Brett to look at Kevin. "You said, 'She seemed fine on Saturday.' It was the kind of empty thing that people say, without really knowing why."

Kevin shrugged and ducked his head in a way that might have been a nod, or might not have been.

Will spoke up then. "I remember that. Yes. Kevin said it."

"We talked on Saturday," Kevin said. "About bulbs. It was overdue to plant any new ones. But she didn't want to bother, because of the condo, you know? Bulbs are what you do when you're going to stick around. Anyway, we didn't talk on Sunday any time. But we did talk on Saturday, so that's what I said. I didn't mean anything by it."

"I think that simple sentence caught in the back of Brett's mind. I think that over the next twenty-four, forty-eight hours, he turned that sentence over and over in his head. Why did Kevin say 'Saturday?' Surely Kevin had seen Mrs. Van Meer at some point the day before, on Sunday. Had he? He's always around. But so often in the background. What if Kevin hadn't actually been around on Sunday. Had Brett really seen him? Or was he remembering a different day, just assuming Kevin was there? If Kevin wasn't there, was he somewhere else? Could he prove he was somewhere else? What if Brett had set up everything to accuse Kevin of murder, and it turned out that he had driven Bonnie to the hospital and spent the night keeping her company there?"

I glanced back at Brett and took half a step backward from the force of his gaze. Gone was the empty, hypnotized look. A fiery hatred burned there now.

But nothing could happen now. I was safe, here in this room with all the others. "So that's when he turned to me. He knew for sure that I was around Sunday night, and he probably heard me tell Will that my husband was out of town. He forged the mention of me in Mrs. Van Meer's will to run the pet trust in order to give me a motive. He told you all that I knew all about it ahead of time, when I didn't. The only explanation is that he was trying to backdate my motive. The will couldn't be seen as a motive if I only found out about it after Mrs. Van Meer's death."

"But that's your word against his," said Will. "That's not proof."

"I know. I convinced Teri, or I think I did, Mrs. Van Meer never had a chance to tell me about the will. If I need to go through all that again, I can. But I truly don't think Mrs. Van Meer ever knew anything about naming me in the pet trust in the first place. I think that all happened after she was already dead. That way, if Brett ever felt like the police weren't buying Kevin as a suspect, he could offer me up. And he did. He stole my pen when I was out walking Reginald and planted it for the police to find. But I wasn't arrested. So he stole my car and staged an attack on Teri."

Brett finally spoke up, addressing Teri. "Are you buying any of this crap? She's a con artist who wormed her way into your grandmother's will, and then her pen was found somewhere, and then she tried to kill you, and now she's making up anything she can think of to avoid a murder charge." It was a good stance for him, even quoting Teri verbatim in a couple places, but the note of hysteria in his voice undermined his credibility.

I didn't pay too much attention to Brett's interruption. Of course, I'd expected him to protest. Who wouldn't?

"She says she has proof," said Teri.

"Proof? We've heard what she has to say! Sounds like a lot of guessing. Sounds to me like she's guilty, and she knows the police are closing in." he said, his voice back under control.

"If that's the case, why not just sit there and let her make a fool of herself?" Teri swung around and stared at Brett. He sank into his chair under the intensity of her gaze. After a second or two, she decided he had been thoroughly cowed and turned to me. She didn't say anything, but raised her eyebrows with a hint of a challenge.

I nodded to her. "So, you wanted proof. It's not, like, DNA or anything, but I think it's proof. Do you all remember when we found . . ." My voice trailed off. I have no idea why I felt squeamish. "Monday morning, when we found the body, er, Mrs. Van Meer, do you remember what happened? We all crowded into the room. Brett was nursing a hangover from the night before. The sight of the body was too much for him, and he pushed his way through us and out of the French doors."

The others nodded along, with two exceptions. Brett had narrowed his eyes and watched me shrewdly. Teri stared at Brett with a look so intense I half expected his head to burst into flames. I could have stopped there, but the others deserved an explanation.

"What Brett did seemed unremarkable that day. But then we learned Mrs. Van Meer died from carbon monoxide poisoning. If there was going to be any chance that the death would be dismissed as natural causes, the murderer had to make sure no one else experienced any symptoms of CO poisoning. He had to air out the room, and he had to do it quickly."

Now everyone in the room stared at Brett, who tried to decide on the appropriate facial expression. It wasn't quite blank, but he hadn't yet landed on anger or defiance or resignation or indignation.

"I have two more questions to ask, and again, I don't know the answers. Everyone saw Brett acting drunk Sunday night. Did anyone see him drinking? I don't think I did." I didn't give them a chance to answer. I focused on Bonnie. "Monday morning, when Brett ran out of the room, you went to check on him. The rest of us stayed on the other side of the room. My impression was that he was dry heaving, which would be possible to fake. Did you see anything that would . . . um," I glanced around the room. My face burned red again, as I realized I had to talk about bodily fluids in front of an audience.

But Bonnie was used to caring for an elderly, invalid mother. It would take more than this to catch her off guard.

"You mean, was there any vomit?" she asked, without blinking an eye. "No, he could very easily have been faking." She looked at Brett with disgust. "Very easily."

"But why?" Ali asked. She seemed more baffled than angry. "Grandma never did anything to him."

I snuck a glance at Detective Tanghal. Frankly, done with the spotlight. If she'd given me any hint of a signal to shut up and sit down, I would've been happy to sit down and shut up. But her face stayed blank. She could have been ecstatic that her case was solved or furious that none of us had told her about Brett's reaction to finding the body or composing a grocery list for when she got off work.

"She didn't do anything to him, no," I said after a few seconds. "But she was planning to sell the house. She had an appointment with her realtor to finalize that Monday morning. And selling the house was something Brett hadn't been counting on, and something he couldn't allow her to do." I looked at Detective Tanghal again, a little pleadingly, before turning back to Ali. "What I'm about to say all makes sense, but it's speculation at this point. I think if you dig into the details of that reverse mortgage—"

"We've got a forensic accountant lined up, ready to start investigating that aspect of the case Monday morning when the banks open."

Thank god, Detective Tanghal finally decided to jump in. And her statement, simple and factual, had a visible effect on Brett. The blood drained from his face, and I don't think anyone in the room missed the significance.

I waited a beat for Detective Tanghal to say more, but she had offered up all she was going to.

"If, about three years ago, Brett had money troubles," I continued, "he could have taken out a fraudulent reverse mortgage against the house of his clients. It was a great short-term solution. He'd get the cash he wanted, and he wouldn't have any pesky loan payments to cramp his style. Like so many other people who get caught up in sketchy financial deals, he convinced himself that he'd pay back the money before the consequences of his actions caught up with him. The Van Meers were old enough to qualify, but in pretty good health. The only danger was that they might decide to sell the house, but they loved it, and Brett couldn't foresee a scenario in which they'd sell up and move."

Ali stared at me. "But then Grandpa died." I got the feeling she'd rather be staring daggers at Brett, like Teri, but she couldn't bring herself to look at him.

"Right. All his calculations were wrong, because your grandmother decided to sell the house. The reverse mortgage was going to come to light. It was going to be discovered when your grandmother's real estate agent got around to running a title check before listing the house. The only other option was for it to come to light after you two inherited the house, or tried to inherit, and that would only happen if your grandmother died."

"But if it was going to come out either way . . ." Ali said.

I shook my head. "If your grandmother had found out about the reverse mortgage, she'd know it was fraudulent, and I imagine it'd be a short leap to suspecting the family attorney. On the other hand, if you found out after both your grandparents were dead, Brett could claim that they'd taken out the reverse mortgage, which is what he did."

Brett sat with his head in his hands, accepting there was no point in fighting any more. Even if he won the day in court and beat the rap, what did he have left? He didn't have the drive to build a new life for himself. He still hung around his childhood friends, working the job his father had given him, and he'd just watched it all crumble.

He stood, a little unsteadily. Officer Hooper adjusted his stance ever so slightly, ready to react. Brett glanced toward Teri, then toward Ali. She was more soft-hearted. She'd forgive him.

"I'm sorry, I'm so sorry. It all got out of control."

Ali stood up from the kitchen stool, one hand on her swollen belly. Will headed toward her.

Brett took two steps toward Ali, arms spread wide. Maybe he intended to grovel at her feet for forgiveness or try to embrace her. As soon as he got close, Ali punched him in the face. Hard. He went down. Hard.

Reginald barked, loudly and sharply, a sound I'd never heard from the sleepy old dog. He shot across the room before anyone had a chance to react, putting his body between Brett and Ali. He kept his rheumy eyes on Brett, with just the hint of a low growl attesting to his alertness. All the humans in the room also stared down at Brett, who lay dazed in disbelief. He put a hand to his split lip but made no effort to stand. Ali shook out her fist, wincing, and looked across the room to Detective Tanghal.

"You saw that, right?" Ali asked. "He came at me. It was self-defense."

Detective Tanghal nodded. I don't think Ali needed to worry about assault charges.

Ali reached down and scratched Reginald's head. "Good boy."

Chapter Thirty-Eight

It felt strange to leave the Van Meers' house, with its giant, fancy rooms, where everyone was on edge because of the murder, and walk into McKayla's cozy apartment, full of laughter and chatter, with her brunch in full swing. Detective Tanghal had assured me they'd only need to keep my car for a short time, and I'd tried not to think about how long that might be as a uniformed officer had driven me home in her squad car. I'd gone upstairs to our apartment first, to freshen up. To my surprise, I found a note on the kitchen table from Jai. "The kids lost, so I'm home early. Went downstairs," with a lopsided heart drawn below the words.

McKayla's door was propped ajar welcomingly, so I stuck my head in without knocking. Ruby stood just inside, listening to some people I didn't recognize. Her mouth was full of something, so she waved when she saw me but didn't call out. As I made my way over, Jai appeared and put an arm around my waist.

"Glad you could join us," he said with a smile. He spoke softly, so that if I'd wanted to bail on the party and pull him upstairs to talk, I could do it. He's such a great guy. But what I really needed in that moment was this atmosphere, the exact opposite of the chilly formality I'd just left. I wanted to drink it all in.

Ruby joined us, and I caught a glimpse of AJ across the room. Before I could ask Ruby what in the world they were doing there, she'd pressed a chunk of some kind of baked good into my hand.

"Eat this. It's amazing."

I was remarkably good at following instructions, and I had the thing in my mouth before she finished talking. It's going to sound lame to say it was a homemade cake donut hole with a cinnamon sugar coating, but it was so much more than the sum of its parts. It was definitely not lame.

"Oh, my god," I managed to choke out as I swallowed. "Is there more of that? I need more of that. Where is it?" Then I blinked, and my brain settled back into gear. "What are you doing here? It's great to see you."

Jai smiled and exchanged a glance with Ruby. "A few minutes after I got home, McKayla came back upstairs. She said she'd gotten overexcited and cooked too much. She asked if I knew anyone I could lure over at short notice with a promise of food."

"And he did!" Ruby jumped in. "C'mon. I'll show you what to get."

I couldn't keep from grinning as we wove our way through the chattering people and into McKayla's kitchen to find more of the donut holes, thank god, along with an entire smorgasbord of other options. I hadn't been even a little hungry, but faced with a bounty like this, I had no choice but to fill up a plate and dig in.

I'd been a little overambitious, so Ruby and I stood in the kitchen and talked for a few minutes until the pile on my plate had dwindled enough to manage while walking. I didn't mention the murder, and she didn't ask. Something about the atmosphere in McKayla's apartment drove away such serious thoughts, leaving me happy and at peace. And I had donut holes.

When we left the kitchen, I scanned the room for Jai, and instead saw Dwayne, sitting on the sofa talking to a woman I didn't know. For a second, my heart skipped a beat, as I remembered McKayla's innocent refusal to believe in our landlord's "no pets" policy. The moment of truth had come at last. Dwayne was in her apartment. And I'd refused to help her that morning. She'd come to me, and I'd turned her away.

Like I said, that moment of panic lasted for a split second. Then I registered that Mr. Cat was curled up in Dwayne's lap, looking up at the big man's face with an expression of adoration.

Dwayne had an identical expression on his face but directed at the woman sitting next to him. The room skewed toward people in their mid-to-late twenties, and she was older than that, but I couldn't have guessed her age with any accuracy. She had bleached-blond hair, but didn't seem overly fussy about it, since almost an inch of darker roots showed, and it fell out of a thrown-together bun. She had a wide smile that pushed her cheeks up and crinkled her eyes in a way that I recognized.

"Is that . . ." I started to ask Jai, who had come up behind me.

"Yup. Mystery solved." Jai grinned as he watched the two humans and the cat on the couch. "McKayla's mom. Anybody with eyes could tell Dwayne's crazy about her. He hasn't moved from that spot since she sat down. Didn't even move a muscle when the cat jumped up."

I had that warm and fuzzy feeling you get when you see people in love. I balanced my plate on one hand and hooked my free arm around Jai's. "Looks reciprocal to me. Good for them." I meant it.

In the end, it took a while to sort things out, but Brett accepted some sort of plea deal. I'm hazy on the details, but he was guaranteed a shorter sentence than he would have risked going to trial. I was relieved. I had not been looking forward to a long, drawn-out court case. Laying out the whole story in front of a handful of people had been nerve wracking enough. Testifying at the front of a full courtroom? A literal nightmare.

Ali and Will had their builder add a six-foot privacy fence to their house plans, and they, along with their new baby, Maya, and their old dog, Reginald, moved into the house as soon as it was finished. I signed over the executorship of Reginald's pet trust to Ali, with no second thoughts. No one looked too hard at whether that part of the will was real or a forgery. I still walked Reginald now and then, but only when his owners were out of town.

I hadn't seen Teri since that Sunday morning, which was fine with me. There had been no reasonable way to hang onto her grandparents' house. She could have raised enough money to pay off the bank, but the real estate market had fallen since Brett took out his loan, and the pay-off amount would have been more than the current value of the house. According to Ali, it all worked out for the best. I understand Teri moved into a condo downtown, and that it suits her perfectly.

Bonnie retired to Florida. She transferred her mother to a nursing home down there and sent Ali a postcard saying how beautiful the weather was all the time. Ali gives it three or four months before Bonnie gets bored and finds a new job.

I've run into Kevin a couple times. I don't know where he's working now, but he had no trouble picking up another job. That spring, Jai and I saw him and his family at a fish fry in the city. I caught up with my cousin Mindy, and then we stood around awkwardly for a minute or two. Kevin and I smiled at each other, and neither of us mentioned the Van Meers or the murder. I still think it was a miracle the police never learned about our connection, and part of me feels like talking about the Van Meers would jinx us.

Jai and I still haven't gotten a dog or a cat. McKayla's assortment of indoor pets has grown, but there aren't any chickens in the backyard yet. We suspect Dwayne has officially started dating McKayla's mother, although I haven't been brave enough to ask McKayla for confirmation. I figure they'll date for a while, and then get married, and then he'll get around to updating his leases to allow pets. Fingers crossed.

Oh, and me? I'm still doing some of the calligraphy and the dog walking and the cat toys, but the big news is that my pet behaviorist business has taken off. Against all odds, the client who died within a week of consulting me somehow landed me more referrals than I can handle. Ali and Will have recommended me to at least six of their new neighbors. It seems like every single condo owner in Teri's building has a dog or a cat with some kind of neurosis. I even heard from the family that lives catty-corner from Kevin and my Aunt Carol. Their pit bull mix is pathologically terrified of their hamster. That will be a long, difficult case, but I'm discounting my rates heavily for them. Nobody deserves to be menaced by a hamster, whatever their ability to pay.

Acknowledgments

I'd like to thank Mark for his incredible patience during all the time I've spent working on The Book. I couldn't have spent nearly as much time in my fictional world if he weren't holding down the fort back in the real world.

And Laura, who's willing to read whatever nonsense draft I send her way, and always couches her criticisms as helpful suggestions or questions, when she'd be justified to go with a simple, "eh, try again."

Thanks to Mom and Dad for making sure I grew up with a love of reading and books. Long before I could drive myself, there was always time for a trip to the library!

Although they do their absolute best to hamper my writing progress, I should still thank Zack, Tommy, Daisy, and Annie for all the love they express even as I'm shoving them off my keyboard.

You wouldn't be reading this without my amazing literary agent, Michelle Hauck at Storm Literary, who saw the potential and championed it all the way through. I'm so appreciative for the whole team at Storm, especially Vicki Selvaggio.

Acknowledgments

My editor, Faith Black Ross, made this book so much better with her great suggestions. Everyone working behind the scenes at Crooked Lane helped pull me across the finish line with their expertise and dedication. Thanks to Dulce Botello, Mikaela Bender, Megan Matti, Stephanie Manova, Rebecca Nelson, Thaisheemarie Fantauzzi Pérez, Julia Abbott, Doug White, and Matthew Martz.

Lastly, thanks to all those lovely people in my life who've let me hang out with their dogs. Lifetime achievement award in this category goes to Tracy.